"Today must be my lucky ...I thought it'd be a massive pain, but two of my objectives found their way into my hands so, so easily."

The final member of the secret Roman Orthodox organization God's Right Seat **Fiamma of the Right**

A Certain Magical

Index

20

KAZUMA KAMACHI

ILLUSTRATION BY
KIYOTAKA HAIMURA

"What do you expect
me to do with useless
information like that?!"

Academy City Level Zero
Touma Kamijou

"And now I have a piece of welcome information for you. I, Lesser, do indeed have a tail coming out of my skirt—but to tell the truth, I'm not wearing leggings under there. I'm only wearing panties."

Member of New Light, a sorcerer's society reserve group that caused the coup d'état in the United Kingdom
Lesser

"…You're trash.
And you're
really getting
under my skin."

"…What do we do?
Where are we even
supposed to run?!"

Former member of Item
Shiage Hamazura

"No...problems.
I'm fine...
So...let's
move quickly,
Hamazura."

Former member of Item
Rikou Takitsubo

"Think of me as coldhearted if you wish. But that's how delicate this situation has become. A single careless decision could lead to countless innocent lives being lost."

Central figure and namesake of the Elizalina Alliance of Independent Nation, **Elizalina**

contents

VOLUME 20

KAZUMA KAMACHI

ILLUSTRATION BY: KIYOTAKA HAIMURA

NEW YORK

A CERTAIN MAGICAL INDEX, Volume 20
KAZUMA KAMACHI

Translation by Andrew Prowse
Cover art by Kiyotaka Haimura

This book is a work of fiction. Names, characters, places, and incidents are the product of the author's imagination or are used fictitiously. Any resemblance to actual events, locales, or persons, living or dead, is coincidental.

TOARU MAJYUTSU NO INDEX Vol.20
©KAZUMA KAMACHI 2010
First published in Japan in 2010 by KADOKAWA CORPORATION, Tokyo.
English translation rights arranged with KADOKAWA CORPORATION, Tokyo,
through Tuttle-Mori Agency, Inc., Tokyo.

English translation © 2019 by Yen Press, LLC

Yen Press, LLC supports the right to free expression and the value of copyright. The purpose of copyright is to encourage writers and artists to produce the creative works that enrich our culture.

The scanning, uploading, and distribution of this book without permission is a theft of the author's intellectual property. If you would like permission to use material from the book (other than for review purposes), please contact the publisher. Thank you for your support of the author's rights.

Yen On
150 West 30th Street, 19th Floor
New York, NY 10001

Visit us at yenpress.com
facebook.com/yenpress
twitter.com/yenpress
yenpress.tumblr.com
instagram.com/yenpress

First Yen On Edition: October 2019

Yen On is an imprint of Yen Press, LLC.
The Yen On name and logo are trademarks of Yen Press, LLC.

The publisher is not responsible for websites (or their content) that are not owned by the publisher.

Library of Congress Cataloging-in-Publication Data

Names: Kamachi, Kazuma, author. | Haimura, Kiyotaka, 1973– illustrator. | Prowse, Andrew (Andrew R.), translator. | Hinton, Yoshito, translator.
Title: A certain magical index / Kazuma Kamachi ; illustration by Kiyotaka Haimura.
Other titles: To aru majyutsu no index. (Light novel). English
Description: First Yen On edition. | New York : Yen On, 2014–
Identifiers: LCCN 2014031047 (print) | ISBN 9780316339124 (v. 1 : pbk.) |
ISBN 9780316259422 (v. 2 : pbk.) | ISBN 9780316340540 (v. 3 : pbk.) |
ISBN 9780316340564 (v. 4 : pbk.) | ISBN 9780316340595 (v. 5 : pbk.) |
ISBN 9780316340601 (v. 6 : pbk.) | ISBN 9780316272230 (v. 7 : pbk.) |
ISBN 9780316359924 (v. 8 : pbk.) | ISBN 9780316359962 (v. 9 : pbk.) |
ISBN 9780316359986 (v. 10 : pbk.) | ISBN 9780316360005 (v. 11 : pbk.) |
ISBN 9780316360029 (v. 12 : pbk.) | ISBN 9780316442671 (v. 13 : pbk.) |
ISBN 9780316442701 (v. 14 : pbk.) | ISBN 9780316442725 (v. 15 : pbk.) |
ISBN 9780316442749 (v. 16 : pbk.) | ISBN 9780316474542 (v. 17 : pbk.) |
ISBN 9780316474566 (v. 18 : pbk.) | ISBN 9781975357566 (v. 19 : pbk.) |
ISBN 9781975331245 (v. 20 : pbk.)
Subjects: CYAC: Magic—Fiction. | Ability—Fiction. | Nuns—Fiction. | Japan—Fiction. | Science fiction. | BISAC: FICTION / Fantasy / General. | FICTION / Science Fiction / Adventure.
Classification: LCC PZ7.1.K215 Ce 2014 | DDC [Fic]—dc23
LC record available at https://lccn.loc.gov/2014031047

ISBNs: 978-1-9753-3124-5 (paperback)
978-1-9753-3125-2 (ebook)

1 3 5 7 9 10 8 6 4 2

LSC-C

Printed in the United States of America

DECLARATION OF WAR

This is a battle to protect the world and every man, woman, and child living in it.

The environmental destruction of today, caused by global warming and rising sea levels, as well as a shortage of oil and other fossil fuels, can all be traced back to Academy City's peculiar science and technology. Because their advancements in these fields are unbound by any law, if we do not stop the flood, the outcome is clear: All life on this planet will cease to exist.

For the future of humankind and all living things, Academy City must immediately halt and decommission all its active projects around the world. In addition, in order to analyze and solve the aforementioned problems, they must reveal the cutting-edge science and technology that are to blame.

If Academy City rejects our peace-seeking proposition, we will interpret it as a lack of intent to coexist with the rest of the world and deem it an evil entity exposing all life on Earth to danger for no reason other than its own interests.

We hereby set the deadline for a reply from Academy City to be seven PM on October 19, Moscow Standard Time.

Should the only sensible answer not come by then, we will treat Academy City as hostile and begin offensive operations, including the possible use of intercontinental ballistic missiles.

Finally, we will also gauge the United Kingdom of Great Britain and Ireland, a nation with especially strong, friendly relations with Academy City. If they would put all other life at risk for their own gain in pursuit of the sweet nectar of Academy City, then we must fight this enemy nation with all our strength, for our sake and for the sake of our children and our children's children who will walk the long road to the future.

October 18, Sorzhe I. Krainikov, president of the
Russian Federation

PROLOGUE

Skies Reeking of Gunpowder

Shooting_Game.

And so, World War III began.

The following day, October 19, would linger in memory as the day of destiny.

No matter how much whitewashing there was, no matter how well God's Right Seat was secretly pulling the strings to keep various intentions secret, a war once begun does not end so easily.

Everyone looked to the skies over the Sea of Japan.

They were the final line of defense for Academy City. If hostile amphibious assault ships and strategic bombers from Russia ever broke through, the tiny archipelago city-state would be transformed into a sea of fire and blood.

And everyone thought that was exactly what would happen.

Academy City may have possessed science and technology twenty or thirty years more advanced, but it was no more than a *city*, its population, including both adults and children, only 2.3 million people. On the other side was Russia, one of the world's top military powers along with China and the USA. Despite their technological prowess being somewhat lacking compared to Academy City, it should have only been a matter of time before their overwhelming numbers could destroy them.

However.

Currently, on October 30—

A female pilot named Ekalielya A. Pronskaya, part of the Russian Air Force, could feel the sweat staining the inside her gloves as she gripped her flight yoke. But the cause wasn't excitement from her country's supposedly crushing advantage. No—what she had was clearly a cold sweat.

With extreme mobility afforded by its canards, the brand-new, top-of-the-line fighter she piloted was said to be able to fly circles around American-made stealth planes in close combat. As Ekalielya flew hers, moving in tandem with dozens of others of the same model, she earnestly began to regret having entered this airspace.

Wars were always carried out at the whims of military leadership and politicians.

They weren't things soldiers on the field could do anything about.

Sometimes, a soldier needed to be prepared to shoot opponents they never wanted to fight out of the sky.

This sudden, unexpected war made people especially guilty for attacking first, no matter what the reason was.

That being said, it had nothing to do with Ekalielya's immediate predicament.

What she regretted was simply the current combat situation, one where she might die.

"*What the hell are those?*" came a voice over the radio from one of her wingmen, flying another fighter. The pilot didn't even bother using military brevity codes. It sounded like a scared child.

"*Are these even jets we're fighting?! They're freaking gigantic!!*"

The name of their enemy was HsF-00, a supersonic fighter aircraft made in Academy City. They used the same frames as the HsB-02 supersonic bombers, which perhaps accounted for their enormous size—about eighty meters in total length. They tore through the skies at furious speeds of over seven thousand kilometers per hour.

But there was something strange about them.

Fighter craft were generally between fifteen and twenty meters long. Their speed usually topped out at around 2,500 kilometers per hour, too. Both the size and speed of these Academy City weapons were abnormal. The faster a heavy object is traveling, the more inertia works against it. If someone took something that large and tried to mimic a small jet's sharp maneuvers, that alone would be enough to cause it to break apart. And even if it didn't, the enormous pressure would crush the pilot's organs.

"…Hard science, eh?" murmured Ekalielya bitterly to herself.

The *Hs* initials given to Academy City weapons were apparently a reference to how they used the power of rigorously tested science to completely dispel the darkness of impossibility and mystery.

"The power of science? *Nihuya.* They've clearly passed into occult territory here!!"

Just ten.

That was the total number of HsF-00s deployed to the entire Sea of Japan.

Their monstrous speed of seven-thousand-plus kilometers per hour and the monstrous range of their weapons allowed each individual craft to maintain air superiority over a massive area.

Countless smaller craft (smaller compared to the HsF-00, but the same size as the Sukhoi Ekalielya was piloting) flitted around the HsF-00s, which formed the core of the formations that were overpowering the Russian Air Force. The smaller craft's canopies were jet-black, making it impossible to tell if anyone was inside.

"*Did you know that apparently Academy City doesn't have a military?*" the wingman continued. "*Seems like we're fighting something called Anti-Skill, which is supposed to be a police force.*"

"Are you trying to say they shouldn't even have any offensive capabilities? How the hell is that thing a defensive weapon?! It's a stealth craft that can fly to the other side of the world without refueling. It was obviously designed for attacking!!"

"*Did you hear their official reply to the declaration of war? 'We have no need for a bloodbath, but would it be right for someone who has the power to stop this war and tragedy to watch and do nothing?'—Yeah, right! They were more than ready for the killing to start!!*"

They couldn't assume this was the extent of the enemy's strength.

And if they repurposed these weapons they were currently using for defense, they could certainly mount an invasion with them.

As it stood, it was hard to tell which side was being driven into a corner.

Whenever Ekalielya felt like she was ready to give up, strange, persistent images of Russian cities turning into seas of flames filled her mind.

As the irrational phenomenon made her burn with anger, the HsF-00's massive body in front of her made its move.

The real dogfight was about to begin. Naturally, Ekalielya and her squadron had no way of keeping up with a plane moving over three times their top speed. They couldn't even keep the enemy within attack range, much less safely get a lock from behind. After all, their opponent's top speed was over seven thousand kilometers per hour. Even if she pulled out all the stops, the thing would easily get over one hundred kilometers away and then ready itself again.

...It can't be using normal fuel.

Though she admitted to herself that they'd lost in terms of pure strength, she was still a professional soldier, so she continued desperately searching for a way out.

It must have an incredibly short flight time in exchange for that insane speed. If we can prolong this battle, we might have a chance.

But then, forgoing all encryption, the enemy contacted her:

"I'd give up on trying to make this a marathon. My craft is equipped with a system that uses the heat resulting from the friction of the armor's surface as energy. In other words, the faster this thing goes, the more efficient it is. At maximum, fuel usage is diminished by around ninety percent, I think."

"?!"

"And don't assume it'll work on the smaller craft, either...Come on. Our weapons were designed specifically for interception. Why wouldn't we come up with ways to overcome short flight durations?"

As he was speaking, something strange happened in the corner of Ekalielya's vision. She thought for a moment that one of the smaller planes had dropped a missile that failed to ignite, but another plane flew past from behind it, "catching" the missile with joints on its wings. It had just *refueled*.

Others were exchanging metal boxes packed with machine-gun ammunition or flying next to one another like trick flying and performing midair refueling through tentacle-like tubes. These maneuvers were supposed to be absolutely impossible during high-speed flight. It was almost like watching juggling on top of a speeding car.

They'd prepared special midair-refueling craft to eliminate the need to return to base.

By creating an aerial refueling network that stretched from their base to the battlefield, they could realize normally impossible flight duration and combat range.

Ugh…!! Then we have to start with their supply lines…!!

Ekalielya fixed her grip on the yoke, but her idea didn't connect to a concrete plan. The smaller crafts' inhumanly nimble movements were one thing, but the way the eighty-meter-long HsF-00 moved was uncanny.

Regular fighter craft had options for distracting an enemy with irregular maneuvers as well. The Split S, the barrel roll, the Russian-invented Pugachev Cobra—they were tactics to instantly turn the tables on an enemy coming in from behind. But in practice, pilots surprisingly disliked special maneuvers like these.

Actually using these unique and irregular maneuvers created intense g-forces that strained the soldiers' bodies. They already had to deal with a lack of blood flowing to the brain, which impaired their judgment. If they started swinging the nose around and distorting their own vision on top of that…Even if the unorthodox moves did allow them to get behind the enemy, it ran the risk of a really stupid ending: giving their prey a chance to escape before they could mount any kind of counterattack.

However.

The HsF-00's nose wasn't pointed forward to begin with. It would move forward with its body turned ninety degrees and whirl in circles like a spinning top. The way it moved cast doubt on the very assumption that it was a plane at all. It was one thing that the plane didn't shatter into a thousand pieces, but the fact that a living pilot was inside was even more startling.

And on top of all that, the enemy's attacks were precise.

The missiles it fired could swerve many times harder than hers as it chased its target. The machine-gun bullets seemed to fly unerringly into her comrades' wings. And to make matters worse, the craft was even using what appeared to be lasers. Her wingmen had been shot down, one after another, by attacks they had no idea how to evade.

Plus...

"Ahem, hello, can you hear me? This is Ryuuta Kameyama of the Academy City Air Defense Team. Technically, I'm with Anti-Skill—meaning I'm a schoolteacher—but I'm a soldier by trade, so there's no need to feel much guilt about locking onto me or anything. Actually, in my case, I wanted to be an Air Defense pilot to begin with, but there was an issue with my position in Academy City, so I'm just using my teaching license for some necessary certification. That's all."

...She was receiving the enemy's carefree transmissions.

"Now that I've introduced myself, I'll get to the point. I set the missiles' proximity fuse to detonate a fair distance away— Are you still okay? I thought it was a pretty imaginative idea myself, so that you could all eject with your parachutes."

"Augh!! Are you making fools of us, you bastard...?!"

Ekalielya, missing the fact that their radio encryption had been very easily decoded, flew into a rage in spite of herself. The man over the radio, however, paused after a moment of confusion, until he said:

"Damn, is that a lady pilot? I mean, I've heard smaller people get knocked around less by the g-forces, but...Sheesh. Now I really can't bring myself to shoot you down."

Her opponent was basically declaring that he could kill her at any time if he wanted to.

It was a bully's way of doing things: flaunt strange, unknown tech, then scorn those who didn't understand it as primitive savages. The man's bearing made it seem as though he was a refined gentleman, too, which made that overbearing attitude even more conspicuous.

But no matter how much rage seethed within her, it wouldn't make up for the difference in power. Ekalielya's plane couldn't touch the Academy City HsF-00. It was like the Wright brothers' biplane trying to chase down a modern jet fighter.

"Damn this giant-ass fly! I hope the g-forces grind you to dust already!! What kind of pilot doesn't just up and die after all those insane moves?!"

"Well, it's really nothing special. The important bit is that human flesh can't withstand combat maneuvers above a certain speed, right? That's a simple problem. If you can increase your body's durability, that'll let you handle way bigger and faster machines."

"…?"

"My body is currently frozen at negative seventy degrees Celsius. There's a life support device standing in for my internal organs. With this setup, the only thing rolling is my brain's decision-making power. I'm even leaving part of the calculations to the machine; it detects subtle electric currents from my scalp and uses those to direct the plane…Get it? With my hardened body, I can overcome the natural limits dictated by inertia. Well, according to medical professionals, we have to be real careful about half-assing the freezing tech so that it freezes the pilot's body but leaves their ability to think."

A shudder ripped through Ekalielya.

It felt like she'd caught a glimpse of a *fundamental* difference between them.

"Anyway, now that my boring explanation is over, I'll get to the point."

A moment after the assertion, the HsF-00's silhouette began to shift.

Ga-gong!!

The upper sections of its giant main wings detached and fell in behind it, flying like small birds. There were about ten in all. Thin wires or something seemed to be attached to them, and each flitted about independently like stunt kites.

"*These are laser units, meant to penetrate an enemy from many directions at once,*" said the pilot named Kameyama, turning the aircraft and swinging the tiny weapons around like morning stars.

Clear relaxation and contempt crept into his tone. "*You can't run from the speed of light. I'll shoot you down real gentle, young lady, so get ready.*"

CHAPTER 1

Immigration of Good and Evil
World_War_III.

1

October 30.
Even the digital display showing the date seemed to be shivering in the cold.

The car's heater was almost completely busted. Driving a beat-up junker across the snow-covered landscape, Shiage Hamazura felt the chill seeping into his hands gripping the steering wheel. No matter how far they went, there was nothing. Just vast, flat land. The perfunctory asphalt road was buried with snow, too, and mostly invisible. There was so little to go on that if he drove off the road, he probably wouldn't even realize it.

This wasn't a sight that could be had in Japan.

He'd heard the Hokkaido area had some pretty expansive stretches of land, but probably nothing comparable.

It was like a white desert.

This was a western region of Russia.

Apparently, they were close to the border with the Elizalina Alliance of Independent Nations.

In order to escape their Academy City pursuers, they'd ridden a supersonic passenger jet on autopilot to the foreign country. The situation hadn't afforded them much time to prepare, so they had almost no escape funds.

...I can't complain because this thing is stolen, but...Shit. Maybe it's not about whether the air conditioning is working right—maybe our clothes are fundamentally wrong for this. You need way more cold-weather gear here than in Japan...

The car's paint was peeling in places, revealing the brown rust underneath. As he held its steering wheel, Hamazura stole a glance at the passenger seat beside him.

A girl, on the short side and wearing a pink tracksuit, was sitting there.

Rikou Takitsubo.

A girl whose body had been ravaged by the side effects of a drug-like substance called Crystals. Even now, she was limp in her seat, sweating profusely as though suffering from a fever. Hamazura wanted to get her to a doctor as soon as he could, but he knew it wasn't happening. Crystals were top secret for Academy City. Even if he brought Takitsubo to an *outside* doctor, they'd have no way of knowing how to cure her.

These two were on the run.

From the one thing that could have saved her: Academy City.

...There's no way we can fight Academy City alone. Besides, if we completely wrecked it, we'd lose the tech we need to cure Takitsubo. However this shakes out, we'll have to eventually go back to the City and rely on its tech to save her.

However, if they put up their hands and returned to the City like this, neither would win any freedom. The possibility that they'd be killed wasn't low either. Which meant Hamazura had to come up with a plan to guarantee their safety.

...So this is how our fight will go. While we're fleeing through Russia, we find something and use it as a bargaining chip. We advance the talks so it's as beneficial to us as possible until we reach a stage where they'll definitely cure Takitsubo. That's our only option.

"Hamazura. What's wrong?"

"Nothing," he replied with a reassuring grin. "...Was just thinking

we'll need money no matter what we decide to do here. What little we had on us when we left the City won't get us far. It's not Russian currency, either, so we won't be able to use it right away. We'll have to *find* money somewhere."

Selling the stolen car he was driving right now was an option, but Hamazura didn't think it was a very good idea. It wasn't that easy to tell which dealers were shady enough to take a stolen vehicle. If he were still in Academy City, things might have been different, but he didn't know what it was like in Russia.

Besides, he didn't know much Russian. If someone witnessed Asian people speaking Japanese in these parts while they were embroiled in their big war, that alone might be enough to cause major issues.

Which left them with…

"We'll have to steal. Time for a robbery."

"That's…" Takitsubo hesitated.

But that was their only choice.

As if in response to their decision, a small store came into sight in front of them. It was connected to a gas station. They probably sold nonperishables in cans and the like for people driving long distances.

"Wait here," he said to Takitsubo, parking the car a short distance away from the store.

"I'll go earn us real cash."

…Saying it was easy, but Hamazura was actually pretty worried.

First off, this wasn't Japan. The guns didn't work the same way. He had a small handgun on him, but it was possible anyone they set upon would have their own for self-defense—or maybe even a rifle.

To add to that—

It's wartime right now.

Ever since Takitsubo translated a Russian broadcast on the radio for him earlier, Hamazura's head had been filled with words that felt highly surreal.

For Russians, we're the greatest enemy of all. If anyone even suspects that we came from Academy City, we could get thrashed.

War.

That was what they were saying, but the word wasn't clicking for him. For Hamazura, the horrors of war were something that only ever happened in distant places or something that he would hear about from time to time on TV news, but apparently, it was happening all across the world now. It didn't feel real—maybe because there was no time for the news to sink in since they had been preoccupied with fleeing Academy City, or it could have been because they hadn't encountered the misfortune of finding themselves on a battlefield crisscrossed by bullets and artillery shells yet. Academy City had apparently dispatched forces that were assisting in the evacuation of friendly institutions and protecting various facilities inside Russia's borders…but even hearing that news over the car radio wasn't enough to give him a sense of danger.

He didn't know what was going to happen from here on out. But to be honest, Hamazura didn't care who won or who lost, or which side would next grab ahold of the world's reins. As long as this ridiculous war ended as soon as possible and someone who would protect them ended up with those reins, he hardly cared about anything that might happen afterward.

…That summed up most of his thoughts on the matter, but the war actually wasn't his number one concern. In fact, it was quite possible he was only thinking about the war because he didn't want to face *it*—his number one concern.

That he had to rob a store with a clerk in it.

This excuse may have been incredibly self-centered, but this was altogether different than jacking a car or an ATM. Every time he thought about situations where he'd possibly need to use his weapon, he could feel something heavy settling into his stomach.

He checked the safety on the small handgun in his pocket several times, thinking, *I will not, I will absolutely not hurt the shopkeeper! All I need is what's in the register. I'll just hold the guy at gunpoint. Warning shots only after I point the barrel up!*

He repeated what he needed to do in his mind and, in the end, casually prayed for something vague. Right before entering the store, he pulled his parka hood down low and put on a pair of gloves that were in the stolen car.

He opened the door and, at the same time, drew his pistol.

I will not! I will not hurt the clerk!!

And then he saw them.

The female cashier, hands and feet tied with duct tape, trying to speak through her bound mouth.

The man, with a mask like a pro wrestler, pushing her to the floor and holding a knife to her neck.

The man was large, over six feet tall, and he wasn't alone. There were three criminals in total, and when they saw Hamazura open the narrow door, one said something in Russian.

<"Who are you?">

Hamazura, who couldn't understand it, simply replied with the Japanese words he'd prepared beforehand.

"This is a robbery. Hands in the air."

Bang-bang-ba-bang!! Takitsubo heard several gunshots fire in quick succession.

When she turned to look from her passenger seat in the stolen car, she spotted Shiage Hamazura leaving the store and heading her way. It seemed like the robbery was over. He was holding several large beige paper bags in either hand. They must have been filled with a lot of food—a long baguette was sticking out of one bag, and she could see the edges of what looked like a knit scarf and a rolled-up coat in another.

As Hamazura opened the driver's side door and climbed in, Takitsubo asked, "Hamazura. Did it work?"

"The clerk was, like, super-thankful, and she gave me all sorts of free gifts!! She even said she'd fill the car's tank, too!!"

"?"

With a confused Takitsubo inside, the stolen car started moving again.

2

Accelerator was stowed away on a freight train.

The Trans-Federation Railroad.

It was the world's longest railroad. Spanning the entire Eurasian continent, it normally took over two weeks to run from its first station to the last stop. But right now, this specific time, seemed to be an exception. The commencement of World War III made it necessary to transport large quantities of military materiel. Trains were completely ignoring their normal schedules and also traveling at high speeds that disregarded safety regulations.

Either they'd been preparing for this for a while now or they'd pulled out a prototype from a research lab somewhere. The freight train Accelerator was on traveled at over five hundred kilometers per hour—fast enough to rival Maglev trains. The leading car was cone shaped like a fighter jet or space shuttle, and the cars' walls were textured, like the latest competitive low-drag swimsuits.

War... What nonsense.

For a time, Accelerator gave thought to the possibility that the recent hostilities were part of an Academy City machination to chase down Last Order and him, but eventually he came to the conclusion that he was definitely too paranoid. Acts that were *this* conspicuous weren't Academy City's style, which he knew from having worked in its underworld until just the other day. In fact, he was sure they preferred doing things in ways that would keep their dirty laundry as low profile as possible.

They'd put on quite a show in a French city called Avignon, but there must have been *something* that'd forced them to do so, though he didn't know exactly what that something would have been.

However...

...Putting aside whether that shithole Academy City plotted all this,

I still can't deny the possibility that they have some ulterior motive in all this.

Academy City's influence was vast. Normally, they would have taken decisive action before things had escalated to a large-scale conflict. And yet, now there was a war that threatened to bring down the entire science-dominated world. It wasn't bizarre to assume something significant had happened.

What's more, Academy City had answered the provocations. Maybe there was something they wanted so badly that they were willing to go to war.

None of that mattered to Accelerator, though. At the moment, that wasn't the most pressing matter for him.

Damn it...

It was the fact that he wasn't alone.

Next to him was a girl who looked like she was around ten.

Last Order.

A clone made from the somatic cells of the third-ranked Level Five. She'd been used to cause a monster called Aiwass to manifest into the world; an act which was now putting a major burden on her brain. She couldn't even walk around freely because of it, and even now, she was lying there limply.

She always wore a button-down shirt over a camisole, but right now she had a thick blanket on top of all that. It had been in the freight train. Accelerator had found mostly white winter clothes, which he'd taken for himself and put on.

"...Where are we? asks Misaka asks Misaka, looking around."

"On a train."

"What about what about Yomikawa? asks Misaka asks Misaka."

"Not here right now. But you'll see her soon. I promise."

"Okay..." Last Order's words cut off for a moment. "If we were all together, Yomikawa could have made stewed Salisbury steak again, says Misaka says Misaka, kinda disappointed."

"..."

"But this is okay, says Misaka says Misaka, relieved. I finally got to see your face again after so long, says Misaka says Misaka, reaching her hand out."

So she said, but her small hand didn't move.

Her fingertips merely trembled and shook in place.

Whether or not she realized this, Last Order continued: "Let's all have dinner together again, suggests Misaka suggests Misaka. Yomikawa's stew was really good, brags Misaka brags Misaka."

Though she smiled, it looked painful for her just to speak.

...*How did it come to this?* Accelerator, hunched into a ball, clenched his teeth. *What did this brat ever do? Was it bad enough that she deserved to end up like this? She can't even move her own fingers. Why does this kid have to go through this shit?*

The only sound he could hear was the unpleasant creaking every time his jaw grew firmer.

There was no freedom or safety for her here.

Accelerator harbored an intense rage toward something—a vague sense of fate that permeated the world. He knew it wasn't a matter of hating someone in particular. But he still couldn't help but feel angry.

His hand gripped his modern-design crutch handle hard enough to crush it.

A global-scale war had begun. All kinds of people from nations around the world were probably fighting for what was important to each of them.

But.

There was nobody to fight for her.

People across the entire planet were ready to fight with their lives on the line, but not a single person stood up to rescue Last Order, who hadn't done anything wrong.

"...It's bullshit...," murmured Accelerator.

He'd come this far in order to fight against how unreasonable that was. One girl, destined to be destroyed in the process of some plan someone had concocted...To save her, to fight against her cruel fate, Accelerator had thrown away his position, his pride, and everything else to come to Russia.

Go to Russia.

Aiwass—the rule-breaking entity who had once thoroughly thrashed Accelerator—had told him to go there. If he could find something in that place, he might be able to save Last Order.

He didn't know what was supposed to be in this country.

It wasn't even clear how much of what Aiwass said could be trusted.

But.

...I'll do it. Accelerator quietly hardened his resolve...*Either way, I knew I couldn't save the brat if we stayed in Academy City. That means I have to look for other ways. The blabber that came out of Aiwass's mouth doesn't even matter.*

Accelerator was Academy City's top-ranked Level Five. Last Order was a unique specimen that formed the core of an Academy City project. It was possible that Russia would treat them like a threatening strategic weapon and an object of crucial military value. But he didn't care about any of that, either. He wasn't entirely happy that someone might mistake them for agents of that rotten city, but he didn't need to clear up every single misunderstanding. Right now, he had one goal. If anyone got in the way, no matter the reason, he'd smash them to pieces and keep on charging.

Just then—

Grr-gam!! He heard a noise from overhead.

It sounded like thick metal being dented.

The freight train container had probably warped. Accelerator looked up as the noise happened a second time, then a third.

It wasn't just this car.

Even the sound of the train on the tracks wasn't enough to muffle this strange sound, and he heard it coming from various other spots on the train as well. Not only from the ceiling, either—he heard it from the walls and underneath the floor, too.

At the same time, there was an angry shout in Russian and then several gunshots.

The shouts quickly became screams.

Accelerator deduced that someone had jumped onto the freight train during its high-speed transit. There were only so many who could jump onto a vehicle going over five hundred kilometers per hour.

Academy City.

…They've come for us.

"What's wrong? asks Misaka asks Misaka."

He heard a little girl's tiny voice.

Slowly, Accelerator examined Last Order, who was lying on the floor. Number One took a handkerchief out of Last Order's pocket, folded it up, and laid it over her eyes.

To prevent her from seeing a world filled with blood.

"…Nothing," he said, reaching for his electrode collar.

This was the switch that would let him wield his power as Academy City's strongest monster.

"Please don't get in fights like that again, asks Misaka asks Misaka."

"…Yeah, I promise," he said curtly, lying to cut off the conversation.

Normally, Last Order could have severed his connection to the Misaka network and taken all his power. And yet, nothing happened. Did that mean she couldn't even perform a simple action like that in her current state?

Lingering for a moment, Accelerator peered down into Last Order's blindfolded face.

Eventually, he quietly got to his feet.

…To smash every last person who could possibly pose a threat to that little girl's life.

Bam!!

A moment later, Accelerator's slim body flew up, tearing through the steel ceiling and jumping onto the freight train roof.

After seeing the young man appear from the fissure, which now looked like torn vinyl, the assailants backed away a little. They had been atop the freight train, buffeted by incredible gusts of wind.

White powered suits.

Soldiers, all armed with the same equipment. About ten in all.

In contrast to their surprisingly slim upper bodies, their legs were extremely thick. Special models, probably, designed purely for assisting movement. They could obviously move swiftly, but they'd also be outfitted with all the necessary mechanisms to maintain proper balance and soften impacts to compensate for the increased speed.

There was a large variety of powered suits, ranging from those designed for construction work to disaster rescue models. The military ones used for the invasion of Avignon seemed to have been deployed to Russia, too, probably because they were in the middle of a newly hatched World War. However, the models facing Accelerator were clearly different: It was as if their designers had completely ignored development or maintenance costs in favor of simply aiming for the absolute best thing possible. The bigwigs who had dispatched this team must have really wanted this operation to succeed.

Though he was surrounded by heavy weaponry, Accelerator didn't waver.

He looked around with shining red eyes, then spoke softly to himself.

"…You're trash. And you're really getting under my skin."

A Russian soldier trembled with fear.

He had never gone through the harsh training to prepare him for a fight on the front lines. Logistics was his specialty—making sure the supplies necessary for war got where they needed to go. But despite that, he was still a soldier. His resolve wasn't so fragile that he'd hesitate when a gun was pointed at him.

But the scene unfolding before his eyes wasn't something so mundane.

Terrifying white machine soldiers had suddenly jumped onto the freight train.

And then—

An unknown monster with white hair and red eyes destroyed them all with one attack.

Roofs were broken. Walls were blown off. Intense winds were coming in through the gaps. Several machine soldiers were kicked outside. A container car, made of steel at least two inches thick, ripped apart like paper by mere human limbs. This was no regular feat. He knew about Japan's Academy City scientific development of supernatural powers, but seeing it up close and personal was an entirely different story.

"Tsk. That wasn't enough to kill you?" muttered the monster, peering outside. That was all he said after kicking people off a train running over five hundred kilometers per hour. This wasn't an issue of identifying which was the monster. Neither was in any way normal.

The monster checked around.

A moment later, a wall separating two freight train cars tore open, and a giant machine soldier jumped through. It had appeared directly to the monster's side—but the white creature wasn't bothered. It waved a hand, and the mechanical soldier's armor, which weighed who knew what, was blasted into bits and blown away.

Something the machine soldiers had been carrying was lying at the monster's feet.

Probably loot that had been stolen earlier.

The object was a suitcase made of duralumin. The battered remains of handcuffs were hanging off the handle. It had originally been attached to the Russian soldier's wrist, but a flick of one machine soldier's finger had easily torn the chain off.

The monster headed for the suitcase, but the Russian soldier couldn't stop it.

If the monster turned its attention toward him, he was sure he'd die. It was like he'd been thrown into a small cage with a predator.

The suitcase was locked, but the monster opened it as easily as one might open a wallet. Or rather, it *was supposed to* have had a lock on it—but the monster had used brute force to crush the locking mechanism itself.

"...What's this?" muttered the creature.

The Russian soldier hadn't been told what was inside. And what came out of it were dozens of parchment pages. On them were inscriptions written in old ink, bringing to mind eerie curses or magic circles.

It was a meaningless sham. Some people might have held vague anticipations or anxiety toward magic charms. But would they think that following the instructions would actually cause a crazy demon to emerge in real life? For example, if a murder occurred and an eyewitness seriously claimed that a demon did it, what would everyone else think?

However...

The military's higher-ups probably hadn't ordered him to carry a handcuffed suitcase stuffed with something useless in it. And machine soldiers that looked like they were from Academy City had come for it...

What is going on here? thought the Russian soldier.

Had Academy City fallen for a diversionary tactic concocted by Russian officers?

Or...

Was the parchment in that suitcase actually so valuable that an Academy City special forces team would do everything in their power to steal it?

"...That's interesting," muttered the monster to itself.

An insane smile rose to the creature's lips—and that, above all else, seemed to be a sign for the Russian soldier that it wasn't just any ordinary parchment.

"This operation was as important as recovering me, Academy City's strongest Level Five...Can't exactly see the effects yet, but this might be connected to those *other laws* that shithead was talking about."

3

And Touma Kamijou was in Russia as well.

It was late October, but everything around him was already

covered in white snow. A few centimeters of accumulation wasn't enough to completely stop public transportation, but it was rough on his basketball shoes and feet. There were spots where the stuff had melted into cold water that soaked through his shoes, and a stinging chill tormented his fingers.

He was wearing his school uniform. Normally, that would have been inconvenient, but now, he was actually impressed at the wide scope of environments that it could handle…Of course, maybe that was because it used Academy City–made textile technology. He certainly would have been happier to have a coat, but he couldn't ask for luxuries in a situation like this.

War…

It was a word that was hard to process if someone suddenly brought it up. According to Queen Elizard of England, the way this happened was "unnatural," even after taking into account current international politics. If it was likely that the Roman Orthodox Church and Russian Catholic Church were cooperating behind the scenes, then did that mean Fiamma of the Right was the true mastermind pulling all the strings?

Was that really all there was to it?

The officially stated reason was simple, and it would be easy to cling to that, accepting it at face value. But didn't Academy City seem way too eager to answer with military force? They'd dispatched huge amounts of troops and unmanned weapons into Russia as soon as the war started. Almost like they'd been preparing for this for years…

What was actually happening backstage?

Kamijou was close to the center of this war, but he was just a high school student. He couldn't figure out anything about what was going on beyond the surface.

But.

If stopping Fiamma would stave off the war for now, he could see what he needed to do. Besides, stopping that man's plans was linked to an extremely personal reason Kamijou had for fighting.

A certain girl named Index.

She had the special trait of having completely memorized 103,000 grimoires, but other than that, she was a totally normal girl. And someone was after her vast stores of knowledge.

Fiamma of the Right.

He had stolen the Soul Arm needed to freely extract the knowledge from Index at a distance. When he activated it, Index's mind and body had suffered immense strain, and she fell into unconsciousness.

In order to save her, Kamijou needed to defeat Fiamma as fast as he could and destroy the remote-control Soul Arm.

That was why he'd come all the way to Russia, where Fiamma of the Right was apparently hiding out, but...

"...Why are you here again, Lesser?" Kamijou asked heavily.

Some might have understandably stared blankly when hearing the name *Lesser*. She was a member of a British sorcerer's society reserve force called New Light. When the second princess, Carissa, had used the Curtana Original to initiate a coup d'état, they were the ones who had secretly dug up the Curtana and transported it to her.

Her skin was white, and her stature short. She was probably somewhere in her teens. Her long black hair was tied into braids at the tips. Her outfit consisted of a jacket on top of a lacrosse uniform, but the thing that stood out most was probably the "tail" coming out from her rear. It was like a flat chain running through a clear tube. After adding in the arrowhead-like tip at the end, she had a somewhat mischievous air about her.

When they'd met before, Kamijou was pretty sure it had been as enemies.

Those ill feelings had faded once the coup d'état ended, but that didn't make her unexpected presence in Russia any more sensible.

Lesser, while swinging the tail she was so proud of left and right, replied to her companion's reasonable question.

"Hmm? Well, it's not because the British royal family ordered me to, or because I have a grudge against Fiamma of the Right, or because I want to be part of the Kamijou faction, or anything like that."

Her tone was incredibly offhand.

"But if you dying here would be against the United Kingdom's interests as a whole, then we figured we might as well be supporting you...I wonder if it's okay to say *we*? Bayloupe might grab my butt again..."

In the middle of her response, she fell into talking-to-herself mode...He'd gotten a sense of it when they first met, but Kamijou deduced she had some extremely self-centered thought processes.

Without a care for whatever Kamijou might think of her, a mean smile made its way onto her youthful face. "Well, you can just think of it as the two of us using each other. Considering you can use a pro sorceress for combat, it's not a bad deal for you, is it?"

"...I forget, but are you even that strong? I seem to remember you fleeing all over London that night with a weird bag in your hand."

"Shall I send you flying to prove it? Necessarius can't give you any backup, right? Maybe you should value me a little bit more. Oh, yes—when it comes to purely using the Jarngreipr, I'm better than Bayloupe. As long as there's no Gjallarhorn involved, I'll never lose," said Lesser, adding that she wouldn't be able to whine if it was a real fight. "Also!! These Steel Gloves have been powered up!! Ta-daa—the Lesser Special Custom! Red laser things shoot out from the tips, see, and these bladed fingers can grab anything they're not touching, no matter how far away it is, and swing it around!!"

"...I didn't ask for any of that..."

"You really don't think I'll be of any use in a fight, do you? Maybe it's because the coup d'état came off as so flashy in comparison...," muttered Lesser, downcast, before apparently deciding to appeal in a different area. "Besides, it would be easier for you in a lot of ways to have someone who can speak Russian translate for you, right?"

"Wait, before all that, I snuck into Russia in secret. How did you get that information...?"

Right after the coup d'état had ended, he'd told Elizard and Stiyl he'd be going to Russia, but he never gave them a concrete method or schedule for it. How did Lesser know where he'd be despite that?

Actually, as someone who had marched into Russia alone without telling anyone, suddenly meeting up with a friend was pretty pathetic. Maybe this wasn't the time to be saying such things, but he still couldn't help feeling that way.

Lesser seemed to pick up on Kamijou's troubled face. "Ha-ha. Were you feeling guilty about Index, asleep in the cathedral in London? You said you'd do your best to save her and everything, and the very first thing you do is meet up with another woman."

"Guh...?!"

"And now I have a piece of welcome information for you. I, Lesser, do indeed have a tail coming out of my skirt—but to tell the truth, I'm not wearing leggings under there. I'm only wearing panties."

"What do you expect me to do with useless information like that?!"

"Go behind me!! And flip it!! Forget about all your old flames!!"

"Everything you're saying warrants me punching you in the nose, you know!!" shouted Kamijou, blue veins popping on his temples.

But Lesser, without responding or giving up, cheerfully swung her tail around and asked, "Besides, how are you going to look for Fiamma of the Right in this big country?"

She made it sound like she suspected he didn't have any clue what to do.

"Russia is really big, you know. It basically connects the Eurasian continent from west to east in a straight line, and not many countries have more than nine time zones. This place seems far too large to randomly bump into a particular person."

"Or so you'd think."

"?" Lesser gave the unexpected answer a blank look.

In response, Kamijou said, "...How many sorcerers do you think I've fought until now? At this point, I'm slowly getting used to how they do things."

4

The Strait of Dover.

A thirty-kilometer-wide waterway between the United Kingdom and France.

A sea full of bloody history, and a place that became a crucial strategic point whenever the two countries' relations worsened, ever since long ago. And that sea was once again about to guzzle the blood of many lives.

"Puritans and Knights' combined-force deployment complete."

Kaori Kanzaki nodded quietly in response to the voice.

At the moment, they weren't standing on land. They were on a boat.

Giant hundred-meter sailboats made of wood dotted the sea. All were magically reinforced ships, tougher than normal warships and with greater maneuverability to boot.

One could call it a strange sight to behold. Not about the sight of so many sailboats, but that a war between sorcerers had escalated into something so massive.

"Times really have changed, haven't they?" Agnes Sanctis asked from where she stood next to Kanzaki.

The petite young woman held her palm above her brow as if in a clumsy salute as she looked out over the water. "I hear they're calling the coup d'état in Britain the *British Halloween*. And they're treating it like one of the world's seven great mysteries, like Nessie and the Nazca Lines. People sure are tough, eh? It might not be something they can understand logically, but they'll accept it eventually, even if time is the only thing pushing them."

"Though it doesn't appear that any have realized it was actually due to something called sorcery." Kanzaki slowly sighed. "Besides, the fact that Japan's Academy City is scientifically developing strange supernatural powers is somewhat known. The principles are completely different, but it means people have just a little bit of tolerance. They'll figure that something like it exists somewhere out there, so maybe it was actually close at hand."

Though as she said that, she could feel something tugging at her, deep in her throat. To stabilize the faction that they called the sorcery side, general awareness of the science side had been a big help. If not, there might have been a much more severe panic. Something had burrowed its way inside without anyone knowing, and it had Kanzaki a little on guard.

"In any case," she said, trying to change the topic, "if they get through us here, it's a straight line to London. I'd like to avoid skirmishes as much as possible, but if the French faction attacks, we must hold the line at all costs."

"But we know they're basically one hundred percent coming, right?" replied the small nun in command of her own unit, sniffing. "The UK and France were in an extremely dangerous and tense situation even before the coup broke out...And though I am absolutely loath to admit it, it's all thanks to the elites in the Roman Orthodox Church. It was already a hotbed, and then World War III broke out. Plus we're getting glimpses of Roman Orthodox and Russian Catholic shadows behind it. France *not* attacking the UK is an impossibility, eh? Can't say whether it'll be Orthodox vanguards or if France will try to put an end to the historical and magical conflicts between it and Britain, though."

It happened just as Agnes was speaking: She received a transmission from Agatha, a nun working under her.

"Intervention confirmed from the French side!! They're on their way— Please take caution!!"

A moment later:

All at once, the waters of Dover, locked perpetually in gentle waves, hardened everywhere past the French national border. It was like ice was spreading in the blink of an eye, cracking as it froze over the seawater.

"Salt?!"

"Rotten bastards. It looks like their plan is to give themselves suitable footing while robbing our ships of their mobility!"

Shadows ran like arrows.

Not just one or two, either.

More than a hundred—perhaps a thousand—sorcerers were running across the hardened white waters in a straight line from the French border toward Kanzaki and the others. At this rate, it would be a slaughter. Like orcas forced up onto land and made into fodder for a murder of crows, they would be crushed.

If their ships were rendered useless, over half the combat force Kanzaki and the others had assembled would essentially be eliminated.

But they couldn't roll over without a fight.

The Born Again Amakusa-Style Crossist Church's sorcerers, Kanzaki first and foremost, excelled in close-quarters combat. They jumped down from their ships, moving to intercept the French sorcerers.

And then Kanzaki noticed something strange at her feet.

"?!"

Hastily, she jumped to the side.

A big hole suddenly opened up in the salty ground she'd just been standing on. If she'd been a split-second late, she'd have fallen into the sea. And had she been robbed of her ability to move, they would have undoubtedly focused their attacks on her.

…*We knew we'd have to fight them with all our strength already, but if it's going to be like this, too…?!*

Now that the ships couldn't move, staying on them would be disadvantageous.

But alighting onto the salt ground would give their opponents the initiative.

It was a difficult situation no matter the case, but then—

"Is this all it takes to make you flinch? I thought you were a force to protect our United Kingdom."

A woman's voice rang out, overflowing with an intimidating presence.

A moment later, a thin film spread over the salty ground as though coating it over. This time, it wasn't from France's side.

The phenomenon widened in one breath to cover the entire sea, encroaching upon France from the UK's side.

They'd secured their footing.

Kanzaki tightly gripped her sheath, and the sheath sent over twenty French sorcerers trying to surround her flying into the air.

As it happened, Kanzaki looked toward the woman's voice.

She was standing there.

Clothed in a scarlet dress—their nation's second princess.

5

Fiamma of the Right.

Leader of God's Right Seat, a secret Roman Orthodox organization. The Church was said to preside over two billion followers worldwide, and naturally, he'd been the one manipulating its various branches.

However, Vento of the Front, Terra of the Left, and Acqua of the Back—the other members of God's Right Seat—had been defeated one after another or had otherwise voluntarily parted ways with the organization.

At a time like that, in order to replenish the diminished combat strength, what would *he* try to take advantage of?

Specifically, within the Roman Orthodox–Russian Catholic alliance?

"And what I came up with was: the Russian army," said Kamijou as he walked through the snow. "Obviously, Fiamma doesn't think of anyone as a friend. Maybe he only wants to use them like a bulwark, something that'll buy him some time so his own plans don't get interrupted. But he'll exploit everything he can. If he wants free rein in Russia, it would be easier and look more natural to move around people already in Russia instead of inserting a Roman Orthodox group. Which means that if you keep track of where the Russian army goes, you're bound to catch a glimpse of Fiamma's shadow. If we keep tabs on whatever's odd about the military's movements, we'll run into him."

"You were saying Fiamma entered Russia to look for Sasha Kreutzev, right?" Lesser asked.

"I don't know why," admitted Kamijou, honestly holding up the white flag at the question, "but if that was *really* all he wanted to do, then he wouldn't have a reason to go to Russia personally."

"Huh?"

The notion seemed to overturn the very premise.

"Fiamma could have simply given orders to the Russian army and the Russian Catholic Church and made them search this huge country. He could have sat in an armchair by a fireplace and waited for results. But he didn't."

"Which means...he's after something else, too?"

"Something he has to be there for personally, like to touch it or something."

As Lesser listened to what her traveling companion was saying, she peered at his face.

She couldn't quite tell if he was stupid or smart, but she had to admit that kind of judgment probably came down to a matter of specialization. The boy couldn't show how insightful he was unless it was on a very limited scope, like a jigsaw puzzle, where he had to fit pieces together. People good at video games had reflexes and kinetic vision, but in other fields—like hand-to-hand combat, for instance—they couldn't put those skills to good use. His case was most likely something similar.

In fact, it was more than likely...

For him, the girl sleeping in that cathedral in London was probably a "piece" of the puzzle.

"But we're in the middle of World War III right now, remember? Military operations are happening all over Russia, big and small. They probably didn't expect China and India to side with Academy City, either, so they panicked and sent troops there, too. How can you pinpoint exactly which of those things are connected to Fiamma, out of all that chaos?"

"Fiamma would definitely try to hide his plans," Kamijou answered. "He would take advantage of the Russian army but keep it a secret from them. Any missions that seem perfectly reasonable at first glance but then reveal a completely different nature after a tiny change in perspective, like with an optical illusion—those are the suspicious ones...For example, an operation where mixing in the word *magic* seems like it would cause some wild chemical reaction."

"And that's what led you here?"

"If it didn't, I wouldn't have come all this way," muttered Kamijou, setting his sights beyond the white snow-filled scenery.

"...Wait for me."

6

The Elizalina Alliance of Independent Nations.

Several nations that had rebelled against Russian hegemony and gained independence had formed this alliance. Like the EU, it had a common currency, and the passage of citizens and goods among its member countries didn't require a passport.

From a Russian standpoint, this alliance was a thorn in their side, and even before the war, they'd always considered invading if they could find a casus belli. And now, with the present turmoil distracting everyone, that opportunity had arrived.

"It seems like the Russian army is trying to set up a base near the border," said Lesser, possibly having gathered information from nearby residents beforehand. "Their basic composition is all-in-one vehicles armed with missile launchers and grenade launchers. It looks like they're planning to lob explosives into the Alliance borders from thirty or forty kilometers away."

If they had a range of forty kilometers, that meant their weapons could reach an area that was larger than all of Japan's Academy City combined. Plus, those armored vehicles would be deployed not only inside the base but around it, too, making their actual attack range as a whole twice, possibly even three times that of the nominal number.

"But that's not what they're really after."

"..."

"If they seriously wanted to bomb Alliance territory, they would ask the air force to lend a helping hand and use attack fighters or bombers. Then they could virtually ignore firing range entirely. They'd be able to instantly turn every last patch of ground into a sea of flames...They're trying to use weapon specs as a distraction. Those bases were never actually needed in the first place."

And then it happened.

Greeeeee!! A shrill roar passed them by overhead. The sound was different than a normal passenger plane—it was unique to supersonic speeds.

However, the source wasn't the engine of a Russian Air Force military craft.

It was the opposite. Hostile supersonic bombers made in Academy City were tearing through the Russian sky. That being said, their current goal wasn't to set cities on fire but apparently to drop supplies and weapons, one after another, for constructing bases directly on the Russian mainland.

Normally, airborne units weren't used like that.

True, if it was possible to airdrop everything into the middle of enemy territory and build a stronghold there, that would provide clear advantages...but only if those strongholds could be maintained. In practice, it would be nigh impossible to secure the land routes needed to transport large amounts of goods, so even if such a fortress was created, it would become isolated in a very short time.

But Academy City had solved this problem with brute force.

Their supersonic bombers could rip through the skies at over seven thousand kilometers per hour. Boldly passing over the Russian military's air defense network, outrunning any interception aircraft with overwhelming speed. The planes were monsters, and they swiftly but surely supplied the strongholds with a huge, steady stream of goods. Thanks to that, hastily constructed Academy City strongholds already dotted the vast Russian nation.

"That really is something," said Lesser as she beheld this technology of a world far removed from her own, sounding somehow laid-back. "Did you hear? When Russia declared war, Academy City apparently said they didn't have any reason to fight, but that it wasn't right to stay silent if there was a way to stop the conflict. If we're purely comparing each side's weapon strength, Academy City probably isn't too worried about their matchups."

Kamijou was silent for a moment at Lesser's remark, but eventually, he offered, "...Wouldn't Russia want to shoot down those big aircraft at any cost? They're insanely strong and keep scattering enemy weapons around." While looking up at the military aircraft passing through the air every twenty or thirty minutes, he said, "Even cats and dogs would know from the engine sound that this place is a major avenue. Despite that, the Russian base only has surface weapons and no runways for jets, right? I haven't even seen many Russian jets. Something's off."

Was the conviction in Kamijou's statement because he belonged to the science side?

Lesser was technically a combat professional herself, but when it came to science-based warfare, she didn't have much insight to add.

"How did you figure that out?"

"From a map," said Kamijou, showing her a folded-up paper map that could be bought anywhere.

Lesser frowned. "You can figure that out just by looking at a map?"

"No. It's not like I'm a professional soldier. As if I could possibly figure out what's going on behind the scenes just by looking at army formations." He shook the folded map. "If a seriously important military operation was going on, they wouldn't be selling maps like this in the first place. In fact, they're apparently rounding them all up in a bunch of other regions. But there weren't any restrictions like that in this area. It was oddly easy to get, given the scope of the base. They don't want people to think the base is important. They loosened the security on purpose. But that was why it stood out."

"Oh," said Lesser, her reaction not quite making it clear whether she was impressed or not really listening at all. "Does that mean Fiamma is in that base?"

"Actually, I'm not sure there's even a base to begin with."

"But there's still some of the Russian army there, right? How are you going to get in?"

"Well…"

As Kamijou was about to explain, they heard a car engine from far away. It thrummed quite deeply. This wasn't a passenger vehicle—it sounded more like a big truck.

Upon examination, he was able to see several large vehicles in a line driving across the white snowfields in the distance. He couldn't tell their exact models, but their vital spots were reinforced with heavy-looking metal, giving them a somewhat warlike impression.

If that was all it was, the scene wouldn't have been unusual. It was wartime.

But something was obviously strange.

The front and rear vehicles…

Those two were carriages, drawn by two horses each. And the horses were made out of silvery metal. It wasn't that they were wearing any kind of armor—they were horses completely made of metal running across the snow.

The carriage also wasn't mundane wood or cloth. It was covered by an outer shell that resembled a Western suit of armor.

This time, Kamijou was the one who frowned. "What are those?"

"Are you all out of science explanations to brag about?"

"Not the trucks—those weird carriages. What part of them says *science* to you? Did the Russian military develop some kind of horse-shaped pet robots with their unique technology or something?"

"Hmm. I believe those are Sleipnirs, made by the Russian Catholic Church. I've heard they were developing legs for moving across snowfields."

"…Which means we're up against sorcerers again, huh?"

"As for the trucks, they probably just borrowed them from the army. Sorcerers don't need to know much about cutting-edge science or technology to simply drive them."

For the moment, Kamijou decided to imitate Lesser and lie

prone on the snow, but when the stinging chill came through his non-waterproofed clothes, he quickly bounced back up.

Lesser gave him a look that was both amused and resigned. "If you're not going to do it right, you're just going to seem more suspicious."

"Yeah, I get it, but...," said Kamijou, breathing puffs of white air. "You said the Russian Catholic Church, right? I wonder what's in those trucks. Soul Arms they can use in the war, I guess?"

He hadn't asked the question thinking he'd get an answer. However, Lesser had a few unexpected words:

"Would it be residents?"

"?"

"Look," she said, taking the map out of Kamijou's hands and shaking a finger in the general direction of where the "suspicious base" was. "They want people to think there's a hastily made base here for the purpose of attacking the Alliance, right? Wouldn't people have been living there before they built it?"

"..."

Kamijou's eyebrow twitched.

Whether or not she noticed it, Lesser continued in a carefree tone, "By the way, that line of trucks escorted by those Sleipnir carriages are heading this way. Once they get past us, they'll reach a concentration camp for political prisoners. I don't know what excuse they're using for the eviction, but...If they're taking those people's homes away like this, the Russian Church must not think very much of their lives. They might have forced nearby residents to leave so they could start up a base they made in secret."

"There's more than one settlement?" Kamijou peered at the map from next to Lesser. "How many were originally where they planned to make the base?"

"About eight, with around twenty or thirty people each. Seems like most of them are uncultivated and not very developed. It might be a tight fit, but with that many trucks, they might get all of them inside— Hey, wait, where are you going?"

Lesser involuntarily called after Kamijou, who had unexpectedly walked off and left her behind.

He was headed for a log cabin nearby. The entire area had nothing else of note all the way to the horizon, so maybe this was meant to be a resting spot, like a mountain lodge.

For whatever reason, the unoccupied log cabin was furnished with a single four-wheel-drive vehicle. Judging by the markings on its side, it technically belonged to the Russian military. Did that mean this log cabin–like building was for observation or keeping watch over something? After nearing the vehicle, Kamijou didn't think twice before smashing the window with his elbow and unlocking the door from the inside.

The glass shattering made a very loud noise, but Lesser didn't shrink away.

In fact, she sighed, appalled. "…What on earth are you getting that toolbox out for? You're not planning to save those in-transit residents, right? With just that L-bar?"

"We don't know how many people we're up against, and we have no idea what kind of magic they'll use. A situation like this won't be so easy that we can just dive in headfirst and hope for the best, right? It's not like I want to jump into a battle for fun, or anything."

Noticing that he didn't deny he would try to save the in-transit residents, Lesser pressed her index fingers to her temples. She'd been under the impression since the London coup d'état that this kid had a very important screw loose in his head somewhere.

…Still, that's exactly why I'll probably have a chance to get him to work for Britain. Simply a matter of wooing him the right way. Mm.

As Lesser was privately confirming her own objective, Kamijou stuck the L-shaped bar into the snow. Taking sturdy nylon twine out of the toolbox, he glanced at his cell phone's screen and the analog clock that he went out of his way to use, then put the twine around the bar in the ground.

"?"

He stuck an iron stake a short distance away, then tied the twine to it as well, drawing it taut. Lesser frowned.

…A ground survey?

That was the first thing she thought of, because she possessed the knowledge and skills to know that in large magic rituals, you needed to gauge an exact direction and align the magic circle's size exactly with your objective.

"What are you up to anyway?"

"Can't you tell? I'm measuring the direction. Specifically, for the air route."

Kamijou stuck several more stakes into the snow, drawing the twine around each one, close to the ground.

"Right. So you're *not* going to make a big scene with an L-bar in your hand?"

"Come on, you're treating me too much like an idiot. How many people are they using just to escort that convoy? Why would I walk over there and pick a fight with a bunch of professional sorcerers? And professional killers, too. What is that, an introductory paragraph for a character in a kid's manga? There's no way I can beat guys like that in a fight…My right hand has a special power, but they could overwhelm me with their numbers, and then I won't be able to do anything."

"In that case, what do you plan to do?"

"First, I want to ask something. These Russian Catholic people don't care about the lives of the residents they're transporting, right?"

"If they did, they wouldn't be bringing them to a concentration camp. I know Japan is too peaceful to understand the concept of such a place, but can't you at least imagine what it's like inside?"

"Well." For some reason, Kamijou grinned. "That's fine, then. Maybe this will work."

"Like I said, what are you planning on doing?"

"Nothing too difficult. We're just using everything we have available."

After he finished pulling the twine around several more stakes, he pointed overhead.

Lesser looked up without argument and saw a thinly stretched condensation trail.

7

Brasche P. Marhaisk frowned.

He was at the front of the prisoner escort truck convoy, controlling a small, eight-wheeled carriage hitched to a Sleipnir. The carriage was covered in silver metal plates in the shape of a pill bug, looking like it was armored.

Still, his expression wasn't due to a bad mood. To increase the durability of the escort vehicle, the driver only had a single thin, horizontal slit with glass in it to look through, so it wasn't just Brasche—basically all armor drivers made this sort of face, whether magical or scientific.

White snowfields stretched out as far as the eye could see. It was almost impossible to tell the asphalt and the ground apart.

At a glance, it would seem like a driver could ignore the road and floor it. However, that wasn't actually how it worked. The problem was the snow. No one could tell from its surface how deep it went. It wasn't possible to see if there was a thick fallen tree buried in it, either.

Brasche wanted to avoid at all costs breaking the eight-legged horse Soul Arm by tripping over something carelessly. After all, Russia was nothing if not big. Its urban areas were some of the most developed in the world, but on the other hand, empty spaces were *seriously* empty. In fact, this area was about as unideal as a desert when it came to bad places to be stranded.

And if someone opened a map, the only thing worth writing about this place was "there's nothing here." Since it hadn't been updated for years, you'd never know what was where. Which meant he really didn't want to veer off the thin road partially hidden under the snow.

"How many more hours until the camp?"

A bored-sounding voice came in from the trucks comprising the convoy.

Over a magical Soul Arm, of course.

"Our population density is way too high, damn it. It's like a sauna in here."

"Why not open a door for ventilation?" answered Brasche, not sounding like he cared much. "In about ten seconds, you'll be begging for the heat to come back."

Just then, a shrill noise shot by overhead.

An Academy City supersonic bomber.

The HsB-02, was it? They'd gotten reports that those things had changed Avignon, in France, to a lake of molten rock. They seemed to be focusing on transport missions right now instead of bombing runs, but they weren't the sort of thing that anyone could remain calm about while they were flying overhead.

"*Damn it. What's the regular Russian military doing? Can't they use SAMs or something?*"

"They go at seven thousand kilometers per hour, remember?" replied Brasche. "Even if they locked on and fired, the missile wouldn't catch it. Academy City seems to think the fundamentals of aerial warfare are beneath them."

"*What about MiGs? Sukhois? Aren't the air force's bigger jets good enough to take on American stealth planes?*"

"I don't know. You're asking the wrong person about science."

Brasche leveled a baleful gaze at the bomber in the air.

…Thanks to Peter's interception spell, the age of sorcerers flying in the sky has ended. If not for that…

If that plane had been loaded with bombs, Brasche and the others might have been dead at this exact moment. It'd be a problem if it scattered light, small, airborne tanks with parachutes, too, but when the bombers weren't doing their *real* job, it made Brasche feel a lot more humiliated than relieved.

"(…Bullshit. You'd better watch out.)"

It happened a moment after he muttered to himself.

Ba-gam!!

Suddenly, roiling flames burst up on their transport route.

"?!"

It was only about three hundred meters ahead. Frantically, Brasche ordered the Sleipnir pulling the armored carriage to come to a halt. The entire convoy stopped on the road.

It should have been an empty stretch of snow all the way to the horizon.

However, a log cabin sort of building was there, perhaps for people who ran into trouble like engine stalls during their journeys. The explosions had occurred right next to it. Brasche carefully scanned the area and saw what seemed like a four-wheel-drive vehicle there.

And then the explosions continued.

This time, the log cabin itself was blown to pieces. The only man-made object on this vast field of snow had been blasted apart.

These weren't mere bombs.

The explosions continued along a straight line, as though running along the ground, for over three kilometers. White snow immediately whipped up, followed by the ground lighting up orange. The crust of the earth, melted by enormous heat, made it seem as though a volcanic eruption had cut a swath through Russian lands.

"What the hell?! Are we being bombed?!"

Normally, Brasche wouldn't have been able to answer his comrade's words.

But one time, he'd heard something along these lines: that Academy City's supersonic bombers had once carved a square out of the map of a city called Avignon. That there existed weapons with terrifying destructive power that took advantage of the air friction born of their seven-thousand-plus kilometer-per-hour speeds.

"They finally did it, the bastards…!!"

An unpleasant sweat washed down Brasche's spine. The convoy, composed of several trucks plus armored carriages, would be easy pickings from the air out on this snowfield with nothing else around them. There was nowhere to hide, and the huge lumps of flying metal could easily get a radar lock on them.

"Hey, can we use an Opila to make it so they won't target us?!"

"We can't take our time setting one up," answered Brasche, recognizing once again the sense of danger he felt. "This is bad. We'd better bail out. If we stay here, they'll slaughter us."

"*They're* bombing *us!! Unknown Academy City superweapons!! If we get out of our vehicles, we'll have no protection from the explosions!!*"

"You saw that power!! With only the Soul Arms we have on us, they'll reduce us *and* our vehicle to smithereens! We should make it so they don't aim for us instead. If we hide ourselves in white camo and spread out over the snowfield, there's a good chance we'll live!"

"*What do we do about the people from the settlement we captured?!*"

"Leave them." Brasche picked up his trusty staff and headed for the armored carriage's exit. "Either way, we were bringing them to a concentration camp. Who cares if they end up as fodder for the bombings?!"

Meanwhile.

What Touma Kamijou and Lesser were hoping for was quite simple.

"You said the Steel Gloves you've got have been improved, right? Something about the blade fingers not having to touch—and being able to grab anything you hit with that red laser thing even if you're far away?"

"Yes, but what about it?"

Kamijou pointed overhead in response to her question. "Then could you grab that for a sec?"

"?"

She followed his instructions, still frowning.

"Wait a minute. One more request. If you, like, stick the gloves into the ground, is it possible to go a little farther away and then make them move with your mind?"

"...That sounds like such a pain..."

"You can't?"

"I can," said Lesser, sticking the Steel Gloves upside down into the snow and walking a few meters away. From there, she slowly channeled mana into the Soul Arm and *grabbed* the distant object.

Yes:

An object flying high at an altitude of ten thousand meters, racing ahead at over seven thousand kilometers per hour—a supersonic bomber.

A moment later.
The Steel Gloves, dragged by the supersonic bomber, divided the Russian land in two.

It was a simple matter of air resistance.
Ripping through the space close to the ground, which was mostly air, at over seven thousand kilometers per hour, created an enormous amount of energy.

With a tremendous roar, a line of orange light about three kilometers long shot through the white landscape, tracing the supersonic bomber's flight route. The ground, melted like magma, threw all the white snow into the air. Likely unable to withstand the friction midway through, the line of destruction crawled to a stop just as the Steel Gloves fell to pieces.

Lesser was the one who was surprised.

"Ooooooooooowaaaaaaaaaaaaahhhhhhhhhhhhhhhhhhhhhh?! M-my-my Steel Gloves!! My Lesser Special Custom, the only one of its kind!!"

"Hmm. That re-created the Avignon effect pretty well. Maybe the Russian Catholics will be nice enough to let it fool them."

The carriage–truck convoy, protected with a durable magic spell, was being abandoned in the middle of the snowfield. Kamijou saw a group of tough sorcerers, the likes of whom an average high school student wouldn't have stood a chance against, running on foot to get as far away from the convoy as they could.

If he'd simply faked an aerial bombing with some explosives, things might not have gone this well. Kamijou was an amateur who couldn't tell the difference, but explosives came in several varieties, and the way they detonated and the sounds they made were all different. For example, an explosion using propane gas or gasoline wouldn't have matched that of a bomb and might have clued the guards in.

However, bombings using air friction were a product of Academy City's special technology. Even when compared to a list of domestic Russian weapons, there wouldn't be a single comparable reference.

That was why it'd worked as a deception.

Whether professional sorcerers or hardened soldiers, it was possible, at least once, to dupe them.

"If they were transporting something they had to protect with their lives in those trucks, this plan probably wouldn't have worked so well. But they don't give a crap about their guests, so they were sure to abandon them in a crisis."

"...You seem to be feeling very accomplished about something, but those Steel Gloves belonged to me!! How are you going to pay me back for breaking them like that?!"

"How much do Soul Arms cost exactly anyway? Do they even sell them?"

Kamijou, asking offhand questions, broke into a run toward the convoy about three hundred meters ahead. Lesser followed him, muttering under her breath.

It seemed like residents who had been living in the area where they planned to construct the base had been all crammed into the trucks.

Kamijou had gone around to the back of one, but he couldn't figure out how to get the door open. He tried shaking around the big metal mechanism he found, but it didn't budge. Lesser had mentioned Russian Catholic sorcerers could have been driving, so thinking they were using a magical lock, he touched it with his right hand, but it had no particular effect.

Then, Lesser reached out from beside him. With a surprisingly simple motion, she easily pulled open the truck door.

The eyes of hunched-over men and women of all ages greeted them.

Some were frightened, others confused.

They feared that the convoy had arrived at their decidedly awful destination—and wondered why it hadn't been Russian Catholics who had opened the truck door.

Kamijou tried to speak to them to set their minds at ease, but he didn't know the slightest bit of Russian. He considered using hand and body gestures, but he gave up on that. Next to him, Lesser sucked her teeth.

"Can you tell them we're escaping and ask for their help?"

"I can't be bothered, honestly," noted Lesser. "This act doesn't seem to be for the United Kingdom's benefit."

Kamijou pointed haphazardly back at the snowfield. "If you don't do it soon, those Russian Catholic sorcerers will realize something's up and come back."

"…"

Lesser made a face but seemed to have decided to comply without further argument. Seeing her turn to face the people in the truck, Kamijou went over to another of the trucks. The mechanisms on the doors were the same, and this time, he opened it himself. It would have been a pain to explain over and over again, so he used gestures to instruct them all to go over to where Lesser was.

"How are we going to run away?"

"We can use the trucks. There are probably adults here who can drive, right? In any case, I want them to go to the nearest town."

"…Well, that's fine. It's just that I don't see much in the way of concealment magic on them. These vehicles will look like they belong to the Russian military, and Academy City's tanks have been deployed inland, so I hope they don't get attacked."

"We'll take the carriage in the front. The one that resembles a pill bug covered in metal plates." Kamijou gazed at the small carriage. "That seems like the best thing to keep people from seeing our faces from the outside. I'm clearly Asian, and Lesser…I can't really tell myself, but I'm sure British people and Russian people have pretty different features and stuff. We'll want to hide our faces as much as possible. That armored carriage would be perfect for heading for that base, too, but…there's a problem I wanted to ask you about."

"You're not about to say you can't drive the carriage, are you?"

"If there's a high school kid these days who can say with a straight face they know how to drive a carriage, I'd like to meet them."

"Well, if you're going to put it that way, I'm only in middle school," said Lesser, nevertheless taking the lead and heading for the armored carriage. She seemed to be rather confident about it.

As Kamijou began to follow her, he felt a sudden tug at the hem of his clothes.

He turned around to a little girl.

She seemed to be trying to tell him something, but she also seemed to understand that the words she and Kamijou used were fundamentally different.

Kamijou slowly removed the small hand grabbing his clothes but, unable to think of any way to get his point across, decided to speak to her in Japanese.

However, his voice never got a chance to come out.

A woman carrying a baby, who appeared to be the girl's mother, hastily took the girl's hand and pulled her away from him. He couldn't understand what the mother was saying either, but hostility and fear filled her eyes.

…World War III—Japanese people from Academy City are Russia's enemies, huh…?

He felt something dig into him, but without letting it enter his expression, he used Japanese to say everything he wanted to say.

"One day, when I'm in trouble like you, you can just repay the favor. So don't worry about it too much."

A quick honking noise came from the armored carriage. Impressed at the horn being no different from a normal automobile, Kamijou ran off toward its call.

8

The armored carriage's interior couldn't exactly be called *comfortable*. It wasn't cold, thanks to an air conditioner–like Soul Arm set to regulate the temperature inside, but instead, the air was thick with the smell of sweat. Hemmed in by thick steel, they couldn't see outside either, making it feel oddly claustrophobic.

Inside the parked armored carriage, Lesser had slipped cleanly into the driver's seat. Nothing exposed there, either—it was totally covered in metal plating. Only the reins connected to the metal horse, the Sleipnir, reached through a slit.

"Wow. I figured it would be muggy in here, but not *this* muggy."

"...Does this air-conditioner thing only have two settings, or what? I bet if you turned the dial just a tiny amount, it would get really cold really fast. Well, before that happens, it would probably break if I accidentally touched it with my right hand."

"Hahhh, screw it—I can't stand this! Time to undo my shirt buttons and air out my skirt."

"Bfft!! What's wrong with you?! I don't understand why you suddenly do this stuff!!"

"I'm trying to use my sex appeal, so react to it already!! Just push me down, get it over with, and that's one vanguard down for the sake of Britain!!"

"Hah! I bet she doesn't even know what any of those things mean, and she's still running her mouth with a smile on her face! Let me give you a piece of advice as someone who's-ever-so-slightly wiser—you're really *seriously* saying some dangerous stuff right now! Be more careful next time!!"

Fool! You fell for it!!

The little devil Lesser, shaking the tail coming out of her miniskirt, gave a wicked smile, as though she'd found a way to counterattack.

"Okay then, fine, I hear you loud and clear!! In that case, let me prove to you just how serious I really am!!"

9

And on the Strait of Dover battlefield, a girl from the Born Again Amakusa-Style Crossist Church, Itsuwa, sensed something cold run down her spine as she clenched her spear in both hands.

"Hah, hawahh?!"

"?! Wh-what's up, Itsuwa?"

Itsuwa slowly and nervously looked away from Saiji Tatemiya, who was startled at her strange behavior, and said, "N-nothing...I just had a bad feeling, for some reason..."

10

Nothing the late-bloomer was anxious about was happening, of course, and Lesser, gripping the Sleipnir's reins, was sullenly driving the armored carriage.

"I was a little scared at first since this was a Russian-made metal horse, but the basics seem the same as a normal carriage."

"A *normal carriage*, she says..."

Kamijou and Lesser were riding a Russian Catholic armored carriage, which probably helped ease their nerves somewhat. Still, he didn't think they'd be able to get into a highly guarded fortress like this.

After Lesser had driven the thing for about thirty minutes, she suddenly stopped on an empty snowfield.

"We're getting close to the fortress's defensive perimeter. To be frank, if we go any farther, we'll end up getting showered with missiles and grenades. The defensive Soul Arm installed in this carriage probably won't be able to hold up against all of it."

"I see a bunch of other ruts in the snow that are about the same size, though. Well, I guess I knew it wouldn't be that easy. For now, it's enough to know the base lets similar 'carriages' inside. It's definitely not your normal military facility."

"A *normal* military facility, he says..."

The fortress itself was only about ten square kilometers. It was nominally a front-line base adjacent to the national border shared with the Elizalina Alliance of Independent Nations, but it probably wasn't operating as a regular installation. It was where Fiamma was secretly advancing his schemes.

Furthermore, there was a defensive perimeter extending about forty kilometers all around the fortress.

Naturally, it wasn't ringed with high barriers like the Great Wall of China. The system consisted of a series of observation towers covering all directions that would radio in as soon as they spotted any suspicious figures, then direct tons of artillery onto that location.

"...Which is why they kicked out all the residents from an area even larger than Academy City itself."

"Still, this region is mostly wilderness. Even with all the villagers together, I don't think you'd have more people than a Japanese hamlet."

The comment was enough to remind Kamijou once again how enormous in scale this country called Russia really was. Someone could look all over the Japanese archipelago and not find any stretch of untouched nature that was comparable in size.

"Anyway, what are we doing now?" Lesser asked from the driver's seat. "If we set foot inside their defensive line like this, we'll be fodder for missiles and grenade launchers in no time. The carriage isn't maneuverable enough to evade them. Don't we need to consider our options? Then again, I doubt they left any obvious blind spots open."

"Not necessarily," Kamijou answered, his tone somewhat tense. "Remember what I said before? Fiamma is using the Russian army for his own ends, but he wouldn't have revealed the details of his magic-related plans. It's like how he pretended there was some noble cause behind starting World War III—he must have built a secret route for bringing in magical equipment. There's gotta be one."

"And if we can find that, we can get inside the fortress without anyone knowing?"

"Most people on the Russian side don't know about magic. At the very least, normal military guys probably can't use it for battle. That means finding that route'll be easier than marching in from the front, right?"

"...Maybe, but Fiamma of the Right is a force to be reckoned with, right? Isn't the story that he's the leader of God's Right Seat? I get the feeling that even just his traps and followers will be pretty high-level, magically speaking."

"And that's where I come in, right?" Kamijou grinned and wiggled the fingers of his right hand.

A power called Imagine Breaker resided there—one that could cancel out any and all preternatural powers.

"Professional soldiers armed with rifles and bombs aren't exactly the kind of people I should ever be fighting. Group combat against a large number of Russian Catholic sorcerers is a no-go as well. To be honest, I was right at the point of worrying that I wouldn't be able to get into my groove…But this is where it starts. Finally, this is where I can really take the stage."

Touma Kamijou looked straight out the armored carriage's slit-like window.

And toward the shadow of the facility that stood near the distant horizon, he whispered:

"…I'm coming for you, Fiamma."

11

In the depths of Moscow stood a middle-aged man in an extravagant military uniform, the kind that no actual soldier would ever wear into battle. He was inside a building that almost looked like a palace but was actually a fortress officially registered to the military. The man, his uniform adorned with numerous decorations, had always believed he'd been at the very bottom of Russia's shadows. But it seemed that was no longer the case.

Other men in similar uniforms were gathered here as well.

Aside from their clothing and records, they all held similar positions to him.

"…The Russian Church's patriarch…The world seems to have broadened significantly in an undesirable direction."

"We instigated this war as they wished, but I wonder—can we repel Academy City's troops?"

"A surprising number of people have sided with Academy City.

The benefits of their science and technology must have been great, to have created a line this wide."

"For all intents and purposes, this is escalating into a conflict between the Roman Orthodox–Russian Catholic dominion and the rest of the world. Not gaining India's or China's support hurt us."

"I can't see what Academy City is after. Putting this much military force on display, including their unmanned weapons, can't possibly bring them any advantages."

"Would you say they have goals other than simple interception and defense, then?"

"Maybe it's our silos."

"Even if everything else falls, we must not allow those silos to be taken. With Academy City's technological power, they might be able to activate them without the proper codes. And it's possible they'll *bring it in* from outside."

"Which would mean…"

"I'd like to propose that we consider activating *It*."

Everyone present fell into a stony silence at those words.

They'd had this same discussion among themselves several times already. Those words had such weight, though, that even given the dire situation, they hesitated to give a concrete go-ahead signal.

Eventually, while glancing at the stack of documents on the table, one among them spoke up:

"The Kremlin Report…"

INTERLUDE ONE

Academy City had gotten very busy in its own right.

In a girl's dormitory room, Mikoto Misaka was sitting on her bed. Her roommate, Kuroko Shirai, wasn't here. She'd apparently been summoned for some sort of job, fulfilling her duty as a member of Judgment.

School, too, was closed today. And not exactly because a typhoon had made landfall.

The possibility was apparently slim *so far*, but there was still a nonzero chance that Russian warheads or bombers could appear in the skies above Academy City.

Incidentally.

Academy City and Russia seemed more than willing to have at it, but the Japanese government was taking a rather passive approach to the war. It made sense—Japan didn't have its own military, so even if someone suggested they go to war, nobody could really snap to it and say *Yes, right away, sir*. With Russia acting as though this was a global-scale war, the US's so-called deterrence wasn't working, either.

With no chance of victory in a real clash, the Japanese government was even trying to pressure Academy City to quickly accept Russia's demands in order to avoid a full-scale war.

In response, Academy City had offered a very simple video.

It showed a ballistic missile blowing up outside the earth's atmosphere.

It wasn't just one—or even two.

Over thirty shadows flew past at once, and Academy City's interception weapons shot every one of them down.

"We will not make any demands of you."

During a mobile 1seg broadcast, the Academy City press secretary had this to say:

"However, we also have no responsibility to protect anyone beyond our own allies. Russia has already launched ballistic missiles without warning. Thankfully, we confirmed that none were loaded with nuclear warheads at this time, but we do not know when that taboo will be broken as well. We'd like you to use your own judgment to make the decisions you feel are right. Still, the nation of Japan also possesses Aegis warships and PAC-3s secured through massive tax investment, so we don't believe this will be a major issue."

…It's practically a threat.

Academy City had essentially said that if Japan interfered, they would remove Japan's cities from its air defense network. The American-made interception systems the Japanese Self-Defense Force had, in desperation, procured were certainly excellent, but they were incomparable to ones made in Academy City, which was said to have science and technology twenty to thirty years more advanced than the rest of the world. Even a child could understand these devices couldn't guarantee 100 percent precision. And how huge a tragedy it would be for even one shot to make it through.

It was almost like Academy City was using Russian-made missiles to make a threat, but most people thought of the issue this way: *I don't care; just please don't drop it on my head.*

Thanks to that, large throngs of citizens were apparently all over their politicians right now, telling them not to provoke the City to ensure that their own cities and towns remained safe zones. The immense flood of public opinion prevented the politicians from doing anything, and meanwhile, Academy City continued to do whatever it wanted.

The contents of the declaration of war had been revealed to the entire world, and Mikoto had viewed it online herself.

However.

It was a fact that she was strangely dissatisfied. Academy City was using indirect threats to stir up the masses, while continuing to claim to be allies of justice who would protect the people—staying clean, never getting their own hands dirty. This image of absolute integrity was eerie, as if everything had been whitewashed with bleach. Eerie enough that it made her think things would be stranger if there *wasn't* something at the bottom of it all.

Something...

Mikoto glanced away from her mobile device and looked at her cell phone.

The phone had her Croaker charm attached to it.

She'd dialed the number of a certain spiky-haired boy several times already but hadn't gotten any sort of response at all. And just the other day, he'd said that he was in London during the coup d'état.

She'd thought it was some kind of joke at the time.

But what if...?

What if he hadn't come back to Academy City yet?

Mikoto decided it was worth investigating.

After the outbreak of war, the City had restricted usage of the District 23 airport by civilians. Plus, considering the timing of the coup and the war, maybe it was difficult to return.

Academy City: seemingly detached from all the disturbance outside it, but actually the centerpiece of a world war.

If that boy was on the *outside*, the danger he would face shot through the roof. In that case, she couldn't very well sit back and do nothing.

CHAPTER 2

Opening Offensives and Counteroffensives
Angel_Stalker.

1

As she was walking over the white snow, Lesser was clicking together some small metallic parts.

"...Hmm. Even with all my spare parts, I can't make the Lesser Special Custom...I'll have to revert it to the old Steel Gloves. I should have bloody documented at least the custom-made one's theoretical values. There was so much trial and error, and I added so many parts while testing that even I can't figure out the balance distribution anymore..."

As Lesser muttered on, she suddenly peered into the snow.

"Whoops. There it is—there's just the thing!"

Kamijou had no idea what she was doing, but after pausing his stride with her, he learned what she was looking at.

He'd thought the snow was about a foot deep, but following Lesser's gaze revealed a cavernous hole that was clearly over three meters deep. It was like a tunnel made out of snow.

"It was probably a ditch shaped like a V before. With all the snow piled up over it, it looks flat from above."

"...But weren't there transport trucks and stuff driving toward the base over this normally?"

"To begin with, if the snow had piled up as usual, it would have changed shape to match the V. They used sorcery to change the accumulation and hardness. I'd bet that if a passenger jet landed here, it wouldn't even budge."

Kamijou glanced at his right hand. "…We won't get buried alive as soon as I touch it, will we?"

"Who knows? Just to be safe, you might want to keep your hands off the walls," said Lesser offhandedly before sliding herself into the cavern.

As Kamijou tried to follow her, she suddenly stopped and said, "Oh, great…If I'd slipped and fell on the snow, I could have opened all sorts of routes, like naturally falling into his arms or showing him my panties."

"I get it. You're queen today. Just get moving already."

A train line ran through the inside, two paths stretching far into the distance alongside it. On the tracks, a distant cargo train was stopped, about five cars linked up. No electric lines or anything were visible, so maybe it had a diesel engine.

"So this is how they secretly got what they needed inside."

"I'm surprised," said Lesser, her expression puzzled. "Fiamma of the Right wiped out the pope of Rome and Second Princess Carissa with one hit, didn't he? I didn't think he was the type to be obsessed with creative methods for maintaining secrecy. I always imagined someone who would simply clear away anything he came across that he didn't like."

"He *is* the one who used his authority as God's Right Seat to impel the Roman Orthodox Church to act and set all sorts of things in motion without doing any of it personally, you know. This is actually more normal for him. If he ever came out to deal with something directly, it would be a sign that his curtain fire had thinned out."

For Kamijou, finding a freight train was a windfall. After all, it was thirty or forty kilometers until the base. No matter how much they searched for shortcuts, if they had to walk over the snow because they had no means of transportation, they'd run out of stamina before even confronting the man.

"Still, if we start up the freight train ourselves, they're sure to notice us."

"So we'll wait for its scheduled move. Over here. Let's hide in one of these containers."

As Kamijou made that suggestion, he moved toward the container linked to the first train car. The door was openable from the side as well. After sliding back the iron door like the rear seat of a minivan, Kamijou and Lesser climbed inside.

Lesser watched his pants pocket closely, then said eventually, "By the way, I've been wondering this for a while—what is that frog strap you have there?"

"It's called Croaker. I don't really know more, though."

"...A fanciful mascot character you don't know much about...? I smell another woman's hand in this. I may need to alter my strategy. I should take the initiative and wipe it out..."

Lesser was mumbling to herself, but after quickly checking the inside of the container, her expression slowly changed into something more dangerous.

"Hmm. Judging by the symbols, most of these must be Crossist-type Soul Arms, as expected. I can't tell exactly what they're used for, though," she said, her eyes having quickly gotten used to the darkness. "I have to say, you seem like you're used to this."

"...Well, during the coup, I had to stow away on a freight train filled with Knights all the way to Folkestone."

"Oooh. Come to think of it, Florice was talking about that. She was saying if she ever saw that Japanese person again, she'd whoop him real good."

"Oh. Why *did* the Knights capture her anyway?"

As they were talking, they started to hear several footsteps and voices from outside. They cut their conversation short and strained their ears.

The people outside seemed to be speaking Russian, so Kamijou didn't understand them, but it sounded like they were opening several container doors to load extra cargo. Kamijou and Lesser tried to squeeze behind a pile of Soul Arms, thinking the people would open the container they were hiding in, too, but it turned out that there was nothing to worry about. The lead car's engine roared to life without the door to their car opening. With a *clunk* and a shake, the freight train began to move.

"...Are those Russian soldiers? Or sorcerers?"

"I can't say for sure, but probably the latter. It's highly probable they're from the Russian Catholic Church. I heard them complaining about the Soul Arms they were loading."

Two people, hiding out in a freight train container.

With each passing second, the train drew ever closer to the mysterious fortress's center.

And...

"...Wow, it sure is hot in here. It seems like the effective temperature in closed spaces generally rises because of your own body heat."

"You're not airing out your skirt in here. I forbid it."

"I wasn't going to. That was only effective at the right time as a surprise atta—"

Lesser suddenly broke off what she was saying.

An instant later, Kamijou realized why.

She'd just figured *it* out: That because of her sweat, the sports shirt she was wearing had turned see-through. And that her bra, with such little surface area that a spy couldn't even hide a small computer chip in it, was visible.

But Lesser didn't blush or try to cover her chest with her hands.

"No!! My secret weapon—now it's been wasted. I was going to save this for the best possible moment...!!"

"Why did you even come all the way to Russia?! I thought there was something up when you were airing out your skirt before, but—no, that can't be true!"

Kamijou was trembling, but in the meantime, the train was closing in on their destination.

After about twenty or thirty minutes, it reached the base's central area. The train stopped, and as they began to hear Russian again from outside, Lesser spoke up.

"Let's get out."

"Huh? Shouldn't we wait until they leave?"

"You're really dumb about certain things, huh? They were using this freight train to carry cargo, right? They're sure to pull stuff out of the containers next. And then we'll definitely run into them. We have to leave before that, or we'll be in trouble."

Now that she mentioned it, that was true, but it still took courage to jump out where people were clearly moving around.

Kamijou opened the container's sliding door a tiny crack. Peeking out, it seemed like nobody was nearby, miraculously. Several wooden crates were piled up on the flat snow's surface—if they could pass through while using them as cover, they could probably keep themselves from getting caught.

...*Getting cold feet now won't help.*

"Guess it's time to go," he said, widening the door gap a little bit more. Then he wriggled through the opening and exited. After dropping down to the ground from a height of about a meter, he immediately went behind the pile of crates and hid. Lesser followed after him. Her movements were limber, like some sort of carnivore.

As they were doing that, the work of unloading cargo was proceeding on the other side of the stacks of crates, making Kamijou feel like he was surrounded by footsteps and talking voices. He was intimately aware of the sweat coming out of him every time he heard one of those sounds.

"Think positively," said Lesser, her expression cool in contrast. "If they're being noisy, they won't notice if we make a little noise."

The exit to the makeshift train platform was at a spot about ten meters away from the stack of crates. What looked like a staircase leading up was visible. The platform was under the snow, so this probably led up to the surface.

From here, they'd head to the heart of the fortress Fiamma had made.

That would have far more eyes about, incomparable to this unloading area, and it would be more dangerous as well.

They couldn't afford to trip up here on a lower difficulty level.

Attentive to his surroundings, Kamijou was about to head for the exit when…

…he bumped into a Russian sorcerer.

The young man was older than Kamijou but probably nothing more than personnel for unloading the cargo, as evidenced by the crate he was carrying in both hands. The event seemed to be unexpected for him, too—he was staring at them blankly.

For Kamijou, the fact that he had his hands full was a silver lining.

It delayed the sorcerer's reaction for a mere instant.

And in that instant, Lesser moved.

"‼"

It was an incredibly cold act. Without a sound, she closed the distance and thrust her arm up at the sorcerer's defenseless throat. A sharper impact than what could be delivered with an ordinary punch struck him, and his body crumpled. Rather than catch the falling sorcerer, Lesser reached for the wooden crate he'd released.

Only a minimal noise escaped, and the work continued around them as though nothing had happened.

An unpleasant chill shot through Kamijou's fingertips.

"Please be careful."

With just that, Lesser lowered the box with a slow motion. Then, after tying some kind of wire around the young man's ankles, she rearranged some nearby crates to form an enclosed space and hid him in the middle.

"…H-he's not dead, is he?"

"It would have been easier to kill him. Then I wouldn't have had to use a valuable detainment Soul Arm like Dromi."

The ankle wires apparently had the effect of blocking *all* body movement. After smoothly explaining, Lesser got the sense that Kamijou really did live in a different world than her.

Meanwhile, as she moved her tail, fluttering the hem of her miniskirt, she thought, *This tactic doesn't seem to be very effective, so maybe being straightforward and racking up points instead will be more efficient in the long run? No, no—I am sexy; I must be!*

After they climbed the exit stairs and emerged onto the surface, they found themselves inside the base proper. A few hundred meters away, they could see what looked like an iron fence barricade.

And.

The base was about ten square kilometers in total. Its center, an area measuring about seven kilometers, was raised quite a bit. The height difference looked to be about twenty meters…which made it look like a huge sheet of snow was casting a giant shadow.

"Standard doctrine would dictate that you want to make your base flat…"

"Maybe that just goes to show this isn't your standard place."

There was a large entrance in the "wall" of the giant slope, maybe for getting cargo inside. That was where Kamijou and Lesser began their infiltration.

Inside, it looked like a European castle. Not, however, the kind decorated with glittering silver and gold treasures. It was a damp space, made of stone, like a place for locking away prisoners.

Fortunately, they didn't run into any lookouts or patrols on their way.

Perhaps Fiamma himself had forbidden anyone from entering.

"Ngh!"

Kamijou grabbed Lesser's shoulder as she tried to proceed.

They were in front of a door.

Peeking in through the slightly open gap, he saw a vast empty space on the other side. He couldn't tell what it was for. But he certainly remembered the voice he heard coming from inside.

"…It's Fiamma. Didn't think we'd run into the big boss right away," whispered Kamijou, and even Lesser stiffened with nervousness.

It was like a church undergoing renovations—a modern steel frame ran here and there over the old-fashioned stone construction. Fiamma was idle on that frame. An out-of-place high-class table and chairs were set up there, and that's where he was seated. On the table there was a thick open book that had a faint light emanating from it.

Nobody else was there.

Only Fiamma's voice was audible.

So was that book a communication Soul Arm?

"*It is necessary. This is a space. Meaning both coordinates and volume are important.*"

Kamijou's heart stirred at the voice. It'd been a while.

"*I have no interest in Russian palaces. If all I wanted was to sit on the throne, I wouldn't have smashed up St. Peter's Basilica, would I? To me, this place is more important than Moscow, and that's all that matters. Though it does take some time for news about the current state of affairs to reach me, which is a problem. Nevertheless, I cannot leave here if I am to go forward with my plan. Not when considering it from the viewpoint of Project Bethlehem.*"

"*…*"

Kamijou carefully maintained his silence. If he didn't put his mind to it, he'd probably cry out and charge in this very moment.

"*I know that. This was not a battle any of you wanted. And I'm not talking about World War III—I'm talking about the greater movement at play, of Academy City and the Roman Orthodox Church opposing each other.*"

They were quite far away, but perhaps because nobody else was around, Fiamma's words reached Kamijou's ears. On the other hand, that meant they were in danger of their own words reaching him. Kamijou's tension only grew.

Who on earth was Fiamma talking to?

"*If Academy City wins, an age controlled by the science side will be ushered in. If the Roman Orthodox Church wins, it will be the start of an age of magic. But either way, there is little for the Russian Catholic Church to savor. Even if an age heralded by sorcery does come, if the Roman Church is in a leadership position, then the Russian Church will lose its footing.*"

Kamijou thought about this as Lesser translated the Russian for him.

But then his thoughts were interrupted—he'd spotted something.

Another Soul Arm on the table.

"*That was why you acted at such an early stage. To reap the greatest profits once this great war ends by aligning yourselves with the faction that will bring the most benefit. In that case, you should hand over the investigation results soon. Give me the reports from the Russian soldiers I sent out everywhere.*"

It was a small, cylindrical item.

It had several ringed metal fittings on it, making it look almost like a padlock with a dial.

The Soul Arm that remotely controlled Index.

The object that was causing her to suffer in unconsciousness.

If only.

If only he could destroy that…

"*Yes, that's right. That's a good boy… The Elizalina Alliance of Independent Nations? Yes, if Sasha Kreutzev were there, it would make sense that we couldn't find her despite searching all over Russia.*"

Kamijou leaned forward in spite of himself.

But then someone covered his mouth from behind.

It was Lesser.

Then, with her other hand, she delivered a sharp blow to his side. He tried to cough in agony, but he couldn't even do that with his mouth clamped shut.

Strength began to fade from his body.

"*No, they're still sorcerers serving on the front lines. Regular soldiers wouldn't be able to properly deal with them. Although, if they get shot and killed, that would be troubling in its own right. The Russian Church? No, Annihilatus is useless, too. I don't know if they were unconsciously pulling their punches against former colleagues or if their specs are simply that low, but the fact of the matter is that they still haven't captured her, even at this stage… I'm loath to say it, but I'll have to do it myself. If it brings more certainty to my plans, it's for the best.*"

His body still pinned down, Kamijou glared at Fiamma through the gap in the door.

He hadn't noticed them.

"*…And one more thing. Your plans don't involve you stopping at* *bishop, do they? The patriarch is the highest authority in the Russian Church, right? But at this rate, you won't assume that position during your lifetime. That's what I'm talking about. If you want to use me for your own purposes, start working hard enough to convince me to want to use you. If you still plan on being oddly parsimonious and waste my time with worthless offers, I will cut you away without a second thought and find someone else. Understood?"*

Closing the thick tome as if to cut off the conversation, Fiamma left the book there and grasped the Index remote-controlled Soul Arm.

Kamijou hadn't noticed until now, but there was a steel window-like object right next to Fiamma. Fiamma flung it open and sunlight shined into the dimly lit room. He nimbly jumped through it, making his exit.

The remote-control Soul Arm had been one step away, but now it was out of reach again.

As Lesser uncovered Kamijou's mouth, he whipped around to face her.

He was very close to grabbing her by the collar.

"(…What's the big idea?! He was right there!!)" he hissed.

"(…What were you planning to do?)" she hissed back. "(There are over two hundred sorcerers in that room!)"

Kamijou stared at her blankly.

He hadn't noticed at all.

But now that she'd told him, he took another peek through the gap between the wall in the door and saw several things here and there in the vast space, deeper in the dark, that looked like the glint of eyes. Maybe they were doing some kind of work, or maybe they were standing by as Fiamma's bodyguards.

"(…If we had marched right in, we wouldn't have reached Fiamma. If he's the kind of person you say he is, he would have had his men stall us and escape through the window anyway.)"

Lesser spoke each word slowly, quietly, in order to soothe Kamijou's agitation.

"(…He mentioned the Elizalina Alliance of Independent Nations. And Sasha Kreutzev. He sent an order for Russian soldiers to stand down, so he might be trying to make contact with Sasha alone. If you want to steal that Soul Arm, we'll just have to head him off. As long as we can catch Sasha Kreutzev before he does, we'll be able to take time to plan a surprise attack against him.)"

"(...Damn it,)" Kamijou forced out in a huff.

Fiamma of the Right. He was exactly the kind of person to manipulate all these people just to cause global turmoil, then watch the fallout from on high. Kamijou knew he wouldn't be able to get to him that easily, but still...

"(...Anyway, let's look for Sasha,)" he continued at a whisper. "(If Fiamma wants her, it can't possibly be for anything good...And besides, I need to settle the score for what he did to Index.)"

2

Shiage Hamazura drove the stolen car.

They'd gotten food, funds, and fuel. Now, it was finally time to "fight" Academy City—by finding a bargaining chip to guarantee his and Takitsubo's safety.

"...But what should we even be looking for?"

"Since we're at war, it might be a blessing in disguise that Academy City soldiers and weapons will be hanging around in Russia, too. Hamazura, maybe we should attack from that angle."

"You mean we should seize brand-new military weapons and stuff and use the technology to negotiate?"

"We could also monitor Russian military movements to offer Academy City as intelligence."

Hamazura was the one who had brought it up, but none of it actually felt very real to him.

Who could blame him?

He had a wealth of experience, but at heart, he was nothing more than a delinquent kid. Even with words like *soldiers* and *weapons* getting thrown around, it didn't have a sense of reality for him. And he didn't have any clue about how exactly one would cut a deal with a massive global power like Academy City.

Meanwhile, Takitsubo, who had peered into the depths of Academy City's darkness, was giving him advice.

"Hamazura. Think about what Academy City wants from this war."

"Huh? They're worried Russia will invade, so they're trying to defend the City, right?"

"If that was all, they wouldn't have to mount an offensive into Russian territory. They could simply focus on building a comprehensive line of defense in the Sea of Japan. Normally, no one would be able to intercept so many bombers and ballistic missiles, but Academy City can. While they buy time with their defenses, they could gradually manipulate the global economy and put enough financial pressure on Russia that they had to stop the war."

"...You mean Academy City has another goal in mind?"

"And since we know that, we should head for the heart. Imagine a set of balanced scales. You might only be a small weight, but if you can take a position where you can tip them no matter which side you're on, you'll be able to make any demands of Academy City you want."

"..."

That meant they'd have to dive straight into the battle raging between Academy City and Russia. They would hurl themselves at the issue and hope they came up with information. The strategy could literally shave years off their life, but if they didn't do it, they'd be giving up one of their only chances.

"They were really going at it around here, too. The Elizalina Alliance of Independent Nations, was it? We should be close to there. Maybe we start searching in that area."

"...Yeah, we should, Hamazura..."

"? Takitsubo?"

Hearing her hoarse reply sent a bad feeling down Hamazura's body. He spared a glance toward the passenger seat, then, without thinking, hit the brakes.

Something was wrong. Her face was drenched in sweat.

"Hey, what's the matter, Takitsubo? Are you all right?!"

"No...problems. I'm fine...So...let's move quickly, Hamazura."

This was no joke.

Anyone could see her condition wasn't normal.

Takitsubo was still was suffering from the ill effects of Crystals. The fact had been thrust before him again, but that didn't mean he could do anything about it. Would it be better to bring her to a hospital after all, even though he knew it wouldn't help? If he had an *outside* doctor look at her, they wouldn't have any idea how to cure her. And even if they did, he was worried about who would take custody of her. It was wartime, and to begin with, neither had so much as a passport—they were both illegal immigrants.

But.

He didn't want to do nothing. He didn't want to leave her like this. For emotional reasons more than logical ones, he wanted to reduce the strain on Takitsubo's body as much as possible. Then what should he do? To find a bargaining chip to negotiate with Academy City, they'd have to enter the heart of the conflict and obtain useful information. That was the only way.

As Hamazura was anguishing over it, he heard a soft rapping nearby.

Someone was tapping on the driver's side window with a fist.

He turned to look and saw a tall Caucasian man standing there. Probably Russian. Without thinking, Hamazura drew his pistol and kept it pressed against the door so the man wouldn't be able to see from his perspective. As stated previously, Academy City and Russia were not on good terms right now. The fact that Hamazura hailed from Academy City, Japan, meant there was a possibility of harm coming their way.

The pistol still hidden, Hamazura carefully opened the window.

The tall Caucasian man said:

"I've done tour guides in Japanese for sightseers before. Do you understand what I'm saying?"

"What are you supposed to be?"

"It looks like you need a doctor."

The tall man gestured with his chin to the passenger seat.

Hamazura found himself taken aback at the question. The man smiled and continued, "How about some *give-and-take*? Our settlement is out of generator fuel. It's below zero, and at this rate, everyone will freeze. This thing's got a diesel engine, right? If you would be so kind as to give us the fuel stored in this junker, I can bring the young lady to see our doctor. What do you say?"

3

Had tanks really ever gotten any more comfortable?

The engine was loud, and the smell of fuel and exhaust mixed with the sweat and grime to create an incredibly foul stench. Of course, with five old guys packed into such a cramped space, maybe any environment would have been uncomfortable.

Antseka S. Kufalke, sitting in the commander's seat, sighed.

They were in central Russia. They had no manual for deploying troops in this area in a defensive outline to protect themselves from foreign enemies. Defense was meant for places closer to the border, and many plans, depending on the situation, anticipated preemptive troop deployment inside the *enemy's* borders.

They'd never calculated for an enemy that could push in this far.

Nevertheless, Academy City's ground forces were on the move. Against all odds—to devour them from the inside outward.

"...Damn it. It's still falling," grumbled Antseka bitterly, aiming his gaze through the gap in the hatch to the white skies. "*Deploying the bare minimum defensive weaponry to protect the peace*, my ass. Those are top-of-the-line vehicles that we might get zero kills on even if we had an entire platoon charge in—and they're sprinkling them around like promotional fliers. The enemy is clearly prepared for invasion and occupation."

"Students make up eighty percent of their population of 2.3 million, right?" said one of his colleagues in the tank, finding it uncanny. "How can they rival Russia's forces like that? The troop counts make no sense. Did you hear? Apparently, there's nobody riding in those tanks, but they can move around anyway."

Antseka's brow furrowed even more deeply. "It's an absurd rumor, but I get the feeling they could pull *anything* off."

No sooner had he seen an Academy City supersonic bomber soar through the skies than a huge line of parachutes fell down in a line along its route. This time, they weren't airborne tanks. They were probably materials for constructing a simple base.

Their bases came in several stages.

They were everything from "log cabins" assembled from multiple steel plates to shelters made from quick-drying reinforced cement. Those, what were they called, power suits? Their armor weapons assembled these bases at a staggering pace, and the bases were deploying all over Russia like cockroach nests.

What's more, Academy City seemed to dislike letting outsiders lay hands on their technology.

Which meant these various fortresses must have been installed with mechanisms to be blown up or collected afterward. Unlike the Russian soldiers, who had their hands full with fighting, Academy City was already thinking of what would happen after the war was over.

"We'll never see the end of them," spat one of his colleagues. "While we're putting together a plan to attack a base that suddenly cropped up in front of us, they put a base behind us, too, before we even realized. Then, while we're sitting around scared, they put down another, this time to disrupt our supply routes. Their speed is too much. Even criminals fleeing through the night wouldn't be this fast."

At first, they'd tried shooting down the parachutes. But it didn't have any effect. They could punch holes in the fabric with their anti-aircraft and machine guns, but then they'd sprout glider-like wings or deploy even more parachutes. It was limitless.

It gave Antseka and the others a very blunt, clear impression.

They wouldn't be allowed to fight on their own terms.

And they weren't idiots, either. In terms of combat experience, they were head and shoulders above Academy City, which persisted through technology. If it came down to a pure shoot-out, they were confident they could at least achieve fifty-fifty results. They'd force the battle into a stalemate and hold off any further encroachment of their homeland that way.

However.

It wouldn't turn into the exchange of gunfire that they knew so well.

It wouldn't become a battle of seasoned tank veterans.

Academy City's peculiar tactics were absolutely impossible under normal circumstances. The materials necessary for the bases—the time and manpower needed to construct them—and the resources and energy needed to maintain them: No one could look at these conditions and call it realistic to build one base after another deep in enemy territory, all the while linking the facilities together with supply lines. It didn't take a soldier to understand—any observing journalist could take one look at it and point out all sorts of problems.

And despite that.

Academy City had overcome those flaws with the brute force of their technology.

With normally impossible speed, the supersonic bombers were constantly dropping vast quantities of materials and fuel. With extreme swiftness, the powered suit groups accurately assembled the materials as they landed. The situation got more ridiculous the more you thought about it. It wasn't possible to keep up without first rewriting the textbooks soldiers used during their training.

"What should we do, sir?" asked one of the younger crew in the tank, though still certainly a middle-aged soldier. "We'll run out of fuel and ammunition soon. Those bases have sealed off our escape route and supply route. I wish the strategists would come up with some sort of radical plan to counterattack."

"At this rate, we'll wither away before any tank battles even begin," grumbled another soldier, disgusted.

The first time one of the supersonic bombers had dropped all those parachutes, their team had tried to prioritize stopping the enemy base's construction. But shooting down the parachutes was ineffective, and the powered suits that'd landed slightly ahead of that evaded their shots with incredible mobility, then used massive shotguns that could have been for bunker busting to mount a precise counterattack.

The enemy's odd movements had thrown their forces into confusion, and in the meantime, the bombers had dropped additional materials and airborne tanks, one after another. The next thing they knew, a very wide gap in combat power had sealed off all of the Russian force's options.

By this point, Antseka was well aware that they'd fired pointlessly.

If he'd known they'd come out with these tactics from the start, he might have been able to conserve ammunition a little more calmly, but pointing that out now would get them nowhere.

As he recalled the situation in his mind, one of his colleagues looked in his direction.

"It's clear we'll have to surrender. But I can't stand this being over without us doing anything. Let's at least blast one of them in the end. It might be a drop in the ocean, but if we don't whittle down their forces even a little, this country really is done for."

Antseka looked up at the white skies from the gap in the hatch.

Even as they talked, several bombers tore through the Russian sky at over seven thousand kilometers per hour, dropping innumerable parachutes in straight lines.

"Hey, if those were big bombs to take out pillboxes and not resupply materials, what do you think would have happened to us?"

"..."

An unpleasant silence fell upon the inside of the tank.

He was right. That was exactly what the supersonic bombers were meant to do. And that might have been a simpler way to shut Antseka and the others up for good.

Why was Academy City purposely adopting such roundabout tactics?

Still looking up at the sky bitterly, Antseka spat his next words.

"Humane weapons usage, is it? The bastards are treating us like fools."

4

The Elizalina Alliance of Independent Nations.

Kamijou and Lesser had reached its interior. Since it was war-time and the country was on the verge of invasion, they'd expected the border to be in a state of high alert, but they mostly just walked on in.

"It's not an island nation like Japan or the UK. If countries neighbor one another on land, you can enter them fairly easily."

"But that was a little *too* easy. With the way things are going, we should have gone in expecting to be shot."

"They probably don't have enough time to bother doing that. Besides, didn't you sneak across a bunch of borders to get to Russia?"

"Actually, I just kept hitchhiking here and there, and eventually, I ended up in Russia. I don't know exactly how it happened."

"…Hmm. Maybe they just weren't able to talk to you, making it a big adventure…?" muttered Lesser.

They were in a plaza-like place, and all kinds of people were coming and going around them. They seemed to be of various ethnicities, not just from one homogenous group. And while he couldn't understand much of their words, it felt to him as though several languages were intermixed here.

"The Elizalina Alliance of Independent Nations was originally a bunch of smaller regions who couldn't agree with Russia's way of doing things that gained independence and formed a country, right?"

"More precisely, it's a group of such nations," corrected Lesser. "This area is landlocked, after all. Even if one country gained independence, they would be surrounded 360 degrees by Russian territory. If that happened, they would end up needing permission from the Russian government for any movement of people and goods. The Alliance is several small countries linked together to escape that kind of indirect control, and they apparently built their own routes out of Russia to eastern European countries…Thanks to that, though, even some among the independent nations have been isolated, particularly from Russia."

Because of the circumstances surrounding its formation, the Elizalina Alliance of Independent Nations stretched long and thin from east to west. Its length was around three hundred kilometers… The chances of coincidentally bumping into someone you were looking for was infinitesimally low.

"Anyway, we've gotta make contact with Sasha before Fiamma does," said Kamijou as if to hurry himself up. "Now, then. How do we go about searching for her?"

"First, let's find an inn we can use as a base."

"Yeah, I guess when we have so much area to search, we might not find her in one day."

"And just one room, of course, so we can conserve our funds. You may assign a degree of indecent implication if you want."

"Are your thought processes basically just locked to that, or what?!"

"You don't want an inn? Then, outside?! W-well, that might pose a problem. Being outdoors by itself is no issue, but given the incredibly cold climate, it might just be boring and difficult."

"…All right. Let's be serious for a moment."

After grabbing Lesser by the back of the neck and heading toward a back road, Kamijou lectured her earnestly for about fifteen minutes. Then, with Lesser's mental state completely clobbered, he dragged her back to the plaza again.

"How are we going to look for Sasha? She's a sorcerer, so if we can spot any traces of her using something strange and mysterious, we might be able to find her."

"A-actually, there' s an easier way."

"?"

Kamijou cocked his head to the side, but a moment later, he realized something was wrong.

The issue was around them.

Four or five men were staring at them, mixed into the crowds of people coming and going. They wore deep-green military uniforms that sort of made them stand out more against the white snow.

"It's the border patrol," stated Lesser simply. "You said it was still too easy before, didn't you? You were right. They're no idiots, either. They don't seem to have a way to get camo gear suited for the environment, but that doesn't change the fact that they're trying to protect this nation."

"W-wait, then what do we do?"

"Do you need me to spell it out? We'll just ask them."

Lesser, saying indecipherable things…When Kamijou gave her a dubious look, she explained again, this time slowly.

"Fiamma was searching for traces of Sasha Kreutzev by using the Russian military, right? That means some of them would have been crossing the border to look for her. Even if Sasha herself was nowhere to be found, don't you think Alliance soldiers would know that the Russian military was hunting her? And the fact that we know the war's mastermind will be trying to sneak into the Alliance—isn't that a bargaining chip they can't possibly ignore?"

5

The Strait of Dover, located between the UK and France, had transformed into a battlefield, with each faction staring their enemies down, face-to-face.

The water's surface was covered by a strange, translucent substance, and atop it, dozens, hundreds, *thousands* of blades were crossing. It was beyond the scope of a simple "battle" this time. This was a clash worthy of the term *war*.

France had the raw numbers advantage, but the UK was the one on the advance.

Kaori Kanzaki was, after all, a major force to be reckoned with. A single swing from her would unleash the power she wielded as one of less than twenty saints in the world, mowing down several sorcerers at once. On top of that, the members of the Born Again

Amakusa-Style Crossist Church around Kanzaki were supporting her at times and using her as a distraction so they could carry out precision strikes, making them a far more effective fighting unit than their numbers suggested.

"Hoooh…!!"

Kanzaki's katana sheath demolished a wide swath of the translucent land at her feet, and as their footing broke and bulged upward, girls in black nun's habits leaped up and staged a surprise attack on the French sorcerers from the air.

They were the sisters from the former Agnes unit. This team, centered around Agnes Sanctis, was performing in much the same way as the Born Again Amakusa-Style Crossist Church. Aside from pure combat potential, their intimate knowledge of their enemy—the Roman Orthodox Church's—battle tactics were also working to their advantage.

However, that alone couldn't defeat the French forces. They didn't have any sorcerers in incredibly unique positions like saints; instead, they bolstered their forces by borrowing enormous quantities of weapons and Soul Arms from the Roman Orthodox Church, an organization that boasted over two billion followers. Their armaments weren't only the archetypical kinds equipped by individuals, like staves and chalices, but also Soul Arm vehicles, which looked like strange tanks with claymores in place of gun barrels and iron-plated suits of armor in place of normal equipment.

When Second Princess Carissa saw that, she said in a fed-up tone, "They're still just warming up. Probing to gauge our combat forces, and all that."

She still wasn't holding any weapons.

Protected by many knights, Carissa exuded an elegant, unwavering air.

In a light tone of voice, she asked a question of the Knight Leader, who was standing beside her.

"Now, I wonder what the French camp's main forces are like. It looks like there are some who seem associated with knights mixed in with their Roman Orthodox Church–based sorcerers. Still, even the knights seem to be at a level that can be filed within the category of Crossism."

"If we're talking about French-bred knights who are Crossists, wouldn't Charlemagne be an appropriate assumption?"

"Or maybe the holy woman, their leader who's been napping in Versailles, swallowed what little pride she had and went crying to the remnants of the Knights of Orleans."

"...You would do well not to underestimate me..."

Suddenly, a voice Carissa couldn't pinpoint interrupted them.

Her eyebrow twitched slightly.

"My pride is not so cheap that I would allow something like that to remain for the sake of my protection. In fact, I am indignant that the issue was resolved by a British mercenary in the first place."

"Well, now. You must still be sleepy, so maybe you should do your morning routine and then come back. You may be confined to Versailles, but your slow response was to blame. Just like this time."

"Ah, but you, too, can do nothing," said the Versailles "leader" in a low voice. *"News that the Curtana Original has been broken reached us as well. We also know that the Second is with Queen Elizard. In other words, you have little power of your own right now. As long as you are outside the United Kingdom's borders, the knights by your side won't have much strength, either. I understand you are the bellicose type, but do you realize how much of a hindrance you are?"*

"Fool," barked Carissa.

A moment later—

Zwaa!!

The knights around the second princess obtained an immense amount of power from the Curtana.

The power supply itself had come from the Curtana Second. Elizard had probably given it some kind of order. But that alone wasn't enough to explain it—as far as anyone knew, the Curtana was only effective within the UK's borders.

"You know how, if I'd succeeded in my coup in the UK with the

Curtana Original, I'd planned to advance into Europe and bury every single one of my enemies?"

"*That can't...*"

"How, exactly, did you think I planned to carry that out? Did you think I would whine and cry about not being able to use the Curtana outside the country?"

There was a massive *thump* sound.

It came from over ten kilometers behind Carissa.

Something was hovering there. An exceedingly gigantic structure. A mysterious object made of dozens of randomly assembled cubes—perhaps it would be best described as a square bubble. Completely removed from rational architectural techniques, it both looked like a castle wrought by human hands and an enormous boulder forced up out of the ground and into the air.

"The mobile fortress—Glastonbury."

Carissa intoned its name.

"By forcibly defining the area around this fortress as part of the British domain, it allows for a rapid extending of the Curtana's effective radius. It doesn't take the enemy's intent into consideration whatsoever. The perfect large-scale Soul Arm for *invasions*, don't you think?"

The tables had completely turned.

The knights, filled with renewed power, drew their swords to defend Carissa.

"This is not a defensive battle of attrition."

The formation of knights deployed to guard Carissa smoothly began to shift to an aggressive posture.

The voice of the princess of military affairs declared what this meant:

"It's mop-up operation leading into our offensive."

6

Kamijou and Lesser walked through the plaza, surrounded by multiple large men. It didn't feel good to be escorted by people he couldn't communicate with and who appeared to be soldiers. He was on pins and needles, and Lesser, who walked next to him, reassured him, her tone sounding bored.

"We'll be fine. The Elizalina Alliance of Independent Nations should want any information they can get on Fiamma, want it so badly they can taste it. They're not going to ship us off to a concentration camp. Besides, the Alliance doesn't have any facilities *that* frightening to begin with."

"...Really? What if they show us to a room with just chairs that have belts on them?"

"Yeah, yeah. If that happens, I'll apologize, wear a baby doll outfit, get on all fours, and shake my butt around for you...Hmm, that sounds nice. You know what, let's do that right now."

"It looks like I haven't lectured you enough, young grasshopper. We'll be making a fuss here, so let's put a pin in that for a moment."

As soon as he grabbed the back of her neck and tried to leave the ring of people, angry Russian shouts rained upon them. Several of the large men already had their hands on their holstered guns.

"Yipes!! I get it, I get it! Damn it, this doesn't exactly feel like a warm welcome!"

"I was joking anyway. I don't plan on providing a free service like that for whoever happens to be around. It probably wouldn't benefit the United Kingdom anyway. I'll be a good girl and follow your lead for now. Leaving aside whether I'll wear baby clothes once we get into our inn room later."

As they continued to squabble, one of the men in the group surrounding them muttered something, seeming incredibly unhappy. Kamijou couldn't understand it because it was Russian, but Lesser interpreted for him.

"He asked if we rescued a mother and her daughters on the trucks in Russia. One girl was a baby, about two, and the other was about ten."

"Ah? We helped a convoy that had trucks and armored carriages in it, but...Wait, there were, like, dozens of people there. I'm going to need some more information."

As Kamijou made a dubious face, the large man continued in Russian, this time spitting out the words.

When Lesser heard it, she frowned for a moment. Then she shrugged and looked at Kamijou. "Apparently, that was his older sister and her daughters."

…If the man knew about this, maybe the people on the trucks had safely arrived in a nearby town and contacted them via phone or something.

Maybe the reason he only had his hand on his holster without outright pointing his gun at Kamijou was because he thought he owed him something.

In the meantime, Kamijou and Lesser were taken to a square stone building near the plaza. Originally, it was one building that was part of a large church, but right now, they seemed to be using it as something else—a military facility.

For an office, a lot of paper documents were scattered wildly around. The positions of the steel desks weren't organized, either. On a whiteboard on the wall, they'd hung a map of the surrounding area. It had different-colored magnets on it—maybe positions of Alliance and Russian tanks or something. The colors on one side were far more numerous.

A blond-haired woman was waiting there.

She was rather skinny. If she'd been wearing a swimsuit, you'd be more worried about her than excited. She directed her slightly sunken-in eyes toward them, then smiled thinly.

In Japanese, she said, "It seems Fiamma of the Right is on his way."

Lesser whistled, impressed.

Did they know each other? Kamijou had to wonder, but it seemed he was wrong.

"…She's the namesake of the Elizalina Alliance of Independent Nations," Lesser offered. "She's like a saint who worked hard to gain independence for a bunch of countries and bind them together."

"It seems Fiamma of the Right is on his way."

Elizalina, the person in question, repeated herself.

The name *Fiamma of the Right* must have been inauspicious enough to the Alliance for illegal immigrants to suddenly meet a person like that.

Not that you could blame them.

He *was* the one who had pulled the trigger on World War III.

If not for that, the Russian forces would never have considered launching an invasion into the Alliance.

"The words came right out of his own mouth at the Russian military base right across the border. I don't think there's much doubt about it…"

After explaining that much, Kamijou felt something was out of place.

"…Wait a minute. You know the name *Fiamma of the Right*, Miss Elizalina?"

That would mean she was aware of the world of sorcery. And to a great extent, when it came to the Roman Orthodox Church.

Elizalina answered almost without moving her lips at all. "Inept though I may be, I am still a sorcerer."

"If she wasn't, she couldn't have responded this quickly to nothing but fragmented reports from her men, could she? She realized how much we were worth and instructed them to bring us to the heart of the country right away. It's obvious just from that that she's someone who knows about magic," added Lesser in an offhand tone.

Apparently, she was familiar with this person named Elizalina's achievements and legends.

"On the surface, she creates a foundation for political and economic national independence, but behind the scenes, she's a powerful sorcerer who repelled every single Russian Catholic soldier who tried to pull off occult sabotage missions. If she fought for real, she might even be able to blow *me* away."

"I'm nothing that amazing. I only proposed a few procedures and helped out. Comparatively, I'm a far cry from my *sister* in France."

Elizalina brushed it off as a triviality. She seemed to dislike it when others flattered her more than they needed to.

She quickly returned to the topic. "Fiamma is a central figure of this war—of this *invasion* encroaching upon our nation. If we have a chance to defeat him now, the threat to our people's lives should decrease quite a bit."

Up until that point, Kamijou was in agreement.

But what came after was another story.

"On the other hand, I don't think I can beat Fiamma of the Right very easily—and not here. It's a matter of the difference in skill as sorcerers. Even if I scraped together everything we have in this country, I wouldn't be able to defeat that man."

A hint of distress appeared on the woman's face as she spoke. She must not have wanted to let Fiamma go so easily.

Now that he was near, she wanted to do whatever it took to escape the threat as soon as possible. Insisting on that—maybe that's what made her a talented politician.

Because what if, even though the situation looked like an opportunity at first, it was actually rife with incredible danger?

"What's most important for us are the lives of the Alliance's people. If by some trick or mischief, those could be lost, then we must avoid combat with Fiamma at all costs."

"You'd let him do as he likes after coming this far?"

The question came from Lesser.

Elizalina shook her head. "No," she answered immediately. "I've heard from my subordinates. Your goal, and Fiamma's, is Sasha Kreutzev. We do know where she is currently. She's right nearby. So close that if I gave the order, we could summon her here right now. On top of that, we're also thinking about ways to defeat Fiamma while protecting our people's lives...Do you understand what I'm getting at?"

"...You'll send Sasha and us back outside the Alliance into Russian territory, then execute a plan to fight Fiamma?"

"Yes." Elizalina nodded. "Think of me as coldhearted if you wish. But that's how delicate this situation has become. A single careless decision could lead to countless innocent lives being lost."

"Nah." Kamijou smiled a little. "We were trying to use you all to find out where Sasha is to begin with. At this point, I'm grateful just for not having handcuffs on me without a chance to explain."

"Despite the difference in scope and degree, you seem to have someone you need to protect as well."

"Everyone does," answered Kamijou in resignation to Elizalina's words, which were also spoken as though to herself. "...I realized it late, and she was almost taken away from me, but I might still be able to make it at this point."

Either way.

They had to find Sasha Kreutzev as soon as possible, lure Fiamma outside the Alliance, and defeat him. For now, there was a chance they could create a more advantageous situation than Fiamma could, but as time went on, the possibility would very quickly deteriorate.

And the chances of rescuing Index would fall with it.

After confirming the situation to himself again, Kamijou faced Elizalina and asked her a question.

"What's the plan?"

"Come this way...Still, this is all rushed, so I can't guarantee much chance of victory."

As she talked, Elizalina headed toward the whiteboard in the room's corner.

And then it happened.

"Indeed. If you're still holding strategy meetings at this stage, you're already too late."

A man's voice suddenly echoed throughout the room.

It was a familiar voice. A voice Kamijou could never forget.

Fiamma of the Right.

The sound's source was the window. Kamijou spun around, and Lesser and Elizalina moved at the same time. Lesser attached a bar magnet to the tip of a retractable, police baton–like object on one of the steel desks, while Elizalina plastered a piece of translucent blue cellophane, normally used to wrap up sweets, to the side of a glass filled with water.

In just a few seconds.

They'd created improvised Soul Arms.

A moment later, flames and water burst forth.

Boom!! With an air-splitting roar, two kinds of attacks rushed toward the window like an avalanche. The glass shattered to pieces. But the voice didn't stop.

"*I was merely saying hello,*" Fiamma continued.

On the other side of the broken window floated a small doll of kneaded flour.

"*This is where it really begins.*"

A moment later.

Ga-gam!!

Touma Kamijou's brain rattled madly.

For an instant, his vision churned. He thought something heavy had hit him in the face. He was on the floor without realizing it, and finally, he realized what it was that had delivered the impact to his face.

It was a piece of debris, a little smaller than a baseball.

Half the ceiling or so had collapsed.

Part of it was on the floor now, dragged down by debris.

Where everything had been crushed, he could see a wall made out of some sort of orange light.

And then.

Something like a giant sword, whose length had to be thirty to forty kilometers, swung down from above, and Kamijou, who was the closest, didn't realize. After all, the base of the sword was so large it seemed like it would disappear beyond the horizon. The blade emitted sizzling noises like it was steaming, and after wiggling from side to side like an ax being pulled out of a large tree, it slowly lifted.

"*It's an awful pain to aim with something so large.*"

The voice was carefree.

As Kamijou shuddered, the huge sword that looked big enough to cleave a mountain range in two continued to rise with ease.

Until it was almost vertical.

And then, Fiamma's sword swung down all at once.

The air shook.

This time, there was no mercy.

Its aim corrected, the giant sword dropped from the sky. The town of the Elizalina Alliance of Independent Nations split in half along a line, and the stone building in which Kamijou and the others were, the spot where its force was strongest, blasted apart into a million pieces.

Clouds sprang up.

Because it had torn through atmosphere and created an air pressure differential, it had created something like an airplane's vapor trail.

A single attack that even affected the weather.

And.

"Oooooooooooooooooohhhhhhhhhhhhhhhhhhhhhhhhhhhhhhhh-hhhhhhhhhhhhhhhhhhhhhhhhhhhhhhhhhhhhhhhhhhhhhhhhhhhhh!!"

A roar.

Touma Kamijou had thrust his right palm directly up.

An awful creaking noise came from the core of his bones.

But.

The boy's utterly normal arm had stopped the map-wrecking attack dead-on.

Did he...stop it...?

Surprise filled Elizalina's face—this was the first time she'd seen the Imagine Breaker in action. Even Lesser, who had witnessed it before, still seemed to have a hard time accepting it. However, there was no time to explain everything. Not even Kamijou could be sure his bones weren't actually broken.

And then.

"What's this? And here I thought you'd learned a little from the British Halloween."

* * *

Suddenly, a man's voice came from right next to him.

Fiamma of the Right.

Kamijou saw the red doll flying straight at him and immediately understood.

There was a gap between the one who had cast the spell and the place in which it had activated.

Just like how Second Princess Carissa had used the Curtana Original and the bunker clusters in tandem, this was a method of focusing someone's attention on a large-scale attack first before driving the real attack right into their wide-open core.

"...?!"

Kamijou tried to get his right hand in position immediately, but his palm had just crushed the orange-colored sword. A tingling, numbing pain was still shooting through his arm and it delayed his response. Taking advantage of the tiny opening, Fiamma reached his hand toward Kamijou with a relaxed look on his face.

A mysterious hand—one Kamijou didn't know the effects of.

"Guh!!"

Elizalina wedged herself between them.

The front of her body was glowing faintly. She probably had some kind of spell activated. A sorcerer with the skills to liberate several countries from the huge nation of Russia and who had continued to exercise her powers behind the scenes. He could assume from her history, among other things, that she could freely use incredible spells.

But Fiamma ignored her.

He mercilessly knocked both Kamijou and Elizalina several meters away.

Kamijou's breath caught.

Fiamma was about to go for a follow-up attack he couldn't even imagine, but then his movements stopped.

The cause was his right arm. Something strange, like a third arm, had sprouted from near his shoulder.

Elizalina's skills had saved Kamijou.

If not, he might have been in two pieces right now—upper and lower.

"I see."

Fiamma tapped his shoulder with his left hand as though impressed.

"The wall seemed a little too hard to break that easily."

Then, two of the tall men who had been serving at Elizalina's side jumped in.

"Beraggi!! Longie!! Stand down!!"

The fallen sorcerer frantically shouted, but they didn't stop. And Fiamma didn't have any mercy with them, either.

"But it's not impenetrable. Don't underestimate me *too* much, all right?"

Sound vanished.

A moment after Fiamma swung his third arm, Beraggi and Longie were knocked straight to the side. The distance hadn't mattered. Beraggi was close, but Longie was clearly outside the third arm's reach. Despite that, he'd been mowed down just the same. They were launched outside the building from a hole in the debris from the initial attack.

Kamijou dragged his injured body upright through sheer force.

"*Fiamma!!*"

"You're the main dish. I need to prepare before I dig into you."

The assailant's gaze was turned toward Elizalina.

An unknown faint light once again emanated from the surface of her body.

But it was clear from the earlier exchange the difference in skill between Fiamma and Elizalina. He'd even pierced through her defensive magic. If he got serious, Elizalina might be killed.

But my right hand can...

Conscious of his smarting arm, Kamijou gritted his teeth.

But can I really block every single one of his attacks?! Can I save Index by constantly being on the defensive?!

Fiamma couldn't care less about their shock and hesitation.

He simply moved—advancing smoothly.

"!!"

But Fiamma's right arm never reached out to grab Elizalina by the throat.

And the reason was Lesser:

The petite girl's hand was now somehow gripping a spear-like object—the Steel Gloves, a magical weapon fitted with four blades like fingers. Lesser had slammed them downward like a guillotine, but…

"Out of the way."

The motion was less of a backhand, more of brushing away a spiderweb.

And despite that, the single hit shattered the Steel Gloves. Not only that, it sent Lesser flying away like a cannonball. Just before she collided with a wall, Beraggi, who had once again jumped inside the building, reached out his arms. He barely managed to soften the impact.

A single moment, earned by risking one's life.

Elizalina, meaning to regroup, rose from where she had been prone with a backward bounding motion, moving her five fingers in a complex fashion. Faint lights dancing at the end of her fingertips flickered irregularly.

When Fiamma saw it, he let out a breath like a chuckle.

"You would use your *right arm* to build a spell against *me*?"

A moment later—

Ba-bam!! A flash of light burst forth.

It came from Fiamma's right arm.

He wasn't showing off his strength—he was acting in a different dimension than that. The motion was almost like swatting an annoying fly flitting about his face. It was a movement to crush both Elizalina's resistance and rend her flesh, no matter what she tried to do.

From the beginning, she had said that, even if she combined all the Alliance's military strength in one spot, they couldn't beat Fiamma of the Right. That was why, when they did set forth to defeat him, she wanted to catch and face him outside the Alliance.

In which case.

Maybe the fact that Fiamma was here, now, had already determined Elizalina's fate.

But it didn't happen that way.

Gkk-keeeeee!! came a roaring sound, intent on contending with him. It was the sound of Fiamma's flash and Kamijou's right hand clashing.

At that time, Kamijou, who had jumped in front of Elizalina, should have accurately blocked Fiamma's hit. The flash of light didn't disappear right away, but it splashed out in all directions as though trying to escape from his right hand. Those splashes should have been mere aftereffects, entirely different from the main thing.

Nevertheless.

The sound was driven away from Kamijou's eardrums.

The flash's aftermath, parried to the sides, this time completely devastated the room's barely standing walls and proceeded straight toward the plaza beyond them. Its trajectory was diagonally upward. Thanks to that, the people standing in the plaza avoided a grisly fate, but the roofs of stone buildings facing the plaza were all ripped clean off and carried away.

Touma Kamijou and Fiamma of the Right.

Two wielders of two special right hands glared straight at each other.

"You're opponent is me. You know why I'm fighting, don't you?"

"What?" In contrast to Kamijou's shouting, Fiamma slowly cocked his head to the side—while glancing at a spot near Kamijou's right shoulder. "I thought I said you were the main dish. You're planning on serving yourself up first?"

"!!"

Lesser, who had been blown away to the wall, moved. After picking up a broken piece of metal from the Steel Gloves, she hurled it at him like a bullet.

Her target wasn't Fiamma.

He'd proven with the last attack that it wouldn't work.

Her projectile struck Kamijou directly in his side. Stiffening, his body doubled over and was knocked straight to the side. A moment later, Fiamma's right hand dropped like a guillotine. The floor melted. A good imagination wasn't necessary to know what would happen to human flesh that came in contact with it.

"...Guh...Argh...?!"

Kamijou rolled, bursting out of the "building," now no more than a pile of broken walls with only the floor and part of the structure barely remaining, and into the plaza. As he writhed on the snow, Fiamma slowly walked over to him. He didn't spare so much as a glance toward Elizalina, who was supposedly his original goal. She wasn't a tactically important target—he must not have thought of her as anything more than an annoying fly to be batted out of the way.

For Fiamma of the Right, there were only two important targets.

The first was Touma Kamijou's right arm.

The second was Sasha Kreutzev.

...Not good, Kamijou admitted to himself. *He's having his way with us. In this state, I can't exactly fight him while protecting Sasha...*

Fiamma still hadn't located Sasha, which was a small mercy. She was apparently right nearby, according to Elizalina, but if he hadn't found her yet, Kamijou had more options.

Or so he thought anyway.

But suddenly, Fiamma came out and said, "Hey, did you know? Modern sorcerers, who came into being at the end of the nineteenth century, generally dislike group action. Even genius organizations, starting with the Golden Dawn, in most cases see internal rifts stemming from personality issues. That's why the Roman Catholic Church made a point of structuring its group combat doctrine around its religious teachings, but...Well, you know how it really is, don't you? Sorcerers see individualism as very important, and that's why the subjective aim of 'magic names' is still seen as extremely important, and why the secret organization called God's Right Seat was born."

"What…are you trying to say?"

"Here's my point."

Fiamma slowly lifted his right hand horizontally to the ground.

As he stood in the middle of the plaza, he paid no mind to any of the townspeople around. Not making any effort to conceal the magic he was using in front of all these people who were smothered by fear to the point that they couldn't even bring themselves to run, he said this to Kamijou.

"Someone in front of you seems like they're about to be killed. From this moment on, hundreds or thousands of blameless civilians will probably be killed in an imminent invasion. In a situation like that, would a sorcerer who possesses power remain quiet and hidden simply for the sake of tactical importance?"

"?!"

Kamijou's body stiffened.

And then he noticed the angel amid the crowds.

A red shadow. A body bound in black belts, an unnatural figure that seemed to be covered in a red innerwear and a mantle. Nobody was paying attention to her, despite her being in the middle of the plaza, perhaps because she had used some sort of magical illusion.

Sasha Kreutzev.

When he spotted her, he unwittingly felt a little relieved, forgetting about the situation up until a few moments ago. The archangel who had parried the saint Kaori Kanzaki with one hand—and who had in the meantime built a spell to "purge" six billion people. Nothing would feel more dependable than if they were able to borrow that power.

But he realized it a moment later.

That was not the archangel Misha Kreutzev that Touma Kamijou knew.

She was no more than the Russian Catholic human sorcerer, Sasha Kreutzev.

She was trying to do something.

She was a professional Russian Catholic sorcerer—and she probably had first-rate abilities.

However.

"Today must be my lucky day."

Fiamma flicked something with his fingers.

With just that, Sasha, who had woven through the crowds with the force of a speeding arrow to attack him, was blasted straight backward, still at her original speed.

"I thought it'd be a massive pain, but two of my objectives found their way into my hands so, so easily."

Fiamma must have been confident that he'd completely stopped Sasha with one attack. Without any particular follow-ups, he turned his eyes to Kamijou again.

"..."

Kamijou quietly assumed his standard stance.

He wasn't exactly knowledgeable when it came to magical combat. But his Imagine Breaker was the only thing that had been able to oppose Fiamma's right arm so far. This wasn't the time to be debating whether he could do it. If he didn't go in now, a great deal of people would be killed for Fiamma's convenience.

One-on-one.

There was nothing he could rely on, nor any weapons to cling to.

And then.

Fiamma of the Right made a strange move.

Casually, he shook his head.

A moment later, something passed by Fiamma, grazing past his cheek. A strange fissure ran through the building wall behind him.

The people in the plaza didn't appear to know what had just happened.

The unreal sight seemed to be one factor paralyzing their judgment.

"..."

But Kamijou, who knew about magic, albeit only on an amateur level, sucked in his breath softly.

Fiamma had just taken evasive action.

Kamijou was surprised at the unknown attack itself, too, but he was more shocked that Fiamma had responded like that.

"Now there's a familiar face," Fiamma muttered.

Kamijou turned around.

He saw yellow.

A woman, eyes adorned with gaudy makeup, piercings all over her face. Her appearance made it seem like she purposely wanted others to despise her. Her clothing appeared to be based on women's wear from the Middle Ages, but perhaps because it was shocking yellow, it didn't come off as outdated in any way. In fact, it almost looked related to super-conspicuous punk fashion.

On September 30, with a spell that used divine judgment, she had almost completely put all of Academy City to sleep. As a member of God's Right Seat, she had shown Kamijou a fight that went above and beyond any he'd known before that.

A clinking noise.

Her tongue was pierced, and a slender linked chain ran through it. The chain reached down to her waist, and a transparent, icelike cross hung from the end. That cross, however, was the one thing different from what Kamijou remembered.

Vento of the Front.

The one who had forced Fiamma of the Right to dodge for the first time was a sorcerer supposedly in the same organization as him.

"It's not like I'm responsible or anything for that brat or the Russian Catholic sister. I just can't stand watching you cause mayhem in the Roman Orthodox Church anymore."

"I thought I'd received reports saying you couldn't use your special 'divine judgment' anymore."

"You really thought that would be the end of me?"

Roar!!

A tempest whirled about.

Two of God's Right Seat.

Two sorcerers from a different dimension, who stood at the pinnacle of two billion followers, collided.

7

Leaning on his crutch, Accelerator glanced around the room.

That stack of parchment he'd found during the fight on the freight train. If Academy City's underworld was undertaking a retrieval operation with the same level of importance as chasing him down, that also meant it was possible these were no mere superstitious drawings.

Accelerator didn't believe a lick in the occult, but he wondered if ancient "magic" was simply today's science and technology.

...*But that's all just me forcing myself to use my own* head *to talk about it.*

Accelerator took just one deep breath.

He sensed, in an incredibly subjective way, that something was *wrong* with this parchment.

A sensation like the core of his chest was under pressure.

It was similar to what he felt sometimes when he was near Mitsuki Unabara. Come to think of it, he used powers that were different from pure supernatural abilities...or so his words and actions implied (of course, there was a non-insignificant chance that it was a bluff, so he didn't have to reveal his hand). Maybe it was related.

Which meant he was curious where they had intended to transport the parchment.

Obviously, Accelerator couldn't understand what kind of information it was just from the parchment. That meant his fastest option would be to extract information from whoever was supposed to receive it. The destination would only be one relay point, of course, and he might not find out who was to ultimately receive it, but in that case, he would keep going from one relay point to the next until he arrived at someone who knew what the parchment would be used for.

If it was a clue to saving Last Order's life, said to be unsavable even with Academy City's cutting-edge technology...

He thought that if worse came to worst, he would simply have to directly attack a military facility, but...

* * *

"Damn. They raided it one step ahead of me."

The air was suffused with the smell of burning.

It probably used to be a Russian Air Force base. The white snow-field had been cut away for several kilometers to pour asphalt into, and it was surrounded by a fence-like barricade. Inside it were several runways and many large buildings made from special concrete used for pillboxes.

There wasn't a soul to be seen.

The fence was torn up, the thick concrete walls leveled wholesale, and the fighters on the runways lying on their sides like toys with fire spurting from them. Even now, as though explosives were still detonating somewhere inside the ruined buildings that held no hint of human life, firework-like explosions that resounded in his stomach were going off sporadically.

Someone was here who knew how to use this parchment, or maybe it was simply a relay point before continuing its trip by air. And now he wouldn't even know that anymore.

Academy City, eh...? guessed Accelerator.

Although it probably hadn't been the regular forces clashing head-on with the Russian military. Their modus operandi was different. This was the work of a shadowy organization from the "evil" world, which had secretly snuck deep into Russia.

He couldn't spot a single cartridge.

Cracks ran through the walls, but the bullets that would have gotten stuck inside had been removed.

Academy City had always tended to avoid letting their technology leak into the outside world. This, though, was altogether more conspicuous than expected.

If taking this position was all they'd wanted to do, they wouldn't have needed to use a group from the underworld. All Academy City had to do was direct the regular forces to mount an offensive on the base.

Did that mean their goal, then, was the parchment Accelerator possessed?

They'd dispatched one retrieval team for the parchment itself, then also committed a separate detachment to its shipping destination, the airport. Survivors might be inside if he searched every nook and cranny inside the base. But they would've at least massacred everyone who knew anything about the parchment or used the shadow group to personally bring them in.

There weren't any hints left here.

It was like his already unreliable lifeline had been cut off, but in his mind right now was not panic, but a question.

...You telling me this parchment is really worth that much?

If it was, how did one actually *use* it?

Was that usage something Academy City wanted to acquire at any cost?

And.

Would it help him, even slightly, to heal Last Order's battered body?

...That shithead Aiwass told me to go to Russia. Is this connected to that? And there was that whole thing about the key being of a completely different "rule set" than Academy City...

He mulled it over, but he had no way of getting any answers.

Setting it aside for the time being, he considered his next course of action.

...I've got no more leads on finding someone in Russia who can explain to me what this parchment actually does now. Which means the next route I can try is Academy City's shadow group. The people running interference should understand how valuable this parchment is.

Accelerator didn't have concrete details on who would have the necessary information, so any combat ran the risk of landing him in a protracted battle. As long as his electrode battery power was finite, that wouldn't be a favorable development for him, but he couldn't care less. If he needed to, he'd crawl through the snow to finish off his target.

It was an extremely combative idea.

Recalling the limp, unconscious Last Order's weight, he let out a grin.

"Not good…"

He thought he'd been hiding it up until now.

He thought he'd decided that no matter how bloody the world he lived in was, this girl was the one person he didn't want to have to pretend with.

…*I'm losing my grip on the brakes.*

He didn't say those last words—because he didn't want Last Order to hear? Or because a slight unease had crossed through the back of his own mind?

Either way, he couldn't afford to call it quits here.

Academy City owned several large supersonic jets. Monstrous aircraft that could soar through the skies at over seven thousand kilometers per hour and arrive on the other side of the planet in just two hours. If the City used something like that to move the shadow group that had attacked this base to another location, he wouldn't be able to pursue them at length. If he wanted to stage an ambush, he'd have to follow their footsteps immediately.

There was no time to hesitate.

And yet, as Accelerator tried to turn on his heel, he stopped.

There were several figures.

The air base was set up on a flat, expansive surface, centered around its runway. Hiding spots were few and far between. Nevertheless, almost ten silhouettes had surrounded Accelerator without him realizing it. Actually, it might have been more than that.

The men and women were largely in their twenties, all wearing the same outfit.

Accelerator frowned. Their gear wasn't cutting-edge, technologically enhanced military uniforms—they were more like a certain kind of old-fashioned religious clothing. He felt the same sort of pressure from them as he did from Unabara and the parchment.

One of their number addressed him in Russian.

"You with Academy City?"

"I should ask you— You're not the ones who attacked this base?"

"You haven't denied it."

The habit-wearing man dropped his center of gravity slightly.

Accelerator took it as a signal that he was prepared for a death match.

"Don't really have the time for this."

Reaching a hand to the switch on the electrode around his neck and retracting his extendable crutch, he continued:

"You don't mind if I finish this quickly, do you?"

8

Fiamma of the Right.

Vento of the Front.

The two monsters of the Church didn't suddenly leap onto nearby roofs or start fighting so quickly that eyes couldn't follow.

Swoosh.

With wordless glares, they smoothly dodged from side to side in an almost relaxed manner. Maintaining equal distance and moving in tandem, they continued toward the center of the snowy plaza.

There were no explosions or flashes of light—nothing so utterly clear-cut to trace the exchanges of their fight. In spite of that, the people below, who were nearly in a panic because of Fiamma's attack, were unable to react save for one thing: The crowds naturally moved away from Vento and Fiamma like so much water overflowing from a bathtub after a giant lowered himself into it.

Kamijou, meanwhile, couldn't move.

He should have been providing backup.

Elizalina, Lesser, and Sasha Kreutzev. He knew he had to help someone back to their feet.

But he couldn't move.

He had no idea when this bomb would go off, and if he tried to mount a rescue right next to it, his mind would naturally be drawn to it. That was the kind of mental state he was in.

Clunk.

He thought a gust of wind had blown through—and then Vento's right hand was gripping something, some kind of hammer with barbed metal wire wrapped around it. It was about a meter long, and its tip was touching the ground.

Fiamma's eyebrow moved slightly.

"How strange."

"What is?"

"God's Right Seat cannot normally use magic. Not unless the spell is perfectly designed for us to use. The divine judgment spell that almost brought Academy City to a complete standstill is kept inside you, but the Soul Arm for supporting its activation should have been destroyed on September thirtieth. And yet…"

"Are you saying you find it surprising that I've caused a strange phenomenon?" said Vento tiredly, lifting her heavy hammer onto her shoulder.

Yes:

It was natural to forget because of each of their incredible achievements, but Fiamma and Vento were both still human. Supernatural phenomena that ignored natural laws weren't things that could be used except through some contrivance. If Vento had grabbed a hammer out of thin air, there must have been a rule or principle that supported such a phenomenon.

In other words.

…Vento can use magic right now…?

Recalling the spell that had knocked out almost every single resident in Academy City, Kamijou paled.

But Fiamma didn't seem too shocked.

"Still, I'm sure you haven't successfully recovered your divine judgment yet. And even if you had, its methodology wouldn't be able to defeat *me*."

"Even your ways of thinking about malice and hostility are twisted beyond recognition. I never thought about using something like that on you."

"Then what will you do?"

"You, of Michael, cannot use your complete power in your current state."

"Indeed. That is why I desire Sasha Kreutzev and the Imagine Breaker."

"That right arm," spat Vento, as if to cut off his prattling. "It must have a usage restriction."

"..." Fiamma finally stopped talking.

In the silence, the only remaining voice continued on alone:

"After bothering to use it on those small fry, it's practically breaking apart in mid-use, isn't it? For sorcerers, wielding supernatural powers is subject to logic. And God's Right Seat have a hard time using any spells other than ones custom-made for them. Meaning that once your stock runs out, you're nothing but a human."

A smile cracked.

It wasn't Vento.

Fiamma's lips had pulled away in a slight curve.

"You think so?"

An eerie, chilling pressure emanated from him into the air around him.

Moving the five fingers on his right arm slowly, he spoke.

"You think you can close the gap with *me* like that?"

"No."

The handle of the hammer resting on Fiamma's shoulder floated a little.

Only a few centimeters.

As she made the subtle motion, she declared:

"This is where it gets good."

Ga-bam!!

A moment later, Fiamma of the Right was knocked straight backward.

Even only a dozen meters away, Kamijou couldn't immediately grasp what had just happened.

The abnormal part wasn't the speed, but the *scale*.

Out of nowhere, a giant structure had appeared, splitting through the snowy earth in the plaza's center—a sailboat, made of translucent ice. It sprang up on an angle and was about forty meters in total length, but its hull hadn't completely appeared. It was forty meters with just what was visible *now*.

With rattling and creaking, the ice cannon affixed to the ship's side aimed at Fiamma.

What blasted out of it wasn't the flames of gunpowder, but instead, fine particles of ice.

The icy attack, the polar opposite of Fiamma's namesake "flame," wasn't composed of a mere cannonball; this was a translucent *anchor*. A clump of ice two or three meters large had stricken Fiamma and careened several kilometers away along with his body.

Ba-grrram!! The sound of the shock wave hit the plaza's entirety a moment later.

Without any attention to the clamor this caused around them, Vento said:

"…Did you know that in Chioggia, Italy, Biagio Busoni was in command of the *Queen of the Adriatic* and its escort, the Queen's Fleet?"

Vento spoke while twirling her giant hammer around in one hand, whether out of some meaning or just a whim. Her voice was low, almost whispering, but she'd probably used magical means to deliver it to Fiamma's ears.

"It was I who readjusted the Ten Rites of the Holy Spirit to bring it to a usable level. Controlling the entire *Queen of the Adriatic* spell wasn't possible, but even I have enough affinity to maneuver *part* of the great fleet."

He heard a jingling.

It came from Vento's tongue.

"Oh, right—one more thing."

A slender chain, like the sort you'd use for a necklace, extended from it, and at its tip hung a cross.

One made of a clear, almost icelike material.

A cross that looked rather like an anchor.

"In Crossism, there are quite a few stories about calming storms at sea and keeping ships safe. The Son of God did, for example, as did Saint Nicholas. By nature, the aspects I must preside over are wind and air, but storms at sea are a combined aspect of wind and water. By going through these stories, I can gain partial influence over water as well…And unlike your complete devotion to fire, I can bring forth more complex and wide-reaching effects."

A blast went off.

It was the sound of the giant ice anchor igniting with Fiamma caught in it, several kilometers away.

It was no mere gunpowder explosion.

The blast wind manifested in the form of an ice stake hundreds of meters long. The ice's tip, sharper than any old spear, expanded in all directions, to form ten thousand, then a hundred thousand tips. They bore a huge hole out of the land, and vast amounts of snow and black soil were flung up into the air. It was fortunate that only plains lay within their scope. With that many of them and with that much power, it definitely would have made Swiss cheese out of any underground shelters.

The people in the plaza probably couldn't comprehend what had just happened. But they seemed keen enough to pick up on the unique energy of battle and bloodlust contained within the icy pincushion that had suddenly appeared. Some even put their hands together, fervently praying for something.

It wasn't clear from here what had become of Fiamma.

Even whether anyone could manage to find out was a mystery.

That's how much sheer destructive power it had.

Vento of the Front.

She, too, had possessed insane strength as one of God's Right Seat, which stood at the pinnacle of two billion followers.

"If you had planned tactics purely to kill me, the result might have been somewhat different. But with your right arm disintegrating as we speak, you can't defend against that attack," she mocked, sticking out her tongue with the Soul Arm on it. "You waste too much ammo, you moron…I guess you can't hear me anymore, though."

*　　*　　*

"Is that so? Then I may have brought more to this than you think."

The voice, its source unknown, put a stop to Vento's banter.

A moment later.

Ka-boom!! went an explosion. It came from several kilometers away—and it was the sound of the pincushion of ice needles shattering apart from the inside. Calling it a volcanic eruption would have been an understatement. The insane force meant the debris didn't even rain down over the ground. All of it scattered, carried off by the wind.

The icy pincushion, now in shambles, blasted away in large chunks in all directions. Directions that included the plaza Kamijou and the others were in. It was like the area was raked with artillery fire. Several buildings were flattened, and the people in the plaza covered their heads with their hands and dropped to the ground. Voices rang out, lamenting the incomprehensible calamity and crying in anguish.

As Vento scanned the distance, her brow twisted bitterly.

There was a flash of light.

It was so far away that Kamijou and the others couldn't see it in any detail. But Kamijou understood. It was an arm. A third arm, that had newly appeared out of Fiamma's shoulder.

"I don't seem able to avoid the disintegration itself, but I have succeeded in stabilizing it."

Something glittered brightly.

Shining, reflecting…There was something in Fiamma's right hand giving off light.

He couldn't see it in detail either, but he had a good guess as to what it was.

The remote-control Soul Arm for Index.

A device that could draw out the knowledge of 103,000 grimoires at any time, in any amount.

"Frankly speaking, there no longer exist any restrictions upon me."

Vento refused to remain silent, however.

Several cannons went off from the sailboat near her all at once. A second anchor of ice lances, then a third, tore through the air, plunging one after another toward Fiamma.

A far greater cannonade than the one that had flung Fiamma several kilometers away earlier.

But Fiamma, at their landing point, didn't even bother dodging.

He only did one thing.

Shake his right arm to the side.

"I don't need brute force."

That was all.

The roaring of anchors shattering split the air. Some of them fractured in midair, while others stabbed into the ground, missing completely. Along with all of it, an explosion several dozen meters wide broke out.

The sight was like some kind of joke. It all went on shaving away hills and rivers—the very landscape itself.

"It ends with a touch, so I don't need effort to break my opponent."

"Shit!!"

Vento hastily repositioned her hammer, muttering something to herself. Maybe she had another trump card in store. Even Kamijou, untrained in sorcery, could sense it was like she was stringing out a cat's cradle very quickly.

However.

"I don't need speed."

A casual voice interrupted all that—by force.

And by overwhelming presence.

"If I swing, it will hit, so I don't need any effort to aim."

He couldn't tell what had happened.

The next thing he knew, Fiamma, who was supposedly kilometers away a moment before, had stepped right up underneath Vento's jaw. A moment later, her body was flying backward.

Fiamma didn't stop moving there.

As Vento floated, her chain fluttered after her. Without difficulty,

Fiamma grabbed it in midair. The motion was so casual it was like snatching a piece of paper drifting on the wind.

With Vento's body still flying.

So naturally.

The slender chain couldn't support Vento's body weight. Kamijou heard a ripping noise. It was the piece holding the chain tearing off. Off of Vento's tongue.

There wasn't time for her to cry out.

The woman clothed in yellow careened several dozen more meters away. She squarely struck the center of the ice sailboat sticking out of the center of the plaza, breaking the giant symbol of cannon fire into two clean pieces, upper and lower.

And at last.

After all that had happened, Vento let out a scream.

"Gaaaaaaaaaaaaaaaaaaaaaaaaaaaaaaaaaaahhhhhhhhhhhhhhhhhh-hhhhhhhhhhhhhhhhhhhhhhhhhhhhhhhhhhhhhhhhhhhhhhhhhh?!"

"It's not like I ripped your whole tongue out. You're exaggerating—It was just a little tear. And your fading defensive spell probably helped you when you hit that boat of yours."

Staring at Vento with absolute boredom as she lay screaming a dozen or so meters away, Fiamma tossed the torn-off chain. He swung the third arm poking out of his right shoulder through the air and shattered the translucent cross into pieces.

Pieces from the broken ice sailboat fell toward the plaza, and the residents in the area quickly rolled out of their way. Fiamma didn't bother glancing in their direction, of course.

"Gh, brgh?! Wh-what…?!"

"It's simple. What I possess is not the right arm itself, but the strength within it. In Crossism, most ceremonies are done with the right. The archangel Michael brought low the leader of fallen angels with his right hand. The Son of God cured the sick with his right hand. The Bible was written with the right hand—and so on and so forth. What I'm saying is that I can freely utilize that many Crossist supernatural phenomena. You figure out the rest. I'm sure you're not *that* dull."

"That's...not possible...That right...arm is..."

"Yeah. It's incomplete. Not normally something I could show off. Still, it's nothing you need to state with such grandiose tones. God's Right Seat...no, this whole world, is becoming something more vague in the same way."

"...?"

"The angel that appeared in an incomplete state during Angel Fall seems to have called itself Misha."

That was the only thing Fiamma said in anything resembling low spirits.

"Mikhail is another name for Michael, the LIKENESS OF GOD. It isn't a fitting name for Gabriel, the POWER OF GOD. Despite that, the archangel named itself as Misha. A name that should have been a role in and of itself, created by God. Do you understand how serious a matter that is?

"Also," continued Fiamma, "supposedly Vento of the Front bears wind, yellow, and Uriel; while Terra of the Left bears earth, green, and Raphael; but this is a deviation as well. Normally, wind applies to Raphael, and earth to Uriel. It's odd that it's anything else."

Vento's expression looked like her heart had stopped.

Her face appeared to say that the mental damage from a pillar in her own mind being toppled was even greater than the injury to her tongue.

"Nobody notices it."

Only Fiamma's words echoed out slowly.

"The world keeps on turning like nothing happened, with no one the wiser. Magic triggers accidentally. Do you understand it now? With it, the four great aspects are beginning to distort, little by little. This world is in a more dangerous situation than you realize. Someone must do something about it."

"You...mean...?"

Vento shook her head, delivering words even she had no confirmation of.

"Are you saying the Angel Fall left aftereffects of that magnitude?"

"I'm saying the opposite. Only because such a large distortion in natural laws existed to begin with did that ridiculous spell activate in the first place...Get it now? Can I stop explaining?"

Fiamma smirked, then raised his third arm high.

An extremely primitive motion.

Dozens of meters still separated them, but considering his phenomenal strength, that offered zero peace of mind.

However, before the motion could complete, Kamijou charged at Fiamma from the side.

"I have no need..."

Fiamma's reaction, though, was truly simple.

"...to turn around."

His arm changed course and swung around.

As if to accomplish its original purpose, it knocked Kamijou to the side. It was like hitting someone with a wooden club—primitive, and therefore, no way past it. Not only his organs but his very spine groaned. Yet, it was strange...if it could crush a giant anchor and destroy an entire sailboat in one hit, it should have reduced a human body to powder.

The role given to it...

Had it automatically calculated and chosen the optimal force with which to bat Touma Kamijou away?

It was different from a saint, who overwhelmed with strength or speed.

To give an analogy to an RPG battle, say you had a list of commands, like *fight*, *defend*, *spell*, and *item*—and also an absurd option that just said *defeat*.

Most likely, Fiamma would respond in the same way against Kanzaki and Acqua as well and dominate them in the same way. Even if he had less speed, even if he had less muscle power, it wouldn't matter. This altogether absolute "strength" ignored all actions taken by an enemy leading up to the very last instant and then defeated them in one fell swoop. It was almost like pushing a giant wall and knocking down a hill of sand made by a child.

Brawling with Fiamma head-on wouldn't get him the win.

But he couldn't retreat, either.

If he left things like this, Fiamma would finish Vento off. He wouldn't necessarily let Lesser or Elizalina go, either. And he'd definitely take Sasha Kreutzev away.

And above all.

In Fiamma's hand was the Soul Arm that controlled Index.

"..."

Kamijou tasted blood—maybe his lips had split.

Ignoring it, he got to his feet again.

He tightly gripped his fist.

"You're an amusing one."

Fiamma glanced his way, keeping Vento well within his firing range.

"How many people have you stood up for? How many incidents have you used that fist to resolve? You really are amusing. I suppose the most amusing thing about you is how you let others catalyze you into putting yourself into dangerous positions and then, in the end, accumulate all the results and rewards for yourself."

"What...are you trying to say?"

"Do you have the conviction that your actions are truly right?"

Fiamma slowly moved his arm.

His third arm.

The incredibly irregular item that probably couldn't be explained by mere magic or science.

"Fundamentally, there's nothing different about my actions, which you're enraged over, and what you've done up until now. I use my right arm to resolve my own problems, and you use your right arm to resolve incidents that happen around you. By shattering all the hard work people have so desperately done, too. Nothing separates our methods. And I have the conviction—conviction that my own actions will bring about an achievement of absolute good."

"...Are you telling me to abandon Index after you've made her suffer so much?" Kamijou shot back, not hesitating for a second. "That's a load of bull. You used the people of the Roman Orthodox Church for your own convenience, instigated a coup d'état in the United

Kingdom by having France put more pressure on them, and you call that *absolute good*? Are you fucking insane?"

"Then you would call yourself good for putting a stop to it?"

"It's not a matter of whether it's *good* or not."

"..."

"Index is suffering. How many people do you think are crying right now because of this shitty war you started? Is it strange to you that someone would want to stand up to you? Is it bad to want to fight for a girl who can't even open her eyes? At the very least, you have no right to complain about anything when you take so much delight in making so many people suffer."

However.

"How amusing."

Chuckling, Fiamma proffered his right arm to Kamijou.

In it was a small, cylindrical device.

The Soul Arm to remotely control Index.

As Kamijou's face changed, Fiamma's cheeks loosened into a grin, and he said:

"Those words—could you still say them in front of the sister you've been lying to all this time?"

Prkk.

Kamijou's shoulders gave a slight start.

Does he...?

"Sometimes her consciousness connects to mine through this Soul Arm. And sometimes, the information I see and hear is transmitted to her."

Has he actually...?

"Now, in this situation, under those circumstances, could you say it again? If I'm mistaken, then you don't have a problem. If you truly feel that way, then why have you kept up this shameless act with her?"

Does he know...?

A cold shudder ran through him.

It wasn't an emotion relating to the crisis he was in.

A certain girl.

He could feel something, like an invisible pillar holding her up, slowly beginning to crumble.

On the other hand…

Fiamma tapped his temple with his normal fingers and, still smiling, said, "You're the only one who understands that which you hide. Only she can give judgment on how she feels. You seem to be protecting her to satisfy yourself, but as for whether that will actually save her, well…I look forward to the judgment she will pass."

His third arm swung.

Kamijou, movements completely blocked by the malicious words, couldn't react to it.

But he wasn't aiming for Kamijou.

It was Sasha Kreutzev, whom Fiamma had knocked down with one hit, who was still lying on the plaza ground.

"Firstly."

The next thing he knew, Fiamma's third arm was holding the short girl's body.

He'd ignored the distance between them. The arm had undulated like a whip, then reeled back in like a chameleon tongue.

"?! Fiamma!!"

"I'd love to have the second, but there is still the issue of compatibility."

After Kamijou snapped out of it and shouted, Fiamma responded in a light tone, almost a whistle.

"I'd like to ensure the angelic medium is sealed, but if I do, your right hand's special effect will interfere. It would probably be hard to carry both at once."

Still gripping Sasha like a bag wrapped in branches, Fiamma turned his back to Kamijou.

"Don't die *too* easily," he offered.

Kamijou ignored them and charged forward.

Fiamma, however, didn't even turn around.

"I need that right hand for something."

An explosion went off.

By the time Kamijou's right hand had canceled it out, Fiamma was already nowhere to be seen.

The buzz returned to the plaza at last, now that the crisis had withdrawn.

As the scenery began to move, Kamijou alone remained still.

The only thing in his mind was what Fiamma had said.

"...But as for whether that will actually save her, well...I look forward to the judgment she will pass."

9

Shiage Hamazura was sauntering about in the snow.

He'd been in a building at first, but he'd lost his patience for staying still and ended up wandering back and forth out in the snow, thinking over what he could do about the weight sitting in the pit of his stomach.

It was a small settlement.

It only had about fifty private homes, all made of logs. Nobody but the people living here could tell the difference between a dwelling and a store. And in fact, *only* those buildings existed out here.

"It looks like treating the girl's symptoms is the best we can do, after all," a tall man addressed him as he was ambling about.

It was the man who had brought Takitsubo and him to this settlement in exchange for the fuel in the stolen car.

His name seemed to be Digurv.

"The drug affecting her is from Academy City, which is several decades ahead in technology, right? A small clinic like this can't possibly know how to cure the underlying condition. The greater danger is us doing something that ends up making things worse."

"Yeah, you're right. I know." Hamazura shook his head, unease coloring his features. "But I haven't even been able to let her sleep in a normal bed until now. Please—just get her health in a more stable condition. I can't stand seeing her in pain."

"Sure, but what are you going to do, ultimately?" asked Digurv.

Hamazura fell quiet for a moment. Takitsubo had said that Academy City might have a hidden reason for such a committed invasion of Russia. If they could find out what that was, then place themselves in a position that could influence the combat situation, they might be able to conduct negotiations on equal terms with the giant organization that was the City.

And searching for it was the only way. Before Rikou Takitsubo was completely out of action, he needed to head for the center of this world war on his own.

Spirits flagging at the sheer enormity of that wall, he decided to change the topic. Glancing around, he said, "Seems kind of busy around here."

"Mm. A nearby settlement seems to have been attacked by Russian forces, but an Asian boy apparently saved them from a truck convoy transporting them to a concentration camp. More people here are runaways than actual villagers at this point."

Were those the circumstances leading to the apparent lack of goods?

"...Will the generator be okay?"

"For now. Normally, we have regularly scheduled shipments of supplies and fuel, but the situation being what it is...The Russian forces are stationed on the roads, cutting off the usual route. To be honest, if you hadn't been passing by a little while ago, things would have gotten pretty bad."

A problem that wouldn't have happened had there not been a war between Academy City and Russia.

"I'm sorry...It's our fault."

For a moment, a ridiculous idea had crossed Hamazura's mind: Could this large-scale war have started because he and Takitsubo fled to Russia? He was fully aware of the fact that they were trivial and didn't nearly have that much value, but he couldn't entirely shake the thought, either.

However, Digurv shook his head. "No, it's not. If I've offended you, then I'm sorry. In all honesty, I get it."

"?"

"The Russian military has been targeting this settlement since before World War III started. The border with the Elizalina Alliance of Independent Nations is a stone's throw away, you know. This is the perfect site to build a front-line base to mount an invasion. We've been in danger of a takeover several times already. It's an awful real estate scam. Things got so bad they've been using the excuse of 'preventing Alliance invasions' to have transport aircraft lay out tons of land mines. Russia might have a way to find all of them and employ machines to retrieve them, but obviously, this settlement doesn't have anything like that."

The idea was unimaginable.

In Japan, a government perpetrating something like that was absolutely out of the question.

"Don't worry about it. We basically treat it like a store point card—the land mines, too. If we retrieve them and give them to an NGO, they'll exchange them for food and supplies. It would actually be safer to set them off where they are, but peace activists seem to appreciate results that are easy to understand."

Digurv pointed to a small house at the edge of the settlement. That was where they threw all the land mines they dug up and stabilized the fuse pins on.

"...Russia really wants to attack the Alliance, huh? What does the Alliance have anyway?"

"Who knows? It might not be an actual threat—the Russian government might simply fear their huge lands fracturing more than they already have. At the very least, the Alliance doesn't seem like it would ever be a military threat to Russia. Whatever the case is, our country can't possibly have the combat strength to fight a direct war."

Just because he was a local didn't mean this man knew everything about the country's circumstances. Digurv's tone made it seem like he'd heard this all from someone else. He was just another person. He couldn't get any news beyond what came on the television very easily.

And then it happened.

Zzzk. Hamazura heard someone's footsteps on the snow.

Digurv turned toward the noise, then immediately shoved Hamazura down onto the snow. He didn't even have time to argue. Digurv pulled on the fallen Hamazura's clothes, then frantically dove behind a building.

"Wh…what? What happened?"

"Russian soldier," answered Digurv in a purposely low voice, putting his index finger to his lips.

When Hamazura, startled, peeked around the wall, a man in his twenties wearing an army uniform was indeed standing on the snow.

The seriousness in Digurv's face intensified. "I thought we had sensors around the settlement to prevent intruders. Did they short out somehow?"

"…Hey, the Russian army is after this settlement's land, right?" asked Hamazura, but then something strange happened.

All of a sudden, the waddling Russian soldier fell into the snow.

Hamazura and Digurv exchanged glances, but the Russian soldier showed no signs of moving after that. After watching for a good thirty seconds or more, they slowly exited from the building's shadow.

Even when they drew near the fallen Russian soldier, no surprise attack came.

When they turned the facedown soldier onto his back, parts of his face had turned blue or purple.

"Frostbite," said Digurv.

With almost-closed eyes, the soldier looked up at his keepers and muttered something in Russian. When Digurv heard it, he glanced at Hamazura.

"Says he wants us to save him. He was waiting at a nearby air base for…*something*, but they were attacked by Academy City forces before it arrived. The cold must have been awful in his indoor uniform."

Hamazura almost grimaced at the mention of Academy City, but worrying about that on its own wouldn't get them anywhere...*Sure are a lot of visitors today*, he added internally.

"...What do we do? Save him? Seems like one hell of an uninvited guest."

"Don't give me that look. It's written all over your face that you want me to save him." Digurv sighed pointedly, then lent his shoulder to the frostbitten soldier and brought him to his feet. Hamazura helped support his body, too, shuddering at how cold his skin felt.

"Hey, will you guys be okay with this, Digurv?"

"I'd take the coldhearted route if I could. But leaving him to die won't change the situation at all."

Their destination was the tiny clinic Takitsubo was also resting in.

Hamazura didn't know any actual treatments for frostbite, but he idly guessed that just carrying him to a fireplace or heater would help quite a bit.

"...*Something*," huh?

As he held up the cold Russian soldier, he suddenly had a thought.

If the Academy City force had a reason other than the obvious war...in other words, if they'd been on a raiding mission to get the *something* scheduled to be delivered to the air base...Would the existence of that *something* be a tool he and Takitsubo could use to cut a deal with Academy City?

Right.

The soldier had said the Academy City force had attacked an air base where *something* was supposed to be delivered.

In that case, wasn't it possible that *something* hadn't made it into that force's hands yet?

Hamazura glanced at the exhausted Russian soldier's profile.

He doubted an amateur high school kid could "elicit information" from a professional soldier who went through daily training and had plenty of experience in actual combat. But in a weakened state like this, maybe there was a chance.

After he started to craft this plan, he said, "...Damn it. I wouldn't be able to face Takitsubo if I did something like that."

"?"

Digurv gave him a dubious look, but Hamazura didn't say anything else.

There was more than one method. There had to be an opportunity to make a deal with Academy City that didn't involve using a stranger's misfortune as a stepping stone.

Carrying this guy someplace warm comes first.

But as they were about to open the clinic door, someone burst out from inside.

It was a girl of about ten. Probably one of the people rescued from the in-transit convoy and not an original resident of the settlement; he could somewhat tell the difference from things like her clothes. As soon as she saw Digurv's face, she began to rattle away in Russian. It seemed to be a message for him, but Digurv was frowning. Maybe she was too excited for her words to get across.

However, as though finally realizing what the girl was trying to say, Digurv's face changed. Entrusting the frostbitten Russian soldier to Hamazura, he rushed into the clinic.

Hamazura didn't know what was going on, but he followed him inside while carrying the soldier.

He was tense.

The building the girl had burst out of was the clinic where Takitsubo was supposedly resting; maybe something had happened.

He had a bad feeling...

But his prediction was wrong.

The situation was even graver than he feared.

"What the hell's going on?! What happened?" shouted Hamazura in Japanese, lowering the Russian soldier to the floor in front of the electric stove near the clinic entrance.

Digurv, who had been speaking quickly, eventually turned around to Hamazura. He was in a whirlwind, like he was about to make an escape through the night.

"...Privateers."

"What are those?"

"They're like corsairs. Originally, it was a name for a military system during the Middle Ages. Government-approved pirates who would prioritize attacking ships from enemy nations, both causing them financial stress and filling their own country's coffers with the gold they plundered. During that time, the pirates would be under national protection, since they're approved by the government. Apparently, a few were even knighted."

"What's that got to do with this?"

"Russia's military uses privateers like that even in modern times," answered Digurv, not paying any attention to the nervous sweat forming on his face, his eyes bloodshot. "Empty units exist in the military. Their official personnel count is zero. Like the name *privateer* implies, most of their missions are to acquire funds by attacking hostile forces. Originally, they needed to carry out operations to disrupt enemy supply lines and indirectly sap their combat strength, but raiding operations targeting lightly armed people were never popular and tended to cause the spread of unnecessary unhappiness, so I also hear they established teams for the express purpose. Apparently, they're now the go-to team for when they need dirty missions done."

Digurv added that he didn't know how much of it was true, though.

"...They gather people mainly from western Europe who have armed forces experience and want to let loose. I even hear they recruit over the Internet. Military regulations don't apply to them, and you can make a lot of money in a short time, so it seems to be somewhat popular. In addition to that, Russia gives them top-of-the-line equipment and pushes the dirty jobs on them—so if push comes to shove, they can immediately disband the team and all its documentation. Any troops that cause a 'problem' are treated as having been thrown in a political prisoner camp on paper only, and then they go back to whatever country they came from. That's how they've built this system where they can smoothly carry out missions that would otherwise earn them criticism from the global community."

"You've got to be kidding me...You're saying crooks like that are on their way here?"

Hamazura looked at the Russian soldier he'd carried in front of the electric stove.

"O-oh yeah, and there's a Russian military ally here. They wouldn't level the entire settlement, would they? They would at least do some checking first."

"We're up against privateers. They don't care about any of that."

Digurv shook his head.

The Russian soldier, too, let out a groan upon hearing the word *privateers*.

After a moment, Digurv said, "They've sent privateers into real combat several times already."

Originally, the Russian military had been after this land to build a front-line base for attacking deeper into the Elizalina Alliance. And they'd even spread land mines using transport aircraft as part of their real estate scheme for it.

"But until now, we've detected them approaching and held out by running away before they started their main attack. I mean, they'd bust up our buildings and take anything worth money, but it was a small price to pay. And we'd always have a chance to manage to rebuild it all."

"Th-then, can't we do that now?"

"...The situation's changed. We're in World War III. The Russian forces have refurbished the privateers' gear. We can't escape anymore. The armored cars they have are far faster than our legs, and their firepower is something we can't deal with."

"This must be some kind of joke..."

Digurv and the others had also said they couldn't run the generator because they had no fuel. Right now, it was possible they didn't even have enough escape cars to fit everyone in the settlement.

They couldn't use their usual methods.

What would happen if they ran out of all other options?

"Away from here is a steel lookout tower that uses magnetism to detect when people are approaching. It's been blown to bits—probably by the privateers. They're already very close; we don't have much time. They don't abide by the rules of war, so if they get inside, they won't bother arresting us or capturing us—they'll slaughter everyone on the spot."

Hamazura glanced toward the clinic's wall.

Were those called AKs? He didn't know the exact model number, but assault rifles with wood here and there were standing up against the wall. He'd been surprised to see them when he'd first brought Takitsubo into the place, but it seemed like they were more common than fire extinguishers in these parts.

But they wouldn't work; running around with things like that was unlikely to lead to taking down the attackers, because they'd know the settlement's circumstances well in advance. Plus, they were probably preparing to one-sidedly massacre the people here.

They had no way to fight back.

Hamazura had used pistols sometimes in back alleys in Japan, but he'd never touched a gun that big before. It probably worked completely differently.

"…What do we do? Where are we even supposed to run?!"

"That's what we're searching for now."

10

In the remains of the Russian military air base attacked by the Academy City shadow organization, Accelerator quietly thought.

Almost ten men and women were standing ready, surrounding him.

And they were a strange bunch.

It didn't seem like they were mere Russian soldiers. Garbed in darkly colored religious habits, they gripped unique ornamental objects resembling swords, spears, staves, and axes in their hands.

Normal thinking named these items impractical weapons. They were anachronistic, by one or two eras, but strangely enough, in the ruins of the base, spurting flames and smoke…they appeared to fit perfectly on a Russian battlefield. He felt the same sense of oppression from them that he felt from Unabara.

There was just something about it…but that wasn't the most important thing.

In his arms was a girl named Last Order.

She was unconscious, her body limp.

If he applied his reflection to his whole body in order to fight while holding her in one arm, he ran the risk of harming her as well. He would have to be careful with his ability usage.

The ability to walk without assistance on two legs.

Deliberate lowering of defensive strength so as not to hurt the girl.

And…

"…"

Thinking for a moment, Accelerator scowled.

And then he went into action anyway.

He concentrated his offensive vector conversion ability into his right hand.

The air thundered and roared.

Accelerator manipulated his leg-force vectors and instantly burst ahead like a javelin. Out of the ten men and women, he closed in on the nearest one.

He stuck out his right arm.

With a strike like a light touch, the habit-wearing man's body flew over ten meters away without much impact.

And yet, even as he careened back, the man spoke clearly:

"*Vodyanoy!!*"

It was spoken like a name.

The group, on the verge of faltering at the sudden whirling injury to their ally, regained freedom of movement at the call. The woman standing diagonally behind Accelerator, directly in his blind spot— probably *the* Vodyanoy—moved her fingers in an unnatural manner.

A moment later:

The snow around her melted, turned into a watery spear, and lunged toward Accelerator.

Neither a bullet nor a bomb—an incomprehensible attack.

A normal person would have stopped moving at the sight of that, then been impaled in the meantime. But Accelerator wasn't shaken. He was a heap of incomprehensible things himself.

He held out his right arm, the only part of him he had applied his reflection to.

The spear burst apart, its water shifting into prismatic beams of *light* flowing from his hand and out behind him. It became a wall of heavy pressure, and it knocked down four or five of the habit-wearing people who were supposedly Vodyanoy's allies.

Accelerator, however, frowned. Even though he was the one who had blocked it.

It didn't make sense to him.

If his reflection had succeeded, the water spear should have plunged toward the woman herself and penetrated her arm. Instead, it had veered off target...and only after degrading into rainbow light.

It was a strange phenomenon. It wasn't water or ice or water vapor. Even he, the one who had caused the reflection, was mystified as to the process that had dismantled it into light.

...*What was that...?*

He felt like something slimy, something caught in his fingers, was escaping.

He'd learned from experience that when he reflected a teleportation ability, queer phenomena would occur in the three-dimensional world, but this was a different sensation from that, too.

But he didn't have time to mull it over.

Vodyanoy must have had her own questions about it. As if to confirm it once again, she purposely created the exact same water spear. As if to observe carefully—as if this time, she'd find a way through to him.

That was convenient for Accelerator, too.

He held out his hand, and once again, the watery spear turned into a rainbow of light.

But this time, something was different.

Part of the seven-colored light nearly grazed Last Order's cheek.

"...Careful."

Boom!! A gut-rattling explosion went off.

It was the sound of Accelerator tapping his foot on the ground and bringing up a huge amount of snow like a tsunami. As it went, it swallowed up Vodyanoy and all the others with overwhelming speed. The snow wall had fired more swiftly than a crossbow, and with a slamming shock wave, it knocked out all his assailants in one fell swoop.

"Figures a right hand wouldn't suit me."

After making sure he'd eliminated all the enemies, he switched off his electrode and thought for just a moment.

What was that water spear?

The way he had to think about the vectors was altogether different from the scientific abilities developed in Academy City.

Different vectors.

Different rules...

Unconsciously, he recalled the parchment he'd obtained on the freight train.

Did he attack this base, or didn't he? Was he from Academy City, or wasn't he? That was how they'd questioned Accelerator. That meant they must not have been the Academy City shadow group, but Russian people...

They might know something about the parchment.

Maybe how to use it, too.

The chances of this being a breakthrough to save Last Order from her critical situation weren't zero.

What a pain...

Now it seemed like he'd have to ask the assailants he'd just knocked out.

He needed to make sure he didn't accidentally kill them.

So he thought, but then he paused and looked up.

An Academy City supersonic bomber shot through the skies. If that were all, it wouldn't be unusual, since this nation was at war. However, the bomber dropped something into the sky over the ruined base.

And it wasn't a parachute. It was fitted with cruising wings, like a more complex version of a hang glider.

He could see a human shape.

He didn't have to think any more than that.

It was an enemy.

He came to the conclusion with but a single irritated click of his tongue.

A moment later, he switched on his electrode and kicked a pebble at his feet.

With an explosive *bang*, the aerial wings were shot out of the sky.

However, the human shape didn't slam onto the ground.

Purple lightning scattered, and the human shape's speed of descent decreased in stages. Even with their wings lost, at the end, they floated lightly down onto the ground.

…They caused the air to explode?

That was Accelerator's idle guess, but it was nothing to be surprised about.

He himself had jumped out of a bomber in Avignon without a parachute once.

What made him curious was the ability that was used.

Electric power.

And an ability Accelerator was *very* familiar with.

"Who is that?"

The person was clad in combat gear colored white to match the snowfields and wore special masklike goggles that covered their face. It wasn't clear where their eyes or nose were. The expressionless mask only featured eight small lenses, fixed in a circle like the face of a clock. The clothing had no gaps in it, so one could store anything inside. Because of that, the visible body build didn't do much good, but as a first impression and nothing more, the person looked like a girl of about high school age.

Crackle.

A strange sense of tension ran through him.

The whiteness of the skin on her ears, which slightly showed at the sides of the mask, and the fluttering of her shoulder-length brown hair gave him an incredibly bad premonition.

Yes.

He got the feeling that this girl was identical to the one in his arms.

"Who the hell are you?"

The figure in white didn't remove her mask.

Her expression wasn't visible.

With only the small lenses—placed in her mask like the face of a clock—shifting place slightly, she answered:

"If Misaka said *Third Season*, would you know who Misaka was?"

Accelerator almost unwittingly caught his breath.

But the girl who had called herself Misaka continued.

"Heyo! Came to kill you, Number One. Misaka doesn't care what happens with this war. Never got inputted with any orders like that. Misaka's goal is only to exterminate Number One. For that purpose, for that goal alone, they went through the trouble of dispatching Misaka from her culture medium."

INTERLUDE TWO

She had wanted to look into it, but this wasn't something she could investigate.

...Well, I guess that much was obvious, though.

Mikoto Misaka looked away from her PDA with a soft exhale.

Until now, she'd always extracted confidential information from the data banks and such, but this time, the situation was different. The security had been strengthened quite a bit. Unexpectedly, the term *war* had started to feel real for the first time.

The data she'd been trying to obtain must have been valuable enough to warrant it.

If the details of operations and such leaked, it would affect many people's lives.

But she'd still gotten more than one thing out of it all—she'd been able to grab several pieces of information unrelated to the war.

Mikoto Misaka had once watched Touma Kamijou's school compete in an event during the Daihasei Festival, a large-scale athletic meet in September. Which meant that she knew his school's name. She used it to consult their attendance data, but as she thought, it seemed he hadn't gone to school ever since the day of that phone call from London.

When she checked his attendance count, she found he'd already gone below the minimum requirement, ensuring he'd get penal courses. Normally, this wouldn't have been possible in their school system...or at the very least, there should have been data that showed traces of confusion or panic into a sudden disappearance of a student. But it just said that he hadn't been to school a single day since then, full stop—and that was abnormal, no matter how she thought about it.

Perhaps it was as she'd surmised: That boy really wasn't in Academy City any longer.

And if the phone conversation was true, he might not even be in Japan.

The war was centered in Russia, and the United Kingdom was, if only somewhat, removed from it. However, that didn't give her any guarantee he wouldn't be caught up in it. And actually, this was a big, planetary war. Safe places were probably harder to come by. Academy City seemed peaceful at a glance, but they'd already intercepted several ballistic missiles. Maybe looking for a safe place wasn't the right move.

...What now? Do I risk the danger and try to get deeper information?

Mikoto began to think about this seriously but then heaved a sigh. She knew the blood had gone to her head. Even if she tried to hack in, if she started in her current mental state, she was sure to mess it up. She'd be better off taking a break, resting her mind, and thinking about what to do next.

The decision made, she switched her PDA to a 1seg TV service.

Like always, a lot of the news was about the ongoing conflict. Many normal programs had been canceled, and though a variety show was on, it felt somehow stilted—they were refraining from using any words related to the war or that might make people think about it.

Nothing she saw gave her any peace of mind.

She considered switching to a browser and watching shows online, but then her index finger, which was controlling the screen directly, stopped dead.

On the news program, the anchor was explaining the situation in snowy Russia. It wasn't a live stream, so it must have been filmed a short time ago.

The edge of the screen showed a small person. A spiky-haired boy with a Croaker cell phone strap hanging out of his pants pocket.

One she was sure she'd seen before, somewhere…

CHAPTER 3
Confront Walls of Doubt
Great_Complex.

1

The invasion of the foreign mercenary privateer unit had begun.

And Shiage Hamazura and the others could do nothing about it.

They didn't seem worried about the wounded Russian soldier, either. It was an all-out offensive.

"This way."

Digurv led them to the clinic's basement. From what it looked like, it was originally a space for storing cheese and smoked meats. Naturally, they couldn't expect a dedicated shelter's durability from it. This wasn't a structure designed for weathering attacks—its only worth was to stay out of sight of the enemy.

After warming up in front of the electric stove, the frostbitten Russian soldier now seemed able to move somewhat. He was focusing on recovering his stamina, having gotten a share of the preserved cheese. However, his face was the definition of gloom. Being abandoned by the army must have been a bigger deal for him than his physical condition.

Hamazura drew Takitsubo's limp form close. He'd never imagined something like this would happen; he'd thought Academy City's back alleys were bad, but it turned out they weren't the only hell. Every place had its own gaping maws of darkness. Hamazura and Takitsubo believed they'd been desperately fleeing here, away from the shadows of their city, but that didn't mean anywhere else was pure paradise, either.

The ceiling began to give off a low rattling noise.

It didn't seem like it was a bomb. It was sort of like a car's engine, but the vibrations were significantly too severe for that.

"What's that? Treads?"

"They might have sent in tanks or something," answered Digurv. "Not many of them. Probably only two. They don't care one bit about standard military practice, after all. They probably didn't bring any foot soldiers along either...Of course, even armored vehicles acting arbitrarily will be enough of a threat in their own right."

As the rumbling continued, Hamazura felt an acute sense of fear but also a streak of doubt. "Reality aside for a moment, what if there *were* troops with antitank rockets behind and inside buildings, waiting to ambush them? Normally, you'd take out valuable cover from a distance, then charge in after that."

"They're not regular soldiers. These units are filled with people who simply want to cut loose and go wild with top-of-the-line equipment. That's why military doctrine doesn't apply to them. Their wanton expression of their humanity might present a vulnerability, but that means they're also far more brutal than robotic units. We're better off not letting them find us."

An awful creaking noise began to come from the ceiling.

The talking ceased. Only the roaring continued, like an active demolition site. They must have been charging in with the thickly armored vehicles themselves, rather than laying down a bombardment. It didn't seem like the proper way to use them.

...They're screwing around.

Still holding Takitsubo close, Hamazura gritted his teeth... *They're waiting until we can't stand the fear anymore and jump out. Once we're out of patience and cause a panic, we'll be like fish in a barrel.*

The privateers were enjoying this, prioritizing the act of killing itself over any strategic objectives. Crying and surrendering would probably be useless. Clinging to them and begging for them to save at least the girl would probably do no good. They'd both end up with bullets in their foreheads for sure.

Vehement rage bubbled up from deep inside him, but he couldn't do a thing about it. If he jumped out in front of the privateers now, he'd be playing right into their plan.

Digurv probably felt angrier than he did. *They* were the ones who had invested everything in this land, not Hamazura. The fact that the privateers were mercilessly demolishing it all for sport must have been amplifying his rage.

And yet, Digurv was still enduring it.

Enduring so that he himself would survive this, and so Hamazura and Takitsubo, hiding in the same place as him, wouldn't be caught up in it.

It reaffirmed to Hamazura the fact that he couldn't take any risks.

However.

That alone wouldn't be enough for the crisis to leave them.

Bk-grr!!

Because suddenly, the ceiling caved in, and the armored vehicle slid inside like an avalanche.

The privateers probably hadn't purposely created this situation. They'd been trying to pass through the clinic without realizing it had a basement, and then the floor had given out.

But that was of no concern to those trapped inside it. A deluge of wooden planks burst forth, sending Hamazura and Digurv falling into desperate rolls. The now-jagged plank edges began to stab into the mortar walls.

The armored vehicle turned out to be an armored car with a fixed turret on the top. It had fallen into the basement at such a sharp angle that the cannon's tip was bent.

"Run!!" shouted Digurv.

The armored car's metal front hatch was about to open.

Hamazura dragged his unconscious charge away. Digurv, who

exited the ruined basement onto the surface before him, took her and pulled her up.

Then, with a bang, the car opened up.

Hamazura and the frostbitten Russian soldier finished their frantic crawling aboveground together at about the same time rifle bullets started spraying blindly. There wasn't anything to be seen of the clinic; the roof was long destroyed—even the walls were gone now. All that was left was an uneven pile of debris.

They'd avoided being peppered with rifle fire for now, but they didn't have time to feel relief.

Digurv, his face white, said, "If we stay on the surface, they'll kill us. Others in the area might find us, and if the guys in that armored car manage to crawl out, it's all over. We have to find new shelter before they catch up!!"

Just then, an explosion went off nearby. Hamazura and Digurv were sent to the ground in different directions.

His eardrums didn't seem to be working right.

From the ground, Hamazura gave Digurv a look. The man seemed to have sustained less damage; still holding Takitsubo, he glanced for a moment at Hamazura, then ran off somewhere as though the situation itself were pushing him. He was probably trying to flee to another shelter, just as he'd said.

...Shit, I don't know where that place is, you know! If you let Takitsubo die, you're never hearing the end of it!!

Hamazura wobbled to his feet. His mind was in a near-complete state of panic. He didn't know at this point where the frostbitten Russian soldier had gone, and he was caught in the terrible stench of smoke rolling by. The old smells—of cooking and cigarettes, of human activity—were all gone. All blown away and replaced with the odor of engine oil and burning buildings.

He lowered himself, and as he hid amid the debris, Hamazura surveyed the area.

Almost half the log buildings were already destroyed, with distinct caterpillar tracks tangling through the snow. They didn't seem to be from the armored car, earlier.

A weapon. Isn't there anything I can use as a weapon...?

He'd never be able to overcome this crisis with nothing but the gun in his pocket.

For better or for worse, only about ten meters away was a machine-gun emplacement. Sandbags were piled up in a semicircle, and a fairly large-sized machine gun had been set up over them. It obviously couldn't have been for shooting down attack helicopters. Maybe, leaving aside its actual effectiveness, they were making an appeal to having countermeasures like it in order to easily stop anyone from passing by overhead.

Naturally, he had no way of knowing how to use a machine gun. The recoil would probably mean the gun would control him rather than the other way around.

But it was better than nothing.

As Hamazura's tension rose to a point where his pulse was so fast he was worried his heart was going to burst, he broke from cover onto the field of deadly white. More stumbling than running, he reached the emplacement, surrounded by several layers of sandbags. It had only been ten meters, but for Hamazura, the distance had been hellish.

The machine gun was fixed in place on a tripod. It was made so the joints could rotate; the three legs' tips were like stakes, which kept it solidly on top of the square concrete sheet. Without tools, he'd probably never get it out.

"Damn it!!" he swore, finally pulling out his own gun. He could still hear blasts going off around him—would anyone notice if he fired a shot?

It happened just as he was thinking about doing it: An armored vehicle with tracks appeared from behind another building.

The distance was about twenty meters. It had a single rotating turret on either side, and their barrels were currently lining up in parallel. It had an antenna that looked like a plate, too—so maybe they weren't tank cannons, but anti-aircraft ones. It seemed like they weren't for firing explosive shells that would bombard an area; they were more like incredibly enlarged machine guns that would fire at more specific targets.

Again, that wasn't normal tank usage. This was not a vehicle made for dashing through the front lines pursuing ground targets.

Nevertheless, it would certainly make mincemeat out of any unarmed human.

Hamazura was so shocked he almost bit his tongue off, but it looked like they hadn't noticed him yet.

It was chasing different prey.

A woman in her thirties, running for her life with a young baby in her arms. A girl who looked about ten fled after her as well. The baby-holding woman's expression had changed completely into overwhelming terror, exhaustion, and humiliation. Hamazura didn't know who she was, but he felt the information squeezing out of the back of his mind. They'd probably been part of the group who had been rescued from the convoy and come to the settlement. He could tell their clothing, among other things, was subtly different from Digurv's and the others'.

The anti-aircraft cannon barrels continued to move slightly, tracking after their backs.

Barrels of certain death; if even one hit, there'd be nothing left to bury.

Hamazura's arms sprang up.

The next thing he knew, he was grabbing the machine gun fixed to the emplacement. There was no time to take careful aim.

He pulled the trigger.

It was fixed to the ground, but he still felt an impact shoot through his right shoulder, like a power tool had pushed back against him. The intense shock rattled his vision, and yet still, he clenched his teeth and kept pulling the trigger.

Sparks flew from the anti-aircraft tank's armor.

With the preface of "if it could hit," the large-sized machine gun packed enough destructive power to deal damage to a small aircraft.

Had the turret's angle of rotation skewed slightly, pushed by the force?

The giant round fired directly after stabbing not into the backs of the fleeing women, but straight past them.

"RUN!!"

They wouldn't understand Japanese, but he shouted anyway, loud enough to be heard over the gunfire.

The anti-aircraft guns didn't stay quiet, either.

Brrrr!! The turrets swung his way, relying on the output of its giant motor. He could feel their irritation at him for getting in the way of their fun. The muzzles, which looked big enough to fit an entire golf ball inside, pointed at the machine gun nest where Hamazura was.

"Shit?!"

Immediately letting go of the machine gun, Hamazura dove to the ground.

The volley came a moment later.

One after another, the sandbags forming a wall burst, sending the black earth packed inside them spraying out. The large machine gun went to pieces. At this rate, he'd lose the wall before ten seconds were up. But if he brought his face out during this tempest of shells, that alone might blow him up.

He was now unable to move—

But then the anti-aircraft cannons stopped firing.

...Did...their gun get jammed...?

His thoughts were optimistic but inaccurate.

These privateers, unlike regular troops, didn't act according to military doctrine.

This was entertainment.

And for the sake of their entertainment, instead of resuming fire with the anti-aircraft cannon, the crew had instead fired one of the surface-to-air missiles attached to the side of their vehicle's turret.

With a jet of white smoke, the explosives flew toward the half-destroyed emplacement.

"Damn it!!"

Goggling, Hamazura leaped to the side, away from the emplacement he'd been using as a shield.

The explosion came an instant later.

His hearing failed.

His body, struck by an intense blast of wind, flew into the air. He landed on the snow, and when he looked around, he was in a place right behind a building. He thought it had been ten meters away from the emplacement. But it wasn't because of any superhuman leg strength. That was just how powerful the blast had been.

His legs trembled in terror.

These privateers were *insane*.

Hamazura and others like him had lived lives nobody could ever praise in the back alleys of Academy City. But these people's morals were so deviant that even *he* was scared. They'd crossed national borders to reach a battlefield out of a desire to kill people—that wasn't normal.

Now that the reality was slowly creeping in, he found himself unable to move.

And then he heard a quiet clanking noise.

"?!"

It almost caused him to panic, and he nearly pulled his gun's trigger without thinking of the consequences, but then he realized something: It was Digurv, carrying Takitsubo, who had come to him. He must have gotten behind this debris via another route. He'd kept the unconscious Takitsubo—he hadn't abandoned her.

Her sleeping face was just enough to prevent Hamazura from losing it.

"Are you all right? I'd rather not have any more sick or injured."

"Wait, weren't you escaping to another shelter?"

"While we were running around trying to stay hidden from the privateers, we eventually ended up here."

...Did that mean their encirclement was closing in? Hamazura felt the inside of his mouth dry out from nervousness. As he considered throwing some of the snow at his feet into his mouth, he asked, "What happened to the other shelter?"

"A few of them were hanging around near the entrance. It didn't seem like they figured it out yet, but if I got close, they might have caught on to where the shelter was."

"Damn it," muttered Hamazura.

Checking again, there were surprisingly few engine sounds. It was probably just the anti-aircraft tank from before. The armored car had fallen through the floor and couldn't move anymore. The small group of soldiers who had exited it were now coincidentally blocking off the shelter.

"What were they like?"

"They were checking everything, from under the roof to behind bunched-up curtains. They were looking under children's beds, looking for anything, even little stashes of money. Also, they seemed angry they couldn't find their targets. Every single one of them is on pins and needles, wanting to kill the enemy."

"...So they're not going to let us get away. Doesn't seem like we can appeal to their humanity, either."

The privateers had blocked the entrance to the shelter, so they couldn't dash into a safe alcove anymore.

Perhaps there'd been no such place to begin with.

Hamazura looked at Takitsubo's unconscious face. A few bangs were caught on the awful sweat on her forehead. He gently fixed them and, strangely, realized that his fingertips had stopped trembling.

He couldn't afford to let her die here.

He didn't want the people who had worried about her to die, either.

He'd had more than enough of being beaten, of never having any power to do anything about it, in Academy City's back alleys.

Hadn't he decided that he would escape from all that?

He felt angry toward this unfair violence. Why did there have to be people after Takitsubo's life in a place like this? Why did nice people who would worry about someone they'd never met before have to be attacked for such a bullshit reason? It was high time they counterattacked, wasn't it? If lives were on the line on each side, then Hamazura had the right to bite back, didn't he?

"...Can I leave Takitsubo in your hands for a just little bit longer?"

"Wh-what are you going to do?"

Digurv might have realized it based on the difference in his complexion and attitude.

Hamazura looked at Takitsubo's face as she rested in Digurv's arms just one more time before answering.

"This is a load of bullshit. I'll reduce them to a pile of metal scrap."

"Just so you know, we don't have any RPGs or anything. They might have lighter armor than tanks, but AKs won't be enough to shoot through that anti-aircraft vehicle!!"

"The point card."

Hamazura said something indecipherable.

Digurv gave him a dubious look, and Hamazura rephrased so it would be easier to understand.

"…You have the land mines you dug up to give to the NGO stored somewhere, don't you?"

2

Accelerator burst out of the base, running through the snow.

Not to hunt prey. Nor to dash toward a destination.

But to run.

Academy City's number one Level Five, holding Last Order in his arms, was running away from something.

Terrified.

His feeling on the matter was sincere.

More than Amata Kihara.

More than Teitoku Kakine.

More than Aiwass.

More than that boy.

In a certain way, the enemy chasing him down was so incredibly terrifying that, in one blow, she would rock the pillar that bore his sense of values.

He heard the crackling of purple lightning bouncing behind him.

It was probably somewhat smaller in scale than the number three Railgun.

But it was much larger compared to the standard Sisters.

He heard a sound like a balloon popping.

A short metal nail, a few centimeters long, had just been launched—at a speed slightly faster than that of sound.

It held approximately the same force as a pistol round.

The nail fired off from behind Accelerator, then pierced his left arm, right in the bicep.

It wasn't that he couldn't reflect it.

It was that he didn't know if he should.

No.

It wasn't that. He simply couldn't decide if it was advisable to let his assailant die as a result of using his reflection.

If he altered its angle, he might have gotten away with not harming the target. But if, by some mistake, he let his habits take over and reflected incoming attacks with intent to kill—the possibility existed. When he thought about that, he couldn't take action anymore.

The strength faded from his arm.

The little girl he'd been holding up floated into the air.

Last Order.

The girl who was supposed to be supporting his mind—her warmth was swept away by the cutting chill of the snowfield.

"Gaaaaaaaahhhhhhhhhhhhhhhhhhhhhhhhhhhhhhhhhhhhhhhhhhhhh-hhhh?!"

A scream rang out.

The deep snow caught Last Order.

Accelerator couldn't even extend his hand to her. Losing his balance, stumbling, he scattered the pure-white snow underfoot.

A laugh threatened to climb up from the pit of his stomach.

Accelerator had given himself a rule.

In the past, for his very own "experiment," he'd murdered many somatic cell clones.

So now, he would never harm any clones like the Sisters or Last Order again, no matter what happened.

For that purpose, until now, Accelerator had been killing and killing, covered in blood. Amata Kihara and Teitoku Kakine—and

Shiokishi of the General Board. He'd been in death matches with all sorts of monsters, and each time, it had chipped away at his body and heart. He'd lost to Aiwass. Following the being's instructions, he'd fled to this snowy land. He certainly wouldn't have received full marks, but he thought he'd been able to protect Last Order's and the Sisters' lives and livelihoods to some extent. He'd been able to believe he was doing what was necessary for that.

And yet, of all the things.

Academy City had worked out a plan to pinpoint and shatter that very thing he held close. A tactic to destroy his motive for combat, his having something to protect even if it meant turning the entire world against him.

They're mad…

He needed to protect Last Order.

He needed to defeat the Sisters' assassin.

No matter which survived, no matter which he protected, Accelerator could not break the rule he had risked his life to uphold.

A "Third Season"? Just to set up this exact situation? To take aim at my trauma? Crush my spirit? For bullshit reasons like that they made even more?! Academy City is a hellhole. I know that now that I've witnessed them from the outside. Something fundamental is totally fucked-up with the people in that city!!

His normal thought patterns weren't establishing themselves.

It must have been proof the assailant's presence was shaking Accelerator's mental state.

Yes, for a tactic against someone with enough power to reflect a nuclear attack, it was having reasonable results.

"Oh? Hmm? Wait, are you thinking you've been protecting Misaka? Nobody asked you to do that, you know. You killed over ten thousand of them, and you think that will make everything right? The thought alone is arrogant."

Those words stung.

Her voice was the same. But the emotion it carried was a world apart.

"Just do us all a favor and self-destruct already. If you break your little rule and fight at full strength, you could've probably beaten Misaka, too."

His assailant's voice reached him from inside the mask with the lenses arranged like an analog clockface.

No fear was in it.

That shouldn't have been possible. Was this attacker confident she could attack him without reprisal?

"Maybe Misaka didn't need to take measures against your electrode after all."

A crackle of purple lightning sparked from her bangs, hanging out of the mask edges. She probably planned to use her electric-based ability for jamming or something. Or would she directly interfere with the Misaka network?

When he thought about that, a little doubt arose in Accelerator's chest.

Last Order.

She was a unique individual who controlled the chain of command for all the Sisters connected to the Misaka network. If this assailant was one of them, one instruction from Last Order should be enough to stop her from moving.

The higher echelons had probably figured out Accelerator was running away with Last Order in tow.

Would they leave this assassination to one of the Sisters, control of whom could be taken over at any time, despite that?

Which meant…

A disguise!!

A moment after coming to that conclusion, Accelerator's legs moved.

Ba-bam!!

Not only the white snow but the ground underneath it broke apart as he shot toward his assailant with unbelievable speed. It was like a shotgun discharged with dirt in its barrel.

Meanwhile, his assailant smoothly, casually, lowered her stance.

His attack, like an uppercut, was dodged easily. But clumps of black earth got caught on her mask and sent it flinging into the air.

Her face was exposed.

And.

This time, Accelerator fell onto the white snow.

He hadn't suffered any particularly strange attack. He just felt such intense resistance to acknowledging the face that had been under the mask.

"Nope."

The assailant.

The girl, her face closely resembling Last Order's but older, something like high school age, spoke without even cracking a smile.

"After all, you're using the Misaka network for proxy calculations. The Third Season Misaka monitors the Misaka network's operation status, which lets her predict your next attack. You'd need a miracle to land a fatal attack on *this* Misaka. This is no time for you to be holding back, is it? If you're going to do this, you'd better come at Misaka with the intent to kill. Get it? Then try killing Misaka. You can't, of course. If you did, all your hard work until now would be for nothing. In that case, want to stay quiet and let Misaka beat you to a pulp? Gya-ha-ha-ha!!"

A disguise.

Special makeup.

She was using some kind of ability.

So Accelerator thought as he struggled to get up, but…

"'I'm scared. Help me!'"

"…!!"

Hearing the girl's imitation, Accelerator stopped. Even as blood dripped from his left arm, pierced by the metal nail, he couldn't even raise his fist up against that voice.

"By the way."

The assailant put a hand to her neck.

There was a very faint trace there, one which he would have missed unless he looked closely.

"Misaka's body contains a sheet and a selector. Even if Last Order sends Misaka a command signal to stop, the device automatically rejects all signals as long as they don't have the permission code from the General Board. Clumsily cling to that girl all you want—it won't stop *this* Misaka."

"…"

The answer offered to him was a very simple one.

Kill or be killed.

That wasn't in reference to Accelerator.

If that was all, he might have given up right there and offered her his neck.

The problem was Last Order. She was now wrapped up in this assassination, too.

This was wholly different from pulverizing third-rate trash. It wasn't a story where he could throw away his life to solve everything, either.

Was there no way to save them both?

No matter what happened, even if he had a gun to his forehead, Accelerator would never kill another one of the Sisters. He couldn't let himself kill them. Even if he turned the whole world against him, no matter how many monsters in bloody darkness he had to fight to the death with, causing pain and suffering to girls with this face was something he absolutely, positively, could not do. He doubted he could put a smile on their faces with all the blood clinging to him, but he wanted, at least, for them to create their own smiles.

And yet.

Win or lose, it would place one of the Sisters in a crisis.

After the experiment, Accelerator knew that if Academy City said they'd kill the sisters, they weren't joking—they would. He didn't have any leftover time to pull his punches and half-ass this, either.

However.

This was.

If this development continued, in the end, Accelerator would probably lose the last part of his self-control.

Even if one of the Sisters died.

"…The Third Season…," muttered Accelerator. "If they really did start a third production schedule and created you, then that means they can make other Sisters at any time and replace them. Cost-wise and ethics-wise, that's the sort of decision they made."

"Yep. And our command tower, Last Order, is no exception."

Academy City was trying to conduct some sort of experiment. He got the feeling Aiwass was involved with the project and that the Sisters' network was being used for it.

"Still, considering the General Board wants to keep constant control over the Misaka network, maybe they wouldn't have had to make the bold decision to make a new one if she hadn't disappeared to begin with. If only you hadn't gone and done all that dumb stuff. It all backfired on you, huh?"

In the end, that was how it was.

This wasn't a retrieval, but a homicide.

If they were going to create a new Misaka network and command tower, the old numbers would no longer be needed. In fact, having two command towers might be an active detriment; that was why Academy City had taken the initiative and decided to kill Last Order.

Even though she'd never done anything wrong.

She'd been made at the selfish whim of somebody else; and now, just for the reason that they didn't need her anymore, they'd kill her.

"What'll you do?"

The assailant smiled.

It was an evil, emotional smile, contrary to the impression the other Sisters gave.

"If you don't want to kill the Sisters, Misaka guesses you'll just have to stand there and get beaten into the ground. But after this Misaka kills you, she'll attack Last Order, too. Well, even if you try to stop me by force, a Misaka will still die! Gya-ha-ha-ha-ha!! Either way, your spirit will die here. I'll play with you until your mind is ground into dust, so let's have fun with it!!"

With those despair-inducing words, the battle began.

The battle to thoroughly demolish all the pillars Accelerator had finally built up to support his fragile soul.

3

Avoiding the Sea of Japan battleground and making an extensive detour in the Pacific Ocean, a Russian Navy submarine had made it to the waters around Indonesia.

They weren't preparing to pull off a surprise attack and fire a ballistic missile into Academy City.

Multiple missiles had already been fired from various angles, but all had been shot down with precision strikes. Most had been intercepted outside the earth's atmosphere, but some had even been blown away by an unknown flash of light not five seconds after launch.

Considering missile development history, this was absolutely impossible.

All sorts of technology was concentrated within the interception systems humanity had developed, but even then, they didn't reach 100 percent accuracy. Generally, the theory for countering ballistic missiles was *supposed* to be centered around political caution so they were never fired in the first place.

Countermeasures to that were for the higher-ups to think about. The current goal of *this* submarine, deployed in the waters near Indonesia, was to cut off enemy supply lines.

Academy City, or rather Japan, was fundamentally an island nation. Unlike Russia, its natural resources were scarce. Nobody expected the battle to get this drawn out, but now that it had, the tactic of cutting off overseas supply routes and quickly depriving the enemy of much-needed materiel became effective.

They wouldn't be wielding their technology in perfect form for long.

Once their stamina ran out, that would be their death day.

That was what the Russian military had assumed.

They had prepared over twenty submarines to prevent even a single transport ship from getting away.

However...

"They're not showing up," muttered someone. No matter how much time passed, no ships appeared.

This strait was like a highway, not only to reach Japan, but for ships from all over the world to pass through. In fact, they'd confirmed vessels from various other nations entering and exiting. However, any transport ships heading to Japan were conspicuously absent.

Were they using a different route? Were they disguising themselves as other nations' ships? They'd thought about several possibilities but never found an answer. All they knew was that without a large quantity of transport ships passing in and out, Academy City wouldn't be able to keep running.

A voice reached them from the communications officer on another one of the submarines in the fleet. Being bored when one had nothing to do applied just as much to soldiers as it did to laymen. The fact that they hadn't seen a single sign of their target was one that, more than necessary, rubbed everyone inside this closed-off sub the wrong way.

"Are they really using ships? Didn't we get reports they're using some crazy aircraft for inland operations?"

"I doubt those monsters alone could carry every single thing they need, including daily commodities. Don't let the shock of their technology confuse you. The fact of the matter is: Sea routes are the most popular method of transporting heavy goods."

"But we haven't seen a single transport ship heading for Academy City. We've even pretended to be pirates to inspect cargo several times but always came up empty. Where are they? They're not on the water or in the air. Don't tell me they're down at the bottom of the sea or something."

"Don't be ridiculous. Submarines have a required maximum size so their sound isn't detected. They can't replace larger-scale transport vessels."

"What should we do, sir? They hit the ball pretty close to the hole."

Saying that was a young communications officer on board an Academy City–made submarine.

They were slipping past the Russian-made submarines deployed in Indonesian waters by a distance of only a few meters each time. Most of their cargo consisted of goods bound for Academy City. The Russians' conversation had been right on the mark.

They indeed had an abnormal size. In contrast to the Russian subs, which were a hundred meters at most, this Academy City unit was easily five times that.

Academy City wasn't situated on the water, but several cooperating organizations had, based on technical intelligence, prepared this secret trick: Once they entered Japan's waters, they would link up with smaller submarines, which would then ferry the goods to harbor.

Another shipmate next to the young communications officer—the navigation officer—replied, in a bored voice, "They haven't actually detected us with radar or sonar. Meaning we officially don't exist."

For a submarine this enormous, the sound of the screw propeller alone would be considerably loud. The noise of them splitting through water would also certainly be detected.

But that didn't happen—because this submarine didn't have a propeller in the first place. The ship's outer surface read the ocean's currents, firing water jets in such a way that it would blend in with the currents' sound to advance forward. It even used the water jets to interfere with the very sounds scattered as the ship progressed, which they couldn't completely erase no matter how hard they tried. All these efforts combined made it impossible for enemy sonar to detect the anomaly.

"But, sir, if we used supersonic weaponry, we could write it off as propeller trouble, not the result of a skirmish."

No expense had been spared in other areas, either—stealth treatments had been applied to the ship's surface, and it also had a mechanism to prevent magnetic detection.

Still, if they rose beyond a certain height, they couldn't deny the possibility that they'd be noticed.

On the other hand, if they stayed below a certain depth, that possibility got very close to zero.

"Our orders are not to sink hostiles."

The navigation officer responded as though confirming this to himself as well.

"We carry out our original mission. For us, the greatest victory is ensuring the safety of all."

4

The land mines were all in one place outside the settlement.

Afraid of the anti-air tank engine noise, Hamazura jumped out from behind the rubble. As he hid behind obstacles—objects barely retaining the buildings' original forms—he advanced across the snow.

There was a small, hut-like structure.

A little wooden building that didn't look big enough to even fit a minivan inside.

After opening the simple door, which resembled a restroom stall's, he saw things piled up haphazardly like stacks of magazines. They were metal plates, pentagonal, like home plate from a baseball field. Other than the ones tied together with rope, cylinders about the size of soda cans were crammed inside, too.

Hamazura groaned. "Here we are…"

According to Digurv, the antitank land mines were the home-plate ones. After grabbing a tied-up bundle in both hands, he placed it on the snow. If he'd known what the land mines were capable of, he'd never have been able to do such a thing.

He unbound the rope and grabbed the end of one of the plates.

A little triangular piece was sticking up from each of the pentagon's points. They were probably the fuses that would detect weight. When he turned it over, he found that the central section was dented slightly, with a tree branch a few centimeters long inserted into it horizontally. It seemed to be holding down a pin-like object. It wasn't an original part; the people from the settlement who dug it out of the ground had probably put it in there as a makeshift solution. Digurv had said these were used the same way as hand grenades. Basically, you pull the pin out, put the mine in the ground, and you're all set.

Then, if anything, even a stag beetle, so much as stepped on it, the whole thing would blow. He had to wonder if there was a tool to control the pin after setting it in the ground.

Hamazura wanted to bring along as many land mines as he was able, but they were quite heavy. He could manage holding two to three at most, probably. If he carried four or five of these things, he wouldn't be able to run straight. He was already at a disadvantage in this situation. His handicap had better be as small as possible.

…Two's my limit.

Just then, a wall from one of the civilian homes relatively close to the hut blew up.

A giant shell from one of the anti-air cannons.

Digurv had said they probably only brought two armored vehicles to the settlement. And the armored car had slipped through the floor and fallen into the basement shelter. If they could just get rid of that anti-air tank, they would be mostly safe for the moment.

Wincing at the blast from the anti-air tank's shot, Hamazura left the hut with the mines in his arms.

Next, he'd have to get close to that vehicle.

He could place the mines in spots he predicted the tank would go to, but that didn't absolutely guarantee it would pass over those locations. He only had so many mines, and what's more, he didn't have the leeway to leave his hiding spot and set the mines right out in the open, so that wouldn't be a very realistic plan.

If he wanted to take it down for sure, the fastest way would be to get close and throw the mines at it. Digurv had only used hand grenades as an analogy, but with this method, Hamazura would actually be using them like that.

Still…

…Running up close is gonna be a really high hurdle.

After all, his opponent had a large-bore autocannon with enough power to mow down buildings, to say nothing of human bodies. If they spotted him, it was over. He would basically be jumping right into the middle of them, taking a risk that would make it easier for them to notice.

He had to say, this plan of his wasn't exactly sane.

But if he didn't succeed, everyone in the settlement would be helpless.

Takitsubo would be killed, too.

Why would he have bothered fleeing from Academy City, then? He wouldn't be able to go back to his old life after finding a bargaining tool and making a deal.

I have to do this!!

Hamazura broke out into a run along the backs of the fallen rubble. The anti-air tank was having fun breaking down all the buildings in its search for prey—they might find where the people of the settlement were hiding quite soon. He ran underneath a precarious, nearly fallen ceiling balanced against a practically destroyed wall.

The sound and vibrations from the caterpillar tracks closed a fist over his heart.

The iron hulk went straight past the broken glass of the window.

Hamazura rested his back against the half-collapsed wall and peered out the window.

It was close.

Only about five meters away.

He reached for the small branch underneath the antitank mine.

If he pulled it out, the land mine would spring back to life. Even the slightest impact would cause it to explode. Naturally, it should ignite if he threw it against the tank.

He took just one deep breath and then set his stance.

Pulling the branch out from under the land mine, he picked himself up off the wall. He leaned out of where the glass used to be in the window.

The anti-air tank seemed to have noticed, too.

But between its giant turrets rotating and a human hand swinging, Hamazura was always going to be faster.

He hurled the explosive, then hid on the wall.

The land mine struck the side of the turret, then went off.

A roaring blast rattled Hamazura's brain.

However, land mines were not the same as hand grenades. They were explosives meant to be used on the ground. Obviously, you could achieve a more efficient explosion if the blast could only go upward, rather than having it spread in all directions.

The antitank land mine Hamazura had thrown was put together in the same fashion.

And that land mine, as it spun through the air, had struck the anti-air tank's turret right on its bottom surface. It had exploded, detecting an impact, but most of the blast escaped in other directions.

It hadn't destroyed the tank.

Hamazura watched as the turret squeaked around and aimed at him.

And then, yet another strange sound went off.

The blast, which had missed its original target, had knocked down building walls that were on the verge of collapsing. Across from the dwelling in which he hid was a small church, the only stone structure in the settlement. The steeple on top with the bell in it came apart and fell toward the tank.

The tank's crew must have realized that as well.

However, before they could run away on their caterpillar treads, the iron steeple hammer swung down onto it. The anti-aircraft vehicle was a hunk of thick steel, so it didn't break just from that. However, the incredible weight on top of it had completely prevented it from moving. The machine-gun turrets couldn't rotate anymore, either.

"…"

For a moment, Hamazura was silent.

All the emotions that might otherwise have been bubbling up within his heart didn't come.

After pulling his head inside the window again, he looked around the utterly wrecked civilian home. It wasn't just a movie set—it was a room someone had definitely just been living in.

And in a rack that had fallen onto its side, he took a bottle of vodka that still hadn't cracked yet.

He left the building and stood in front of the self-propelled anti-air gun.

If it had been a main battle tank, it would have been equipped with light machine guns in addition to its main gun in order to spray suppressing fire at any infantry that got close. However, this was an anti-air vehicle—it wasn't designed on the premise that it would be advancing through enemy lines. No such firearms were fixed to it.

Nothing was left to hurt Hamazura.

He brought his mouth near the small air vent used to supply oxygen into the vehicle, then quietly spoke.

"...Pretty cold today, isn't it?"

It was pure, unadulterated Japanese, but he didn't care.

It wasn't his job to exchange pleasantries with them.

"Perfect weather for roasting some meat."

He rapped on the anti-air tank's roof with the bottle of vodka, and the privateer soldiers frantically burst out of the metal hatch.

Hamazura pointed his handgun at that hatch.

He had no hesitation swinging its muzzle toward them.

5

Touma Kamijou ran about the plaza, which was now in ruins.

The results had been awful.

The professional sorcerers Lesser, Elizalina, and Vento of the Front had been defeated. Sasha Kreutzev had been taken away by Fiamma personally, and the only things that remained of the battle were the scars.

Kamijou was currently giving first aid to the wounded sorcerers. Still, he didn't have much real knowledge. He was just following the others' instructions, since they couldn't move.

"Vento..."

"If you're going to thank me, you've got the wrong person," she spat, sticking her tongue out for want of being able to move her limbs in her current state. "I just don't like how Fiamma does things. I really can't forgive him for causing mayhem in the Roman Church any more than this. In the process, my actions only happened to be to your benefit."

"…"

The voice was hateful, but Kamijou was somehow relieved.

Not everyone in the Roman Church was saying things like Fiamma was. People who would properly argue were part of the organization, too. He'd learned that fact once again, and it lightened his load a lot more than he'd thought it would.

Elizalina, lying down in the same way, spoke to him.

"I never thought Fiamma would be in a state where he could use the knowledge from the one hundred and three thousand volumes."

"Index couldn't completely cover the God's Right Seat spells, though. He's probably using her to clear away his obstacles and be more efficient."

"Do you know where Fiamma of the Right went?"

Elizalina should have been in an ambulance, but she had refused personally. Maybe it was out of regret from magic having been revealed to the masses during the fight with Fiamma. Maybe she wanted to avoid leaving this place during such a difficult phase. Only Elizalina herself knew for sure.

"…Probably a base over the border," Kamijou answered, after thinking for a moment. "He was preparing for something there to begin with. To the point where he evicted all the people living nearby, too. I think he wants to bring Sasha there to try something."

As for what Fiamma was trying to do—that wasn't clear yet.

But his advance preparations alone had already caused this many casualties. Maybe even World War III itself was only part of them. Considering that, it was then possible that whatever Fiamma was trying to do would be even bigger than *that*. Either way, he couldn't stay silent and watch. He didn't want to let something like this happen again.

"I'll manage," said Kamijou to Elizalina after a moment's thought. "I'll do something about him. I have to save Index, too. You all wait here. Nothing says all the crap he stirred up won't turn around and spread back here again."

He tried to burst out then.

But a hand grabbed his arm.

It was Lesser, who had sustained relatively light wounds. She didn't say anything in particular, but he could sense that unless he gave permission for her to come, she wouldn't let go of his arm.

Kamijou wavered a moment, then eventually nodded.

Lesser let go and got up to stand beside him.

"We don't have much time. Let's borrow the Alliance's strength. We'll ask their military for help and get right up close to the base."

"But they're opposing nations, aren't they? Wouldn't that make them even more cautious?"

"The Elizalina Alliance of Independent Nations is a group of countries that gained independence from Russia in recent years. The vehicles they use are all basically the same. If we break through where their border security is thin, we shouldn't have a problem after that."

Kamijou fell silent for a bit. "...Is it okay to get them involved, though?"

"?"

"Like I said before, they're opposing nations. If they'll cooperate, then fine, but if we get found out in Russian territory, we definitely won't have any guarantee of survival. Is it really okay to ask them to help us, in that kind of situation...?"

"We're not the ones who get to decide that," Lesser said without hesitation.

At first, it might have seemed like a haphazard reply, but it seemed to prove that she was used to the politics of life and death.

"The people who would be risking their lives can decide that. At the very least, they should be able to choose how to live their own lives. If they turn us down, we'll look for a different way."

"..."

But Kamijou, once again, fell silent.

Lesser put an index finger to her temple and, in a mildly irritated tone, said, "In the end, it's all probably the same, though."

"What is?"

"Fiamma can say what he wants, but a person's life is for the person to decide, right?"

"...Maybe."

"And whatever you happen to be hiding, it's not like you've been stuck like that forever, right? You're still risking your life to keep moving ahead. As a result, you've saved a bunch of people's lives, and you even stopped the coup in the UK. Frankly speaking, I think that's a life worth being proud of."

Hadn't it been a mistake to hide his memory loss and go on living?

Hadn't everything he'd done to protect Index's smile been complacency?

But she was right.

Kamijou had resolved so many incidents and saved so many lives before now. That was probably praiseworthy, wasn't it? He had gotten to know other people after he'd lost his memories, too. For those people, what did it matter whether he had his memories or not? Either way, it didn't change that he'd fought for their sakes.

"But still...," said Kamijou to himself.

As if to dig a knife into his own chest.

"...Still, wouldn't that mean that I'm not the one allowed to decide whether everything I've done has been good for Index?"

6

The sorcerers of the United Kingdom and France clashed atop the hardened surface of the Strait of Dover. It was nearly a melee, but they were slowly and steadily rallying around the Knights, who had borrowed the power of the Curtana Second and the mobile fortress Glastonbury.

However, when pushed, it's human nature to push back even harder.

The French sorcerers weren't the sort who would calmly calculate numbers on each side and the conditions of the field then just walk away. The more they were pushed back, the more bloodcurdling their expressions got as they utilized a myriad of offensive spells.

Several of the British Knights tried to draw back.

They positioned themselves as if to regauge the distance just a little bit.

Carissa, second princess of Britain, took this as a show of weakness and stepped out onto the front line.

"Oh, bollocks. Those French bastards are going to kidnap me and rape me to death," she baited.

"…???!!!"

Now her knights' pride wouldn't let them withdraw any farther.

Wielding their weapons as though ripping through physical limitation itself, they just barely managed to prevent Carissa from being swallowed up in the French throng.

Meanwhile, Carissa put her hands on her hips and said, "I better not see you holding back on the battlefield again. You *should* have been fighting with that much energy from the beginning."

At that point, the Knight Leader finally used his communication Soul Arm to secretly contact Windsor Castle.

"Yes. Put me through to Queen Elizard! It's extremely urgent!! I would like to ask permission to give Princess Carissa a good spanking!!"

"Would you quit that?! My mother might *actually* focus all the Curtana Second's power on you just so you can do that!!"

Even as they bickered and snatched the Soul Arm back and forth, the battle between the two forces raged on. As many swords and spells intersected, Carissa cast the French sorcerers a glance, then moved her lips.

"Hmph. What a bunch of clones."

The words came out like spit.

"They have a lot of sand grains with passing marks, but they lack decisiveness. Are they planning on using troop numbers as an excuse or something? If this is all they have, they certainly won't be able to deal with a group containing saints and Knights."

Ga-bam!! An explosion went off.

It was above Carissa.

A lightning bolt had shot down from the heavens, aiming to obliterate the second princess.

But she hadn't sustained any injury.

Through whatever means, the nearby knights had lofted their blades and cast the lightning attack away.

"In the end, trying to win from a distance is all the Saint of Versailles can do," Carissa said. "But it's clear you fundamentally cannot leave your palace, even though no seals are preventing you from escaping. Your body was readjusted down to your very organs so that you can't live anywhere but the magical environment inside the palace...by the foolish French powers that be."

The distant Saint of Versailles could probably hear her voice as well.

There was no response.

Even so, Carissa continued. "And after increasing the range on your spells more than necessary, you can't easily land a finishing blow."

Assume a sorcerer has the power of one hundred. If the sorcerer was able to use his full power for attacking, his attack power would be one hundred. But if he combined it with a spell for extending his firing range, the percentage dedicated to attacking would go down proportionally to the increased range.

There were certain spells that could ignore physical distances from the start and deal the same amount of damage to any location in the universe. But the Saint of Versailles's spell had no such trait. It was a typical spell, one whose power would decrease the farther it was extended.

On top of that, the Knights, currently borrowing strength from the Curtana Second, had superhuman abilities to begin with. They were not the sort an enfeebled spell would do anything about.

"Anyway," Carissa said to the Saint of Versailles, who was probably observing the state of battle from afar, "if you don't mind, I'll be getting serious now. Please, twiddle your thumbs and watch us as we land on your shores."

7

The crack of purple lightning cried out across the snow.

The Third Season.

A project executed to put a guaranteed end to Last Order, growing ever more useless thanks to Aiwass's existence, and to get rid of Accelerator, whom the powers that be could no longer rein in.

A series that was different from the twenty-thousand-plus-one Sisters, who came as a single set.

In the end...

"An extra specimen—you could say *Misaka Worst*."

The assailant named herself. Likely in the knowledge that she was an organism that never should have been born, whom nobody particularly desired.

In her hand danced short metal nails, each a few centimeters long. Now and again, with a balloon-like pop, a nail would fire at him at supersonic speeds.

But...

Judging by the electric power she's using, she seems different from a Railgun.

Cornered, Accelerator desperately worked his nearly chaotic mind and analyzed her.

The same method as a magnetic rifle some sniper used. It's simpler than Fleming's left hand; she's using an electromagnet to fire metal ammunition at me.

Even having come this far, he still hadn't used his reflection.

Manipulating his leg-force vectors and conducting short bursts of super-high-speed movement, he was instead taking evasive action to avoid Misaka Worst's aim.

To align with the situation, and to protect Last Order, he wouldn't be able to avoid fighting.

But it was also true that he didn't want to kill this girl if he didn't have to. Even if she'd been created through a different project than the Sisters, even if she was a specimen from a third development project designed to kill Accelerator and Last Order, he still felt an extreme aversion to letting any of these somatic-cell clones die.

It was a cruel thing, but Accelerator couldn't help thinking of what he'd do if it had been Amata Kihara or Teitoku Kakine. If it was a shithead like that, he probably wouldn't hesitate. He'd mercilessly shred them, flinging the resulting pieces in all directions, for the sake of protecting Last Order.

After all, Accelerator was no philanthropist. He wouldn't stop himself from getting into a killing match with an enemy if that lined up with his own objectives. But even still, he absolutely wanted to avoid applying that rule to the enemy who had appeared here now.

And.

Naturally, Misaka Worst had realized that.

She'd realized he was hesitating, and she'd taken advantage of it, working it into her tactics.

Because that was why she'd been born.

"Might want to be careful."

Grin.

With an "expression" clearly different from any of the previous Sisters, Misaka Worst spoke.

Yes—while wearing a smile filled with malice.

"Misaka doesn't have as much power as the original, but even this Misaka can manage to get up to two billion volts. I'd probably be around Level Four."

Roar!! A blast went off.

And the girl's body vanished.

She'd ignited the air by using a huge amount of high-tension current, then used the force to take flight. It was the same as what she'd used to land on the ground from the transport plane.

By the time Accelerator realized it, it was too late.

"Look—one more for you."

He heard the voice from overhead.

And then a two-centimeter-long metal nail shot down at him.

He jumped directly to the side, but halfway through his jump, he lost his balance and fell spectacularly onto the snow.

There was a dark-red wound in his thigh. This metal nail had apparently stopped *in* his body.

"Would you *please* run away some more?"

Misaka Worst stepped down onto the snow, the metal nails in her hand jangling. It was an aggravating noise—was it affected to torment her target as much as possible?

"You killed over ten thousand times, over ten thousand Misakas, didn't you?"

The words cut deep.

It carried a whole different weight than if a complete stranger had been blathering on about it.

The subtle vibrations in the air from her voice caused Accelerator, who could even reflect nuclear attacks, to begin collapsing from the inside out.

"So run away. Beg for your life like a dog. You're not a normal person facing a normal death. The books won't be balanced unless I trample over your human rights at *least* ten thousand times worse. And just so you're aware, that's a minimum number. It'll be more than three times that, with interest."

The skin on Misaka Worst's face twisted from the inside.

Her carefully crafted face distorted like a vinyl puppet in the oven.

The source: abhorrence.

Her insane smile, something more than anger, something more than horror, spread across her face so much it seemed her original face would never come back.

...Don't let her get to you, thought Accelerator desperately, holding back the intense pain crawling out to his arms and legs. *She isn't one of them. She wasn't born for that experiment specifically. She's literally a fake who talks with the same face and body. I don't need to trip up over every little thing she says!*

With a shudder, he felt a strange sensation begin to gather toward the center of his forehead.

Could he apply his reflection to his whole body?

Should he even block Misaka Worst's voice with it? The scales were starting to tip.

However.

"Misaka is the same."

That one phrase.

Just four words put a halt to Accelerator's decision.

"Misaka was born to kill you. She didn't want to be born, but they made it happen. They cut open Misaka's skin to cram piles of strange sheets and selectors inside, all to cut off the signal from Last Order. This wouldn't have happened if it hadn't been for you. If you hadn't made the choices you did, Misaka would never have been born. Even if she had, it wouldn't have been through *this* futureless method. 'It hurts— Help me.' By the time Misaka knew those words, she couldn't say them anymore. Misaka has the right to denounce you. She has a reason to kill you."

And, added Misaka Worst, like a murderous huntress showing off each and every one of her vaunted weapons:

"Misakas are each individual specimens, but at the same time, they're one big Misaka connected by a network. It's not some unique way of thinking that only specimens called Misaka have. Because it's one part of what the big Misaka encompasses."

Accelerator's vision blurred.

It had taken him a moment to realize Misaka Worst had combusted the air to move swiftly and kicked him in the face.

"Why do you think none of the other Misakas, including Last Order, ever denounced you before now? Didn't it seem unnatural to you? Ten thousand people, ten thousand times you kept on killing, and why didn't they ever harbor any hatred? The answer's simple. The Misakas are no saints. The Misakas aren't like those mythical princesses, either, pure and just…It isn't that they decided not to hate you. It's just that the way they handled humanlike emotions was too incomplete for them to understand and express it, so it never come up."

This was her aim.

She wanted to drive Accelerator into a corner.

Which meant he didn't have to care.

It was all an act, and he didn't have to take every little thing as the truth.

However.

What he couldn't bring himself to do was ignore any malice that Misaka Worst—or the Sisters—had for him.

Even if he knew it was part of her strategy, he would get caught in it.

But what if…?

What if Last Order's smile wasn't one of forgiveness—it was nothing more than a product of her personality, formed rapidly by the Testament, and not mature enough to properly recognize and understand negative emotions like hatred or fear? With everything he'd done, he couldn't possibly be so easily forgiven, could he? These apprehensions made him reel.

His blood was trailing through the white snow. It was like someone had drawn a line to trace his movements.

Misaka Worst rubbed the red liquid on the end of her shoe onto the snow.

"Gya-ha-ha!! The Misakas are slowly becoming more human! They'll be able to do all sorts of new things like humans can!! But being more human isn't always a good thing! Many Misakas will come to realize their hatred soon. They'll start thinking they have the right to pursue a just revenge!! All this atonement that you've been so absorbed in until now was nothing but self-satisfaction you were consuming for yourself!! None of it will dampen the Misakas' hatred!! In the future, every Misaka connected to the network will gain human hatred and go after your life!! Will we succeed and kill you, or will they fail, and you'll kill us all? Either way, that convenient future you're imagining will never be real!!"

As she spoke, again and again, her shoe's toe flew.

Each time, blood spurted from several places on Accelerator.

He would have been able to avoid it if he had tried.

He would have been able to counterattack if he had tried.

But he couldn't do that.

The stirrings of the mind needed to do so weren't forming.

Because in his heart, something was close to breaking.

It wasn't just the external damage. Just trying to get angry in order to resist her was about to utterly destroy him.

Destroy him so badly he'd never return.

Maybe even so badly that he'd transform into a greater monster than he'd even been during the experiment.

"If you want to drown in your sentimental delusions and deny what Misaka says, that's fine. But what Misaka has said is already proven. This Misaka, Misaka Worst, isn't like the other Misakas. She had her intracerebral substance secretion patterns purposely readjusted so that negative emotions come to the surface more easily. So that it's easy to read negative emotions out of the giant network. They figured out that it isn't that the Misakas don't possess the emotion of hatred, it's that they do, but they don't have a way to express it...And that goes for all Misakas, including Last Order over there!!"

Misaka Worst's foot abruptly stopped after stomping on his face.

She was watching something.

A short distance away, on the snow, lay Last Order. The effects of Aiwass's emergence had put the young girl's very consciousness in danger. Still buried in the snow, her hand was squirming, reaching out—in Accelerator's direction. As if to somehow protect him from the bloodshed, from the trampling.

Not caring about any realistic numerical values...

...like whether that hand would reach him.

Last Order seemed to be trying to stop his assailant's movements by using some kind of ability, but there was no change in Misaka Worst. She appeared to be using some "countermeasure," and above all, it wasn't certain whether Last Order, in her current ragged state, even had enough spare energy to properly serve as a command tower.

Thick sweat dripped from the little girl's face.

Clearly, something ominous was happening inside her body.

"..."

For just a moment, Misaka Worst stopped moving.

And then her twisted smile broadened even further.

"All right. Misaka will start by taking care of that defective product over there. Seems like it would be more effective."

With a shudder even larger than before, an awful premonition swelled deep within the heart of Academy City's number one.

"The Misakas have been refurbished for the Third Season, plus the network's expansion and redeployment have strengthened and rapidly increased their capabilities."

Jingle-jangle.

The two-centimeter iron nails in Misaka Worst's hand gave off a grating cadence.

"They no longer need a last-generation command tower like Last Order. In fact, now that all the Misakas are going to be deployed, all she's doing is shackling them."

The situation was almost cannibalistic, but if he assumed the Sisters to all be controlled by one giant Misaka network, he could also apply her words and actions to human thought processes and deal with them that way.

Normal humans thought in ways that were convenient for them, too.

The you right now isn't the real you. You have wonderful talents hidden inside you. Draw them out and become the real you. Abandon the old you.

In normal humans, convenient but empty ideas like that came from the mental parts inside the body. The Sisters, however, were a giant network composed of many bodies. The notion of "abandoning the old you" would then come to be used in a physical, rather than metaphorical, sense.

...Right.

Wanting to prevent their spontaneous "advancement" and keep them the way they were now was nothing but pure egotism. Nothing but an idea to take someone's freedom away, much like how a parent wanted their child to remain a child forever.

...So that's what it meant.

It wasn't possible to settle this without letting anyone die.

The following two choices were available:
Kill Misaka Worst to protect Last Order.
Or keep one of the Sisters alive and watch Last Order die.
Metal nails had pierced his body. He'd been kicked in every spot imaginable. He'd been trampled on. And now the spear was pointed at Last Order.
Finally, Accelerator realized there was only one question left:

Was giving up the only thing left he could do?

Ba-bam!! A blast rang out.
It was the sound of Misaka Worst—this girl who had stomped on Accelerator's face and aimed her metal nails at Last Order—being hurled into the air. Her body flew in a wide arc, going a good ten meters during her flight before plummeting to the snow.
Yes.
If the number one in Academy City got serious, such a thing was easy.
Whether it was a two-billion-volt high-tension current, or metal nails flying faster than sound could travel, or one of the Sisters.
One or two insignificant chumps couldn't do anything to him.
"Gah?!"
As Misaka Worst groaned, she saw a figure standing up unsteadily.
Accelerator—like a mirage, bereft of his central core.
Originally, she should have successfully weakened him, then arrived at the chance of a lifetime.
And yet...
"...!!"
Misaka Worst puffed out a burst of air, then focused some magnetic force to launch a shot.
The metal nail, flying faster than the speed of sound, was arced precisely to Accelerator's forehead. He didn't dodge it. He didn't swing his head away or even shut his eyes. Despite that, not a fraction of his skin tore, and not a drop of his blood spilled.
It was due to his reflection.

The metal nail bounced back and penetrated Misaka Worst's arm. Accelerator had had no hesitation, no indecision. As she tumbled, she took out another nail. This time, her aim was Last Order. She reached out her arm, attempting to destroy the core of Accelerator's proxy calculations.

And then the mirage-like Accelerator moved *distinctly*.

Only when he had manipulated his leg-force vectors and approached her, all in the span of an instant, did he bring his fist down onto her outstretched arm.

It broke.

The nail still buried within her arm, he used blunt force to break her bones.

She screamed, searing the air with a high-tension current, attempting to immediately withdraw. However, Accelerator grabbed her leg and slammed her onto the snow.

Wh-whump...!! A tremor dispersed into their surroundings like the venue of a fireworks show.

As Misaka Worst coughed, he swung his fist down again.

Only the sound of pounding meat, creaking bones, and spattering blood continued.

Misaka Worst had evidently brought a way to interfere with Accelerator's electrode, but he never gave her an opening to use it, whatever it was. The intense, continuous agony prevented her from gaining even the scant focus to use her ability.

As he did so, he felt the sensation of something that was inside him now slowly beginning to collapse. He wasn't walking a path that anyone in their right mind would praise him for, but it was still his way of life that he'd crafted with his own unskillful hands—and he could tell that now, he was losing every last bit of it. Even if he made the whole world his enemy, even if he had to fight to the death against other monsters while crawling through a bloodstained world—his wish, his desire, to protect the people who shared this girl's face at all costs, was crumbling.

Except...

It wasn't exactly crumbling.

It wasn't approaching zero.

It was going *below* that.

He himself realized that he was transforming into a far more terrifying monster than what he was when he met Last Order, or even what he was during the experiment.

"Hah, ha-ha."

The next thing he knew, Misaka Worst wasn't moving anymore.

"...It hurts...Misa...ka..." She was managing to inhale and exhale, but several places on her body were torn apart. Her arm was bent in an unnatural direction. Her regular features had swollen. The girls he had to risk his life to protect, one of their number, was at death's door.

"Help me. Someone..."

Accelerator realized that.

He saw the blood covering his hand, and he dropped to his knees in the snow.

"Gya-ha-ha-ha-ha-ha!! Giiyaaa-ha-ha-ha-ha-ha-ha-ha-ha-ha!!"

Only dry laughter seeped out of him.

It was over. He couldn't move anymore. Everyone from Academy City was insane. He couldn't keep up with something like that. And he couldn't make sense of a world that prospered on that sort of power. He was acutely aware of the pitch-black underbelly lurking just behind all the peace and happiness in this world. Exactly the way amiable smiles in television commercials were artificial things created to gain immense wealth, he could no longer believe in any of the *light* or *good* that he'd so idealized.

In any case, this wouldn't be the end.

If they realized that Number One's spirit hadn't broken yet, they would no doubt execute a second plan, a third. Would other Sisters appear next? Or would it be a specimen adjusted to have a body like that brat's? Would they use Yomikawa or Yoshikawa? Or would they use a completely unrelated village or town wholesale, like a disposable tool?

Whatever it might be, this was all he had. After this, his opponent would definitely deliver greater pain than he felt now, and he wouldn't be able to endure it. He didn't even want to fight it. Letting himself be broken now would probably be easier for him. The darkness Academy City gave form to simply wasn't normal.

But then, he heard a stirring.

It was the sound of Misaka Worst, so viciously flattened, squirming on the filthy red snow.

As he recalled it, she'd said she had a plan to use her ability to block Accelerator's proxy calculations.

The beating earlier probably hadn't given her the time to use it.

This time, she might use it to counterattack.

For some reason, Accelerator shook his head, still grinning. He didn't know the meaning behind the act. But he didn't want to move any longer.

Nothing mattered anymore. The pain in his heart had wiped out everything he'd had inside him just a moment ago. With his spirit in tatters, he decided if he was to be killed now, he didn't mind.

However.

Academy City was more insane than even Accelerator thought.

He heard a soft *brrrrkkk*.

It was the sound of a selector, buried in Misaka Worst's body, rupturing.

"...Eh?"

Whatever happened next, the damage to his heart was now at its height.

There was no greater pain than this.

The tormenting mental attacks Misaka Worst had used on him had ended.

That was what he had thought—and that was why his mind, if only for a moment, had blanked.

All his emotional waves had flatlined.

And a moment later—

Every emotion a human could possibly have exploded in his head.

"Kuh, ha-ha?! Gi-ha-ha-haaaahhh!! Gyaaaa-ha-ha-ha-ha-ha-ha-ha-

ha-ha-ha-ha-ha-ha-ha-ha-ha-ha-ha-ha-ha-ha-ha-ha-ha-ha-ha-ha-ha-ha-ha!!"

The impact caused his vision to spin.

In a world where he could no longer tell the difference between colors, only a small reddish hue remained—and spread.

Something had torn Misaka Worst's skin, from the base of her skull to the bottom of her neck.

She was losing an enormous amount of blood.

Meanwhile, the girl, lying on her side, was grinning. A smile that seemed to be her negative emotions having hardened on her face. It was like invisible fingers of malice were tugging at her skin from the inside.

Her mouth opened and shut, opened and shut.

In a hoarse, grating voice, she hissed:

"...This...is...your...fault."

He thought she would spray vomit and excreta everywhere.

"Gfh!! Gah-ha-fhgh!! Gibh, gya-ha-ha-ha-ha-ha-ha-ha-ha-ha-ha-ha-ha-ha-ha-ha-ha-ha-ha-ha-ha-ha-ha-ha-ha-ha-ha-ha-ha-ha-ha-ha-ha-ha-ha-ha-ha-ha-ha-ha-ha-ha-ha-ha-ha-ha-ha-ha-ha-ha-ha-ha-ha-ha-ha-ha-ha-ha-ha-ha-ha-ha-ha-ha-ha-ha-ha-ha-ha-haahhhhhhhhhhhhhhhh!!"

Those Academy City bastards had designed her body so that no matter what her results were, she would be able to put an end to Accelerator's life. So that if Accelerator had wielded overwhelming power but tried to settle the matter without killing her in half-done measures, she could tear whatever remained of Accelerator's mental state into shreds.

Until now, this was how he'd figured they were thinking:

If they could use Number One's trauma against him to weaken and kill him, that was fine.

Even if she lost, the fact that he'd murdered one of the Sisters would crush his mental state.

But he'd been wrong.

It hadn't been that simple.

It wasn't about whether he won or lost.

Whether he won, lost, fought to a draw, escaped, reconciled—this device would always lead to her finishing off Accelerator, no matter what the situation was. That was what this girl, Misaka Worst, really was.

The term *breakdown* seemed apt.

It was a mental term, and what he experienced was strong enough that Academy City's number one believed that he really had died.

And Accelerator's spirit, in fact, had been almost obliterated.

He'd lost the power to interact with other humans as a human.

He didn't want to keep living in this rotten world. He didn't even want to *change* this rotten world. It was too far gone. Too far gone for human strength to do anything about. If he could leave this world, then maybe letting himself sink into the snow was a better deal.

Misaka Worst's body twitched and squirmed, unconnected to her will.

She'd probably lost so much blood in such a short time that the shock was manifesting its effects.

A result the rotten people from Academy City had produced.

Now, having seen the absolute worst ending, Accelerator…

"You motherfuckeeeeeeeeeeeeeeeeeeeeeeeeeeeeeeeeeeeeeeeeeeeeeeeeee eeeeeeeeeeeeeeeeeeeeeeeeeeeeeeeeeeeeeeeeeeeeeerrrrrrrrrrrrrrrrrrrrrrrrr rrrrrrrrrrrrrrrrrrrrrrrrrrrrrrrrrrrrrrrrrrrrs!!!!!!"

…finally screamed and rushed to the near-dead Misaka Worst's side.

His ability was vector manipulation.

The power was one he mainly used for offensive purposes, but that didn't mean that was the only way he could use it. By reading the direction of blood and electrical signals flowing throughout a person's body, he could examine the state of a person's health, and if he really applied himself, he could even perform some medical treatment and first aid.

"Bastards, bastards, bastards!!"

Accelerator's eyes were bloodshot.

A new objective was born.

It was a paltry resistance.

Yes—

"This was what those Academy City bastards were planning, wasn't it...? No matter how I struggled, this kid would die, my mind would be ripped to shreds, and someone in a nice warm room somewhere would sip their wine and smile. Pretty clever of them to tie it all together like that..."

His emotions frothed and bubbled up.

As did the necessary impetus for affecting another human as a human.

"In that case!! I'll wreck everything!! If their plan won't succeed unless this kid dies, then I'll save her and ruin it for them!! You shitheads, you better be watching!! I'm about to wipe those shit-eating grins off your faces!!"

An overwhelming anger.

A clear intent lay in Accelerator's eyes.

"Fuck, fuck, fuck!! You scum, always looking down on me, thinking I only have the power to kill people!! I'm about to show you something you'll never forget!! Just like how I saved that brat from Amai's virus before—even I have the power to protect people, damn iiiiiiiiiiiiiiiiiiiiiiiiiiiiiiiiiiiiiiiiiiiiiitttttttttttttttttt!!"

8

Her blurred vision never shut off, no matter how much time passed.

Eventually, Misaka Worst was able to interpret that to mean she was still alive.

The selector embedded in her body was for refusing signals from Last Order, and she had intentionally set it off. The explosion was an extremely small-scale one, but several broken pieces had gone deep inside her. Normally, there would have been absolutely no saving her; even an operating room in a hospital outfitted with the latest equipment probably couldn't have pulled it off. And with nothing but empty snowfield around, there was nothing anyone could do.

She was a disposable specimen.

It didn't matter if she won; nobody had considered any other use for her. Even in the Third Season project, she was a specimen designed to die before the official network was constructed.

And yet...

...?

No matter how much time passed, a definite death never came.

Only an obscure life continued on and on. Eventually, she also dimly came to the realization that it was because her vitals were stabilizing.

Had she survived?

Had Academy City's plans failed?

Could this have meant Academy City's number one Level Five had been able to overcome a malice that operated on a global scale?

That notion was hard for her to accept as someone fine-tuned to pick up more negative emotions from the Misaka network than normal. But the reality was that she'd lived through a situation that she was pretty sure she had to die from. And with the help of a third party, no less.

Misaka Worst stayed quiet for a while.

For someone built to accept only negative emotions, the silence was bewildering, but at the same time, somehow comforting.

However.

"Gya-ha."

She heard something—an unpleasant noise.

The noise of whatever she'd been about to accept shattering into pieces.

"Gya-ha-ha. No good, no good. Ku-ha-ha-ha-ha-ha."

The waves of the voice were unstable, going high, then low; loud, then soft. The sound evoked a far greater sense of danger than even the sound of something leaking from a gas main.

Misaka Worst slowly turned her head.

And before her was…

"Ihya-ha-ha-ha-ha-ha-ha-ha-ha-ha-ha-ha-ha-ha-ha-ha-ha-ha-ha-ha-ha!! I can't hold it in anymore!! That brat's smile isn't enough anymore!! Gya-ha! Gya-ha-ha-ha-ha!! I wanna destroy all of it! I wanna tear them all to shreds, every single one of them!! All those bastards who get their kicks making stuff like this *and* the bastards happy to benefit from it! I won't leave a single one standing!! Not a single damn one!! Gya-ha-ha-ha-ha-ha-ha-ha-ha-ha-ha-ha-ha-ha-ha-ha-ha-ha-ha-ha-ha-ha-ha-ha-ha-ha-ha-ha-ha-ha-ha-ha-ha-ha-ha-ha-ha-ha-ha-ha-ha-ha-ha-ha-ha-ha-ha-ha-ha-ha-ha-ha-ha-ha-ha-ha-ha-ha-ha-ha!!"

Boom!! A blast went off.

Misaka Worst thought it was Academy City's number one having lost himself and flinging his ability in every direction.

But it wasn't.

She saw black wings.

Wings like a solidification of all despair.

Each of the wings in the pair tangled with the other, crushing each other, plucking the other off. The stirrings of his heart, likely manifesting on the surface in some form. Each time, Accelerator's mouth unleashed a scream. The air tingled and trembled, and she could tell the white lands of Russia were creaking, hurting, from the energetic aftermath. Fissures sprawled through the foundation like a spiderweb, centered around Accelerator's feet in the snow.

Misaka Worst didn't know how far it would expand.

She could have been witnessing the day the world ended.

Maybe what she'd felt just a moment ago hadn't been a mistake.

Maybe something warm like that flowed within Academy City's number one Level Five as well.

But.

This shattered all of that.

What had she started? As she began to realize what she'd done, her entire body began to shake in a strange, awful trembling.

9

The anti-air tank attacking the settlement had stopped moving.

The other soldiers, spread out here and there, were the ones who had originally been driving the armored car. They weren't geared up like they would have needed to be for actual melee combat.

Their proficiency as soldiers aside, a simple comparison of how many people had assault rifles actually showed that the villagers had greater numbers. After all, the things were more widespread than fire extinguishers in these parts.

Each side was stopped in place, their guns aimed at the other battle line.

However, the privateers' armored car and anti-air tank were both destroyed. The fact lifted the spirits of the villagers more than necessary.

After seeing the people of the settlement standing firm, it didn't take long for uneasiness to spread through the privateers. If the strings of tension snapped for either side, and this turned into a shoot-out, there would definitely be casualties on both sides. The privateers probably didn't want to consider that sort of development; they'd come to this battlefield to go on a homicidal safari.

It didn't take long for their morale to break and their hands to rise.

Maybe the very fact that they believed it would save them meant they still hadn't realized the true gravity of what they'd been doing until now.

"...We patted them down and threw them into a usable shelter for now."

Digurv was delivering a report of that nature to Hamazura.

Hamazura had just been putting disinfectant onto his scrapes here and there.

"Oh."

"To be honest, I wanted to break their legs and leave them for the wild dogs. In fact, some are saying they're going to try exactly that. But you're the one who blew up that anti-air gun. They wouldn't have listened if it wasn't you who had asked."

"..."

Hamazura thought for a moment about how heavy the gun in his pocket was.

In the end, he hadn't been able to shoot the soldiers who had come out of the immobilized anti-air tank. No matter how detestable they were, he couldn't pull that trigger. If they'd been about to take his life, if it had been that very moment, he probably would have. Or rather, he wouldn't have had the time to think about it. But back there, he had the time—time to think about how they were people just like he was.

Either way, though it may have been temporary, they'd averted a crisis.

He wanted to stop people's thoughts from becoming bloodthirsty. Most of the buildings were now rubble, but in his view, everyone could still be smiling. Not shooting the privateers who had surrendered earlier would, one day, surely be a great help to the people in the settlement. He was sure it was okay to think that way.

Despite all that...

"Somebody, come here!! It's bad! Way worse than the guys before!!"

Someone shouted in Russian. Hamazura didn't understand it, but it sounded important. He ran there along with Digurv to where many people had gathered in a yet-unbroken building. They weren't just holding out against the cold. There was something that looked like an out-of-date television. It was showing green dots of light on it.

"It's an old-gen radar," explained Digurv. "It picks up metal response reflections and shows them. The closer they are to the middle, the closer they are to the settlement. Things along the ground won't show up."

"What are those three dots for?"

"They're big ones. Maybe over thirty meters long. Doesn't seem like they're fighter jets. Which means..."

"Then what are they?"

"Helicopters."

Digurv's expression visibly shifted, tense.

"Attack helicopters for strafing the surface. We can't tell the exact models, but they're fairly large. If all three are the same kind of attack helicopter, we can't fight them with what we have in this settlement. Grabbing some mines isn't going to do anything about them, this time."

This settlement had assault rifles like AKs, but they probably wouldn't hit helicopters. Attack helicopters had thinner armor compared to tanks and anti-air cannons, but they could move around faster as well. So fast they might even dodge portable surface-to-air missiles unless you fired right behind one.

On top of that, if they could move quickly, that meant they'd be hard to run away from. If you were just fleeing in a car, they'd catch up in no time. He doubted they could endure swarms of missiles and machine-gun-strafing runs from the air.

"...Privateers again?"

"Most likely. If this was an official cleanup operation, they would have attacked with more than just one kind of weapon. Theoretically, you'd have multiple weapons and service branches and deploy in a combined-arms unit to let them cover one another's weaknesses. Tactics like that don't even enter the privateers' minds."

Which meant...that in light of the armored car and anti-air tank never returning, a second wave showed up. If it was true, their tenacity of purpose was really something else. Doubtless they would commit to a fierce offensive, less to retaliate for their comrades and more to recover their own besmirched honor.

"We can't use basements anymore. They're all pretty damaged from the battle earlier. If they fire missiles at us from above, we'll be buried alive," Digurv explained to Hamazura, unfurling a map.

He'd probably already conveyed their general plan of action to everyone else in Russian.

"There's a big forest to the south of the settlement. The leaves and branches will block them from seeing us from the air. We'll just have to run through it, spreading out as much as possible, not clumping together. As long as the helicopters haven't caught on, they'll focus on the settlement."

The bit about "not clumping together" got to him. The helicopters probably had sensors that could detect heat sources and magnetic fields. If they moved as a group, the pilots would realize it was a bunch of people. But by moving scattered, and if the pilots mistook them for beasts roaming the forest, the possibility for survival went up.

But that was all probably superficial reasoning. In truth, all they were trying to do was decrease the number of people who died in a single strafing run.

...We can't get away with zero victims.

Everyone understood that, but they were all too scared to say it.

Hamazura didn't think that was enough. Looking at the map as Digurv explained, he interrupted and said, "...We might be able to win if we use an anti-air tank."

"You want to lay down curtain fire to shoot down aircraft? No, this isn't some Russian military installation. We don't have any weapons like—!!"

As he was about to finish, Digurv caught himself.

He'd figured it out.

Didn't Hamazura *just* put a caterpillar-tread anti-air vehicle out of action?

This time, Hamazura shoved away the map they'd prepared in order to run away and said, "Any heavy construction equipment? Even a power shovel or something is fine! If we can just move all the debris covering the anti-air tank, everything changes!!"

"But we—"

"You want to let yourselves get killed without doing anything?! Anyway, aside from using the anti-air tank, nothing about the plan changes. We'll still move the battlefield away, and we'll still get everyone else to hide in the southern forest! We're better off with as many plans as we can get, aren't we?! Even if I mess up and the anti-air tank blows up with me in it, they might be satisfied they took down a target with some fight in it and go home!! That's a hell of a lot better than doing nothing!!"

Digurv ran toward the building's exit. Hamazura followed behind him.

Apparently, they had an excavator in the settlement to deal with blocked roads whenever tons of snow accumulated.

Hamazura had controlled a heavy construction vehicle like it once when he was robbing an ATM in Academy City.

When they removed the rubble, out came the caterpillar-type anti-air tank.

The treads themselves were undamaged.

However, one of the two turrets set up in parallel was bent way out of alignment. If they fired it like that, they'd be hurting themselves instead. But nobody here had the expert knowledge of how to take one of the cannons off. As a hasty stopgap, they pulled out all the ammunition from the busted cannon. Now even if they fired the cannons, ammunition would only come out of the working one.

"Their accuracy will plummet," said Digurv. "Why do you think they put two turrets facing in the same direction? It's because they almost never hit. Even with rapid-firing cannons made specifically for anti-air, they normally never use just one. They put dozens on a single vehicle, put out a huge bullet curtain in a section of air, and then you can only shoot those down if a few of those hit. That's the kind of weapon they are—"

"I don't need your whining," interrupted Hamazura. "We're not exactly in a situation where we can get top-of-the-line weapons. If there's even a slight chance, that's enough. I'll pass on staring at the sky waiting to be killed, thanks. If there's any chance left for me to affect something with my own strength, then I'm plenty happy."

"Do you even know how to operate one of these things?"

"Using the treads is the same idea. It's probably the same idea as the excavator, right?"

Digurv watched Hamazura shimmy up the dented vehicle and gave a bitter grin. "These things generally need more than one person to move."

"What?"

"Someone to move the vehicle, someone to move and fire the

cannons, and someone to keep an eye on the surroundings and command…You need three people at least. Its specs say it normally needs *five*."

Hamazura stopped moving.

If he tried to do all those things himself, he'd have to stop in the middle of one thing to do another. Evasive maneuvers might not mean much against attack helicopters freely flitting about in the skies, but fighting while moving and stopping just to fire completely changed the tactics they could use and their chances of survival.

"Which means I'm coming, too," said Hamazura. "I'll ask the others in the settlement. If we get two or three, we should be able to operate it. Can't say everyone who hears about this will want to fight—that would be more worrying."

"W-wait a minute."

Hamazura was at a loss.

A different sort of tension ran through him than that which the thought of going to a battlefield on his own gave him.

"Are you sure? You just said it's not a sure thing that we'll be able to win. It's more than likely a busted-up anti-air tank like this won't stand a chance against three attack helicopters, isn't it?"

"Hey!"

Then it happened.

From a different direction, a Japanese voice spoke to them. When Hamazura and Digurv turned around, they both wore dubious looks.

The one who had spoken to them was the Russian soldier who had been suffering from frostbite.

"In that case, count me in. I was assigned to an air base, but before my transfer, I had training in anti-air weaponry like this. You'll have a better chance of winning if an actual soldier helps you out."

"…Wh-what are you thinking?" asked Hamazura somewhat cautiously. "Those privateers are with the Russian army, just like you."

In response, the Russian soldier answered as though spitting out bad food. *"Russian army just like you,* my ass."

"…"

"You two saved me when anyone else would have left me to die. And those guys are trying to exterminate you like you're some kind of bugs...I'm sick of it. Fuck the military. I don't care if they come after me. In fact, I might as well defect to Elizalina. It's more important that I repay my debts. I want to use what I have to help the people who saved my life."

"...All right." Digurv, too, relaxed his shoulders slightly and grinned. "You seemed to be more concerned than anyone else that we'd get mixed up in the fighting. I don't want to leave someone like that out to die. If that's your reason, we can look forward and fight... And you're not the only possibility I'm betting on. We're getting pretty sick and tired of the way the privateers do things ourselves."

When Hamazura heard those words, he silently lowered his head to the two.

He quietly savored how reassuring it was to have people fighting with him.

Then he turned back to the anti-air tank.

The weapon Hamazura had won from the enemy.

The last possibility that might let him save a girl more important to him than his own life—and the people who were worried about her.

Once more, he felt firmly.

That he couldn't afford to lose.

The privateers, that foreigner mercenary unit on a homicidal safari, would be here soon.

10

Something had broken apart inside Accelerator. Something that had been holding him up.

The black wings, symbols of malice, stretched out on and on, endlessly.

But even that wouldn't last forever.

The core of his spirit, the part that caused negative emotions to spring forth, was gone. Neither candles nor lighters could retain their flame without something to burn.

That was when it happened.

Something came up at the edge of his vision.

It was a motorcade. Several large vehicles were driving through the snow. They weren't Academy City's; the level of the tech used was different. Still, he couldn't deny the possibility that the shadow group was disguised, purposely using Russian vehicles.

If that was all it was, he might not have paid it any mind.

The typical, astute Accelerator certainly would have cautiously observed. He'd have been on guard, considering the chance that it was the shadow group. But now, having lost his vigor, things that unimportant wouldn't have been worth thinking about. In the worst case, he might have decided that he didn't care if he was shot dead because of it.

However.

His heart, the empty husk that it now was, had stirred.

The cause came from one of the big vehicles. A man's face, seen from the side, riding within.

It was the face of the man who had defeated Accelerator in a switchyard in Academy City. The face of the man who had stopped the experiment, permanently froze the Level Six Shift project, and saved the lives of a little under ten thousand Sisters. He would stand up for himself no matter how critical the situation, would always save lives in danger, no matter how desperate their position. That was the kind of man he supposedly was.

He should have been in Academy City.

Why was he in Russia, of all places?

And.

That hero.

The hero who would properly save others, unlike Academy City's half-finished number one.

Why was he just trying to pass by, without noticing the threat to Last Order, who was suffering right nearby?

Before he knew it, Accelerator was screaming with all his might.

As he bellowed his throat-ripping roar, he snatched up a boulder buried in the snow and manipulated vectors to hurl it full force toward the motorcade.

The back of the vehicle blew up like a balloon, and the motorcade instantly halted.

He knew he was venting for no reason.

This was originally something Accelerator was supposed to accomplish. Not only had he willfully abandoned it, he was denouncing someone completely unrelated, and he realized full well his anger was misplaced.

However.

"...Weren't you the hero who saved all the Sisters? Weren't you the *real* hero who rescued almost ten thousand clones, every single one of them?"

That man climbed out of the busted truck.

He seemed to have noticed Accelerator and the black wings he was sprouting.

"Then save that brat's life, you bastard!! Why only her? She hasn't done anything wrong—why does she have to suuuffffffferrrrrrrrrr rrrrrrrrrrrrrrrrrrrrrrrrrrrrrrrrrrrrrrrrrrrrrrrrrrrrrrrrrrrrrrrrrrrrrrrrrrrr???!!!"

With a roar, the black wings crashed outward, spreading even more.

He knew he was wrong.

He was perfectly aware, but he couldn't stop his own powers anymore.

Last Order.

The symbol of goodness—but even her smile wasn't enough for him to be able to hold it back.

Academy City's number one.

Through sheer rage, the monster had gone above and beyond that title—and now, his battle was about to begin.

INTERLUDE
THREE

Mikoto Misaka decided to pore over Academy City's data for real.

She'd seen that boy at the edge of the picture in the news from Russia, which meant that her hunch was correct—he wasn't in Japan. And of all the places he could have been, he was just casually walking around the most dangerous place in this war.

Something was up, out there where she couldn't see. Maybe he was out there fighting some grand evil again, his right fist clenched.

Focusing her attention on her PDA screen, she found several pieces of information.

She had a bad feeling about this.

She remembered when she'd been desperate to get any information on the experiment related to the Sisters.

The screen displayed read: "Sightings of Imagine Breaker in Russia and the Elizalina Alliance of Independent Nations."

Imagine Breaker must have meant that spiky-haired boy. She recalled him having once called his ability that at some point.

She scrolled down the screen. Along with several maps, there was some kind of annotation written in small lettering. Several arrows had been drawn on the maps…movements of Academy City forces and weaponry, maybe? Or was it the route the boy had traveled?

"By the notification from the General Board chairperson, response to Imagine Breaker will be different from normal."

The "normal response" was apparently how they clamped down on any factions trying to leak Academy City's supernatural ability development tech to outside organizations. It was a severe methodology, one that tolerated shooting to kill in the worst cases.

However, for whatever reason, it seemed it didn't apply to the boy.

She was about to give a sigh of relief, but it was too soon for that. Hadn't that very incident with the Sisters taught her, to a terrifying degree, how dark the shadowy parts of Academy City were?

"Imagine Breaker is an esper possessing rare value, even throughout all of Academy City. In consideration of that rarity, our objective is to retrieve him alive if possible.

"However.

"Should we discern that the Imagine Breaker will align himself with an organization other than Academy City, our secondary objective is then to swiftly attack him, apply Number Two's treatment to him, and retrieve him inside a life-support system, thereby minimizing further disruptions.

"We have confirmed that Imagine Breaker is currently acting alongside a member of an external organization.

"Should he only be treating them as a temporary guide, we will withhold punishment, but if he crosses the line, we will execute our secondary objective.

"It will not cause a problem, as we have approval from the General Board chairperson.

"In that case, though it is impossible to view details for authority reasons, he has said his 'plan' will still commence."

"…"

Mikoto Misaka fell silent for a while.

She was certainly surprised, but at the same time, she figured that might be the case.

Also recorded on the PDA were specific paratrooper unit personnel, equipment, and operational schedules for attacking the target boy. Naturally, the military's airplanes were ready in District 23, where its aeronautics and space-related technology was assembled.

She turned the PDA off and headed for District 23.

…Once, that boy had risked his life to prevent the Sisters from being massacred during the Level Six Shift project, standing up against a great darkness in Academy City. It may have been that he didn't actually have a good handle on just how terrifying it was. But the undeniable truth was that he'd crossed a dangerous bridge for her sake and the Sisters'.

She had a big debt to repay him.

As she ran, she figured it was high time she paid a little of it back.

CHAPTER 4

Here Begins the Counterattack

Heroes_Congregate.

1

Three attack helicopters provided by the Russian Ground Forces tore through the white scenery. Pushing speeds of about three hundred kilometers per hour, the helicopters were large and heavily laden with ammunition. The sound of their rotors hitting the air was grand as well. Many people associated helicopters with being extremely loud, but military models tended to be quieter than others.

The design philosophies were probably different from their American counterparts, which concentrated on small size, high speed, and little sound. The fact that it took three crew to operate a single helicopter meant they weren't exactly the most commonplace machines. As kings of the sky, they had no need to hide. In exchange, by loading as much ammunition on board as they could, they aimed to deal as much damage to the enemy as possible. That's what these machines were for.

They left air-to-air combat, where both speed and maneuverability were necessities, entirely up to fighter jets like MiGs and Sukhois, and they didn't even consider engaging in helicopter-versus-helicopter combat. Instead, they were designed to blow up all surface targets without fail. That was the sort of specialization they'd been made with. That was what it meant to be an aircraft belonging to the ground forces.

"This is pretty nice. I could get used to this kind of layout," one of the privateer pilots said.

They didn't share a common nationality. No common religion, ethnicity, gender, or age. Even their tastes in food and music were so different it was almost funny.

They only shared one thing:

The desire to kill—and kill one-sidedly.

"This thing's a vaunted prototype that one of the largest militaries in the world was developing in secret. I can't get enough of it. I'm basically living the life of a main character in a side-scrolling shoot-'em-up."

"It's not just a test machine."

A transmission came in from another pilot in their group.

"This is a prototype test on a tactical level—to see whether large aircraft designs are still practical. No guarantee military tactical theories will work with them…And the Russians seem to want them coordinating with smaller helicopters and fighter jets when they actually deploy them into real combat zones. They could have a whole list of shortcomings—namely, people on the ground having an easier time hitting them because of the increased size."

"None o' that matters. We just have to hit them before they hit us. All we gotta do is blast 'em with long-range missiles before we enter their firing range. That's why these things are so big, right? Just like a side-scrolling shmup—we can fire away without worrying about how much ammo we've got left."

As they were bantering, the target location was approaching.

A small settlement where the only stuff piled up was rubble.

The armored car and anti-air cannon vehicle that had gone ahead of them had evidently met with resistance and were now immobilized. But none were indignant about it. They didn't care whether other privateers got captured or killed or whatever. The battle that was about to begin was simply more important to them.

Gripping the yoke so hard it creaked (and while exposing how self-educated his way of squeezing it was), the pilot let out a cry as though excited by the sound of the rotors.

"Ah-ha-ha!! Kill 'em, kill 'em, kill 'em aaaaaaaaaalllllllllllllllllllllll lllllllll!!"

2

A low growl escaped Accelerator's throat.

The motorcade of large vehicles had stopped a few dozen meters in front of him. The back section of one had been utterly destroyed. And he'd seen one boy open the destroyed vehicle's front door and step out onto the snow.

The one.

The boy who had once stopped the experiment that would have been fulfilled through the murder of twenty thousand Sisters.

Accelerator knew he didn't have a good reason to feel anger toward him. His words and actions had no justification, no integrity. Any outsider, from their perspective, would have judged him to be the one in the wrong.

But.

What if the hero, great enough to put a stop to that damned experiment, *was* to die so easily, for such a shitty reason? What if this being who existed for the sake of stopping tragedies, the one who occupied the most important position in Accelerator's mind, lost so simply?

Then, in the realest sense:

This world would already be over.

"Oooooooooooooaaaaaaaaaaaaaaaaaaaaaaaaaaaaaaaaaaaaaaaahhhh-hhhhhhhhhhhhhhhhhhhhhhhhhhhhhhhhhhhhhhhhhhhhhhhhhhh!!!!!!"

A scream.

The black wings burst from Accelerator's back anew. After instantly stretching to over a hundred meters long, he turned them into terrible weapons and swung them down at the Level Zero boy's head.

There was a shattering roar.

The destructive power was enough to cleave a high-rise building vertically in one strike.

Despite that, the boy who was his target didn't end up a clumpy puddle of flesh.

The cause—his right hand.

That one arm, held directly aloft, disbursed the jet-black darkness.

"…"

Accelerator's lips twisted slightly.

What was he thinking, deep down in his heart, about the boy not dying in his first attack?

Without coming to a clear answer himself, Accelerator swung his black wings again.

This time, in a horizontal sweep.

A blow that would have severed any object that existed in the world in two at chest height shot cruelly toward the Level Zero boy.

This one, too, was repelled by his right hand.

But the situation was different. Despite canceling out the black wings, the boy still staggered to the side, as though shoved by the force.

Accelerator knew: That boy had a secret that could cancel out Academy City's top Level Five power with just a touch. But he also knew the boy couldn't deal with attacks that blew away everything in a fixed area, like intense winds or plasma. Either he couldn't cancel out force exceeding a certain level, couldn't deal with abilities applied over an area, or didn't have the strength to cancel out secondary physical phenomena caused by supernatural abilities. Accelerator hadn't discovered the correct answer yet, but he didn't need to understand the logic or rules behind it to know what he had to do to crush this Level Zero boy.

In other words.

I'll use overwhelming force, give him no chance to counterattack, and pound him to bits…!!

A dull, creaking pain assailed the back of his head.

It was like his left and right brain were going to split apart, and something was about to fly out from within it.

This was abnormal.

It wasn't even clear whether it was really Academy City's number one Level Five.

He didn't know what would happen.

He could begin to disintegrate in the process.

But he clenched his teeth. So what?

In this place.

In this situation alone.

He had to rally every last ounce of his strength and fight at full power.

Boom!! The wind roared.

His pair of black wings turned into dozens of sharp stakes, lashing out toward the Level Zero boy as he tried to run in closer. Accelerator wasn't aiming for the small target from many directions—he was laying down a carpet bombing on an area that included the boy.

A shock wave ripped out.

White snow and black earth erupted over ten meters into the air, blocking their field of view. Accelerator could see giant cracks forming in the ground here and there. Seismographs had probably picked up the shaking from far away.

The boy standing in the center of the blast couldn't have been safe.

Even if he could nullify powers with just his right hand, he couldn't have been able to intercept all those attacks without missing anyone.

The damage had definitely been done.

There was no way the Level Zero boy would be saved.

And even the resulting shock wave created by a single one of the dozens of stakes packed enough punch to mash up an unarmed human body.

It should have ended with that.

As he gained victory, so, too, would Accelerator have lost a glimmer of hope.

And yet.

A figure stood before him, swaying beyond the dust of white snow and black earth.

The Level Zero boy was standing.

*   *   *

He wasn't unharmed, of course.

His clothes were stained with dirt. Something red dripped from near his temple. It seemed like his center of gravity was leaning to the side somehow.

But the boy was still standing.

Standing on his on two legs, never breaking.

"Ha, ha-ha…"

Accelerator chuckled quietly.

He didn't understand the logic. The boy shouldn't have been able to deal with that attack with just his right hand. But Accelerator was definitely grinning. He appeared to be enjoying this. It was like he was happy his theory that his attack was absolute had been overturned.

And *that*.

That looked to him like a symbol that he'd easily leaped off the unalterable rails of fate.

"Ha-ha-ha-ha-ha!! Gya-ha-ha-ha-ha-ha-ha-ha-ha-ha-ha-ha-ha-ha!!"

Laughing, Accelerator funneled even greater energy into his black wings.

The awful cracking sound inside his skull got louder.

The Level Zero boy, fist clenched, ran toward Accelerator.

This time, it wouldn't be a warm-up.

This was where the real clash would begin.

3

"They're here."

Digurv, only his head poking out from the anti-air tank's upper hatch, announced it with binoculars in one hand. Hamazura was in the front of the same anti-air tank, sitting in the seat for controlling the caterpillar treads and moving the vehicle—because there was nothing else he could do. The controls were similar to heavy construction equipment like excavators, but he couldn't fully handle expert work like manning the radar or aiming the machine guns at targets.

Peering out the horizontal slit made of reinforced glass to glance at the snowfield, Hamazura asked:

"Is it attack helicopters like we thought?"

"Yeah, a group of three," Digurv answered, without looking in his direction. "Never seen the type before. They're pretty large. Maybe they're doubling as prototype tests."

"Russia's always had a long history of pouring resources into weapons development on large helicopters," the frostbitten Russian soldier cut in from the side.

His name seemed to be Grickin.

"After all, the world's largest transport helicopter apparently has the same carrying capacity as a C-130 transport plane. Russia's the only nation that tries to make helicopters based on those design principles, regardless of what's technologically feasible."

As he listened to Grickin, Hamazura could feel his own face going white.

"If they're huge, that means they're loaded with a lot of ammo and bombs, right?"

His fingers ran over the rough lever in the anti-air tank.

He'd wanted to set himself at ease by confirming that they had troop strength of their own, but it had had zero effect.

"Brand-new prototypes?" Hamazura hissed. "Are we going to be okay? Damn it, we can't fight them in a broken-down anti-air weapon!"

"No, that might actually give us the chance," Digurv explained.

"?"

"It means it's entirely possible these are unreliable prototypes, since they gave them to privateers to test instead of real soldiers. If we were facing attack helicopters that have been proven to be highly reliable on the front lines after countless hours of trial by combat, *then* we'd have had no real chance of winning."

"Either way, this is still gonna be a death match!"

"Here they come," Digurv noted as he peered through his binoculars.

These short words sparked tension within the vehicle.

"...They're probably hit-and-run types, with most of their emphasis on top speed. They can't flutter around, so after they go through the battlefield, they'll probably make a big U-turn before starting a new attack run."

"Which means we're in for a Wild West shoot-out. The only way to win is by trading shots as they go past."

Ba-ba-ba-ba-ba-ba!! They began to hear the giant rotors hitting the air.

Even from the little slit in the driver's seat, Hamazura could see three shadows in the white sky. At this rate, they'd pass overhead in no time at all.

The last thing they wanted to do was let those helicopters get past them.

If they didn't stop the helicopters here, everyone fleeing from the settlement would be killed.

"Here we go!!" shouted Digurv.

Hamazura grabbed the levers for controlling the treads, while Grickin reached for the device that rotated the turrets.

The battle had begun.

When they'd gotten within three hundred meters of the attack helicopters, the anti-air tank's muzzle erupted with fire. In exchange for the cannons' firing rate being somewhat lower than regular machine guns, low *taiko* drumlike beating threw itself against Hamazura's ears.

The attack helicopters split off from their formation with the sound of artillery fire. Orange sparks leaped from one—a round had connected. But it wasn't enough to take it down.

"They've got thick armor since they're so big?!"

"Hamazura, it's their turn! We'll have missiles coming down on us like rain next!!"

As Digurv shouted, Hamazura quickly pulled the anti-air vehicle backward. The steel treads dug into the ground with enough force to spray snow everywhere as they forced the heavy machine where it needed to go.

Caterpillar treads gave the impression of sloth, but this was still a military vehicle. Glancing at the speedometer, it was apparently designed to reach speeds of about seventy kilometers per hour maximum.

However.

The speed of the attack helicopters ripping through the skies was on a completely different level.

"Hmm-hm-hmm!"

Meanwhile, the pilot of one attack helicopter, strengthening his grip on the flight yoke, was even licking his lips. Machine guns or missiles—he could smash that anti-air tank to smithereens with all kinds of stuff. After leaving the airspace, he pulled around in a wide U-turn, raised his speed, and dropped his altitude to take aim at the target.

"Morons! If you survived, you should have just played dead!! Then your chances of holding out might have been a little higher!!"

The vehicle, its anti-air attack having failed, seemed to be desperately trying to run. However, it wouldn't be a challenge for the attack helicopters, equipped with all kinds of sensors. The pilot used his thumb to flick open a protective cover near the top of the yoke, then went right ahead and pushed the red "fire missile" button.

With a trail of white smoke, the little missile sped toward its target. It was too late for it to take evasive maneuvers, and besides, a self-propelled anti-air cannon on caterpillar treads wouldn't have the speed to dodge it anyway. They seemed to be trying to escape into the tall coniferous trees in the woods, but that was pointless.

"Hee-hee!! Now you're toast!!" the pilot shouted.

...But the results he'd hoped for didn't materialize.

It was probably because they'd hidden in the trees. The missile had struck the top of one of them, which hung out like a roof right over the anti-air tank.

Flames and a shock wave rippled out, but even the anti-air tank, with its relatively thin armoring compared to actual tanks, was nearly unharmed. The conifers blown away by the missile broke apart, raining down on their surroundings.

Plus…

"You just gave us an opening, you piece of shit!" shouted Hamazura. "Grickin!!"

Grickin, manning the turrets, pulled a lever. A surface-to-air missile, fixed to the side of the machine guns, ignited and headed for the sky.

The sky that was just a moment ago blocked by trees.

But the SAM shot out from the hole the helicopter's attack had opened up.

"?!"

The pilot's throat dried up for a moment, but the missile didn't fly to him. It penetrated a different helicopter, one who had been preparing for a second flyby.

With an explosion, black smoke sullied the Russian air.

The attack helicopter, now an orange chunk of metal, crashed into the white, snowy ground. There was another explosion, an even bigger one.

But the pilot wasn't sad for his colleagues' demise.

"Rain time."

Using his comm, he prompted the other attack helicopter to join up with him.

"Missiles will get blocked. We'll rain machine-gun fire on them and pump 'em full of holes!!"

The two helicopters veered off in two completely different directions. After a U-turn, they immediately flew toward the forest where the anti-air tank was hiding.

They were set up to strafe from two directions at once.

The anti-air tank frantically hid in some conifers, but the same trick wouldn't work again. The helicopters' sensors had a clear read on something big and metal, and thirty-millimeter Gatling cannons could shoot through those conifers like paper. They couldn't use their cover this time.

But then he looked at the radar again.

"Wha?!" he grunted, confused.

The radar wasn't displaying right. He was slightly disturbed, but he still properly handled the yoke. The Gatling cannon strafing run traced a line into the ground where he wanted it to.

In time with the helicopter's movements, a string of bullets flew out over the white ground.

Several thick trees snapped all at once, and a huge hole opened up in the hunk of metal hidden under them. Not just one or two, either—the bullets were making it into mincemeat.

Boom!! An explosion spread through the woods.

The target was successfully destroyed—at least, it should have been.

Nevertheless, the look on the pilot's face wasn't a good one.

"Hey, what's going on here?" he asked his colleague in a voice that was more angry than confused. "Why are we getting more pings on the radar?! I don't think we hit 'em!!"

If there had only been one anti-air tank in the trees, this couldn't ever have possibly happened. And then a transmission came in from a colleague to answer that question.

"Look—a passenger car! They knew we'd go after them all along, and they hid a car from the settlement in the woods beforehand!! That's why we aimed at the wrong metal indic—?!"

The voice cut off partway through the sentence.

Several orange-colored sparks flew about. His colleague's helicopter's armor had been shot through. Hit by a stream of fire from the anti-aircraft cannons, it exploded in midair.

"…"

At this point, the remaining pilot had the option of going back to base for now.

But he didn't choose it.

The blood rushing to his head was one reason. But more than that, it was because they'd mowed down most of the conifers in the woods. The anti-air tank couldn't hide anymore; even if they tried to throw off the radars with a bunch of other cars, as long as he could visually confirm them, there was no reason to be confused.

"Time…to…die."

The pilot left the region one more time, veering away to a place the anti-air tank couldn't reach, then performed a wide U-turn.

The next run would be the last.

Without cover, this time, this time for *real*, the anti-air tank wouldn't be able to avoid the attacks from above.

"Gya-ha-ha-ha-ha-ha-ha-ha-ha!! You're gonna look like a beehive when I'm finished with you!!"

4

The Strait of Dover.

Atop the solidified water's surface British and French sorcerers fought, but now that the second princess, Carissa, and her Knights had taken to the front lines, the British side was now pushing the enemy back, albeit slowly.

The Knights' power supply from the Curtana Second using the mobile fortress Glastonbury played an especially large part in this. The Knight Leader was also using his spell that reduced personally perceived weapon attack power to zero to great effect. Ignoring normal national borders, the knights' swords were proving to be incredibly effective.

Though they were pushing back the French sorcerers, the Knight Leader's expression was not pleased.

"…Whenever we're winning smoothly, I start wondering if the enemy is setting up for something big. Must be an occupational disorder."

"Well, given who we're up against…"

"…"

The Knight Leader unintentionally sunk into silence at Carissa's answer.

An opponent against whom common sense didn't work. The French tactician—the one people called a holy woman—was one who possessed a peculiar quality unique to France.

The Femme Fatale.

Jeanne d'Arc. Marie Antoinette. Several women appeared in French history who had greatly changed the nation by their existence alone, whether for good or for ill. This tactician was another one of them. It would be an all-too-painful loss were they to execute her unfairly, but it would have been all too terrifying to grant her freedom. Thus, she had been confined by the French government to a basement in Versailles.

Up against a personage like that, maybe it was stranger that things were proceeding according to theory.

Or was his consideration that something was up actually because he'd already been stricken by the Femme Fatale's aura?

"These guys are going to be hard to deal with, too," asserted Carissa in an offhand tone. "If they decide they're being cornered, we run the risk of them committing to acts of violence otherwise impossible during normal military actions. Do you know what the best way to prevent that is?"

"?"

"Gain control of the battlefield quickly, without giving them time to be confused. If our military results are great enough, they'll go past fear. We'll have them dumbfounded."

"I'd appreciate it if you didn't underestimate me."

They heard a voice, source unknown.

It was the "brain" commanding the French sorcerers from afar—the holy woman.

But Carissa grinned.

"Well, maybe if you'd come out here personally, you would have changed things."

Protected by many a knight, Carissa made a declaration.

"But no matter what, you can't leave that basement in Versailles. Small, compact ranged fire from a distance won't be enough to take down our Knights. Use your head all you want—you can't change your troop strength on the field. Using power effectively and raising the upper limit on that power are two entirely different things."

Even as she smiled, the second princess's tone sounded somehow bored.

"Our goal isn't France. We don't have time to spare on the small fry, so unless you want more casualties than you need, make way. Your job is to be the brain, right? I'm positive you know exactly what move you should make now."

"*Heh-heh.*"

And then the Femme Fatale laughed.

"*You know I'm the type to use her head—so I wonder why you never considered the possibility.*"

"What?"

It happened right as a dubiousness came to Carissa's eyes.

Boom!!

The Knight Leader next to her was swept off his feet by a massive impact.

"?!"

Carissa didn't have time to be surprised.

All of a sudden, a woman had flown over to them. One wearing a gorgeous dress, mainly of comfortable white fabric. In contrast to the dress, however, her skin was an unhealthy shade of white, and her eyes were slightly sunken in. The sword she held in her hand was an awful fit for her. It was like a young man who spent all his time reading in the library was wielding a baseball bat.

She was…

Her true identity…

"…The possibility that I *can* actually act. And *that* is France's greatest scheme."

Her gaudy Western straight sword, mostly red and gold, pointed at Carissa.

The first one to respond was the Knight Leader.

"Zero!!"

With that one word, the Femme Fatale's weapon's attack power should have vanished. It should have turned into something safer than a sponge.

However.

"Cute," said the Femme Fatale quietly and simply. "The histories of Britain and France are actually surprisingly ambiguous. Even William I, king of England, was originally a French noble."

She didn't move right away—perhaps because she was confident in an assured victory.

"...And your spell doesn't apply to weapons related to the royal family, does it?"

"Blas—?!"

After seeing the Knight Leader's shock, the Femme Fatale swung her sword.

Its speed exceeded that of sound.

It was probably like the Curtana—a special sword imbued with a national spell unique to France.

Carissa had no way of defending.

The Knights were borrowing strength from the Curtana Second, but Queen Elizard was the one actually holding the weapon. Carissa herself wasn't even receiving its benefits. And even if the knights were to offer their bodies, the Femme Fatale's sword would cleave through all their shields and Carissa with them.

And.

With a shrill *gkkeeeeeeeeeeeee!!*

The blade in Second Princess Carissa's hand parried the blow she should never have been able to block.

The Curtana Original had lost its power with the end of the coup.

The Curtana Second was in Elizard's hand—Carissa shouldn't have had any strength at all.

But nevertheless:

"The Durandal, eh?"

Her body wasn't cleaved in two, didn't have even a scratch on it. As their swords pressed against each other at point-blank range, only Carissa was grinning.

"How?" the French woman hissed to herself.

What Carissa had in her hand was silver metal only a few

centimeters long, but a sword made of light was sprouting from it. Considering the force of the weapon she herself carried, the phenomenon was absolutely impossible. This was France's sword. The destructive power of France itself. To rival it, one should have had to bring out the Curtana, equally a symbol of Britain.

"The histories of Britain and France are surprisingly ambiguous. You said so yourself, so."

"Wh…what?"

"Your king Charlemagne thought the same. Didn't he try to embed fragments of the holy lance in his own sword in an attempt to imbue it with sacred power and value?"

"…You don't mean…?"

The Femme Fatale again glanced at the few short centimeters of metal.

"Is that a fragment of the Curtana Second?!"

"When I fought Mother, the Curtana Original and the Curtana Second clashed. This is a by-product from that time…Still, I hadn't thought it would draw this much power just after passing into distinguished royalty's hands. I can't simply use it for crushing things. I don't like this sword—it's got all kinds of loopholes and secret tricks. I hate it enough to incite a coup d'état, in fact."

A magical explosion went off between Carissa and her nemesis.

Each took distance and repositioned their swords.

"And actually, *me* being able to act is *Britain's* greatest scheme."

5

The action Accelerator took was a simple one: He swung the jet-black wings sprouting from his back from high to low.

However, his target this time was not the Level Zero boy running toward him.

It was the empty white ground in front of him.

A blast.

The intense destructive force whipped up a huge cloud of dust and dirt. A tsunami of earth appeared, over fifteen meters high and over *three hundred meters* wide. Embroiling the very scenery, it lunged toward the boy, aiming to swallow his tiny body whole.

With this, he should have died.

Even if the boy had been wearing a military powered suit, it would have crushed him into a bloody mess along with his composite material armor.

Despite that.

Wham!! The Level Zero charged through the dust cloud head-on.

Struck with rocks but never taking a fatal wound.

"..." Accelerator was surprised at first, but then he figured out the trick.

He had advance information, too.

Academy City's number three Level Five. For Accelerator, Railgun was a fated opponent. And one of the rumors surrounding Railgun was that there was an unknown Level Zero who could deal with her ability with only his right hand.

He had his doubts.

For example, assume he did have a right hand that could cancel out any ability.

But how would he time it?

Railgun's attacks traveled at three times the speed of sound. Her lightning lances boasted even greater speed. Even if it was an effective means of interception, getting the timing right would be a Herculean task. And if he'd gotten the timing wrong by even an instant, he might have died instantly. In that situation, how could he have easily repelled it, over and over?

Seeing this now, though, gave him a rough idea.

In other words, this was...

He can detect the signs.

For example, in Railgun's case, whenever she used her ability, it would spread a weak magnetic field and electromagnetic waves into the surroundings. Paper clips and doorknobs lying around would rattle about. Because of the huge explosion that happened afterward, Railgun herself might not have realized it, but it was exactly like subtle rumbling portending an earthquake. Like an elementary school experiment, spreading out iron sand to see what direction invisible magnetic forces were going in…All those subtle, incidental motions would vividly telegraph the attack Railgun was about to use.

The stronger the ability, the more unintentional aftereffects it would fling around. It was like having a tell in rock-paper-scissors—maybe it gave away the next action they were about to take.

Of course, that wasn't all.

It wasn't limited to just that one variety.

She was nothing compared to Accelerator, but Railgun was still the third-ranked Level Five, not someone to be trifled with like that.

There were probably other kinds.

Take the lightning lances.

They were pure high-tension current, so if he held out his right hand first, then even if her aim was somewhat off, the lightning would naturally be absorbed into that outstretched right hand. It would act like a lightning rod.

Take a sword of iron sand—other than the sword gathered into her hand, iron sand in the surrounding area would faintly react to the magnetic force lines and begin to change shape. In which case, he could use the visible magnetic force lines to predict how the next attack flung out would flow. In certain cases, he could even dismantle the particle sword itself without even touching the actual thing, instead by only touching the iron sand *lines* scattered in the vicinity.

Each time, there was a different method for sure victory. Either it was the power at the very core of his ability—or a subtle side effect derived from it.

Even which thing was treated as more important would change each time.

The important thing wasn't whether there was a method to win. Never relying on a single type of pattern, always reevaluating the problem from new angles, and on top of that, searching for the most suitable way to resolve things each time…Even against another esper, he understood that the same resolution wouldn't necessarily work. He knew that even against one lightning lance, depending on what he chose at the starting point to combat it, he could have to take a completely different path.

That was why his fighting style changed.

He would rely on his defensive capacity to nullify any other abilities to avoid being killed instantly, and then he would take maximum advantage of the little bit of time it bought him, using the information he'd gotten by literally throwing himself at the problem to discover a means of survival.

His way of thinking wouldn't be enough on its own.

His ability wouldn't be enough on its own, either.

Only because both were present could he use these tactics that could just barely reach victory.

In a situation where he was face-to-face with death, the guts to keep his body and mind moving were probably important, too.

However.

The Level Zero himself wouldn't be aware of that.

A basis of judgment, of how to use both the ability itself and the side effects derived from it. And the actual actions taken, the quick changing of tactics depending on the situation…He was probably only using them in conjunction with his reflexes. Even when it came to the subtle fluctuations in nearby metal items against Railgun, he wouldn't be consciously perceiving them; his subconscious would be processing whatever he saw move slightly in the corners of his vision for him. Which meant there was no guarantee of a 100 percent success. In fact, it was highly possible that if he tried to do any of this on purpose, he would fail.

But.

Just the fact that Accelerator had hit him with an attack—and he'd survived—made him a potent force in battle. Even with that special power in their right hand, how many others could have achieved the same results?

The pure ability by itself certainly wasn't that strong.

A comprehensive evaluation might have said it was weak.

And that was why.

This boy knew how significant hard work was in order to survive.

""Oooooooooooooooooooooooooooooooooooohhhhhhhhhhhh-
hhhhhhhhhhhhhhhhhhhhhhhhhhhhhhhhhhhhhhhhhhhhh!!!!!!"""

Two shouts overlapped.

The Level Zero boy leaped into his fist's range without hesitation.

Accelerator similarly swung his black wings.

The boy's tightly clenched right fist flew in to oppose him.

Of the two intersecting attacks, the Level Zero's reached just a split-second faster. Accelerator's face was punched aside, and his balance faltered for a moment. The black wings veered away, failing to hit the Level Zero boy and instead ripping right by him.

The aftermath: A blast wind whipped up, sending both combatants tumbling dozens of meters backward. The two got up on the snow, clenched their fists again, and then dashed in to minimum range, meaning to close their distance to zero.

Something dark and sinister erupted from within Accelerator's chest.

It wasn't only a response to the Level Zero. It was against something more vague, an urge to rail against this illogical and unfair world—his hatred and rage, bursting out of him all at once in the form of words:

"Why?! Why doesn't anyone save that kid?! You're supposed to be a hero! The hero who stopped that experiment with nothing but a fist!! *Save* her, damn it!! If you can do something nobody else can do, then give a little of that to that brat already!!"

With his roar, an even greater power escaped his wings, whipping around furiously.

As it did, he could feel something ripped apart, tearing off inside his heart.

He couldn't stop anymore.

Not even remembering Last Order's smile could restrain his violence.

"The fact that a shitty villain like me has been trying to stand up for her this whole time is insanity! I'm the wrong person for it, no matter how you think about it! There's no way I'd ever be able to be a hero! No matter what, the only thing I can choose is a resolution covered in blood! Why did I have to do all this shit?! If a hero like you had come running to the rescue, I wouldn't have ever made this mistake in the first place!! And that brat would have never had to suffeeeeeeeeeeeeeeeeerrrrrrrrrrrrrr!!"

Swinging wings and fists, even as they each tried to kill the other, the Level Zero boy probably didn't understand why things had come to this. Just as Accelerator was shouting without really understanding what it was he wanted to say, obviously, nobody else would be able to.

For just a moment, the two were silent.

Their gazes averted, glancing toward a little girl fallen some distance away.

And...

The black wings expanded even more.

The wings partitioned into over a hundred pieces, and they flew at the Level Zero from every direction imaginable.

An explosion and a shock wave went off, and even the foundation rattled.

*He has to be dead now...*thought Accelerator. *It simply wouldn't make sense if he wasn't.*

And yet.

"How...?"

An unintentional groan escaped him.

Eventually, it turned into a huge scream.

"How did that not kill you, Mr. Hero?! If you don't die now, everything is going to be ruined!!"

Words came back to him, from the mouth of the nearby boy who clenched his fist, which was dripping with both their blood.

"...You don't need to be a hero."

Several footsteps echoed on the snow.

Fist and wings crossed.

Several attacks hit their mark, pounding through air, and blood splattered.

"I'm just a Level Zero! Do I look like some kind of superhero to you?! Good guys? Bad guys? Don't give me that bullshit. Do you have to pick a side to save anyone?! Someone you don't want to cry is crying right in front of you! She can't even ask you to save her—she just has to bite her lip and endure it!! Isn't that enough for you?! Enough for you to stand up for her?! You don't need some special position or reason!! That's all you need for it to be okay to be her shield!!"

Each time he shouted a word, the boy's power grew.

He wasn't directing it only toward Accelerator, either.

It was like his words were dispelling the hesitation that existed within himself, as well.

"I really don't know why you want to protect her or how you've hurt others until now. But if you wanted to protect that girl, then be proud of it and protect her!! Be proud of how you want to save her, right here and right now!! It's your life—*you* decide!! If you want to personally keep her safe, then do it, and if you want to abandon her, then I'll take everything off your hands. But what the hell is it that *you* want to do?! Are you okay with that? You'd rather praise someone you barely know and give them what's most important to you? Can you really be satisfied with all that?!"

An explosion went off.

Chaotically, the black wings swung.

Earth and snow were blown high into the air. But the Level Zero boy didn't go down. Against an enormous attack that would have buried him altogether, he had twisted himself into a weak spot where he would barely miss a fatal blow, then charged in, ever onward.

A shuddering chill ran through Accelerator's spine.

Until now, he'd thought the scariest part of this Level Zero was his constantly adapting tactics against powerful espers. He outwitted them in ways they hadn't realized were possible, ran in head-on, and beat their little blind spots with his strong fist. He'd thought *that* was the scariest thing about him.

But he was wrong.

The scariest thing about him wasn't anything that complicated.

It was the desire to never give up. Staying in the fight, no matter what happened, always hurtling straight toward the enemy, no

matter what—that, Academy City's strongest Level Five finally realized, was the scariest thing he'd ever seen.

And as proof:

That attack...

Accelerator audibly gulped.

Relatively, it was really weak, but a human body shouldn't ever be able to endure something with that much force!!

That didn't matter.

It wasn't mundane logic that lay at the core of his fear.

The most important thing—the most fearsome enemy—was close to him now.

Come to think of it, Accelerator recalled suddenly.

When they'd clashed like this at the switchyard, during the Sisters-consuming experiment, didn't it strike him then, too? That the scariest thing about the boy was how he'd always get up on his own two legs when he shouldn't have been able to stand, never giving up?

"You be the one to choose..."

The Level Zero boy, just like the switchyard covered with too much blood to do anything about, stepped right up to Academy City's strongest Level Five.

"Will you keep protecting her yourself, give everything to someone else and run away, or ask for my help?!"

That fist.

Clenched more strongly than it ever had been.

"I don't care if it's arrogant or what—you choose something that *you're* proud of!!"

A thunderous roar split the air.

It was the sound of the Level Zero's fist striking Accelerator directly in the face.

The power of those black wings, acquired after pushing forward on the path of "evil" and after several coincidences, would not work against him.

They would not.

Because, in the first place, were there really ever any shackles forcing Accelerator to walk the path of evil?

Something he had to defend, no matter what happened...

Last Order's smile—that wasn't something that had anything to do with their relative positions, was it? If he wanted to truly protect her, then didn't he have to jump over the fences of mundane good and evil?

Maybe this was what it meant for someone to try so desperately to live while following in someone's footsteps. Not because they were good or evil. He'd never thought about any of that from the start—so maybe that was why Accelerator, a "simple evil," couldn't ever catch up to him, no matter what.

In that case.

As Accelerator fell backward, he had a certain thought.

And he felt an illusion lurking within him shatter.

And:

The sorcerer Lesser, who had been traveling with Touma Kamijou, had been watching the battle as well.

From a magic perspective, the mysterious assailant's black wings held a terrible significance. But the scariest thing of all was still Touma Kamijou, who had brought even those wings into submission.

Just now...

Lesser internally reviewed once again what she'd just witnessed.

...That boy. The black wings had split over a hundred times, and he just...grabbed one and twisted it...?

The boy's right hand seemed to have the power to cancel out any supernatural or paranormal abilities. But it had conditions and limits. When it came to incredibly immense amounts of power, he wouldn't be able to cancel it all out; there also seemed to be cases where it wouldn't do much more than simply block it. In fact, it had taken him some time to fully cancel out the special large sword Fiamma had used.

Logically, a situation where he couldn't cancel something out should have been a disadvantage for him.

However, just now, that boy had used that disadvantage as an advantage, purposely grabbing one of the black wings that he couldn't nullify. And then, by twisting it, he had ruined his attacker's balance, creating a safe zone within the net of a hundred wings unleashed equally, which left him just barely enough space.

Elimination and interference.

A unique power he could use differently by aligning it with his opponent's strengths.

Did that mean this cruel war had only amplified the boy's power?

However.

…Could he have really overcome the situation with only that…?

Even if he had "grabbed" that immense force with his right hand, she still didn't think that would be enough for him to pull through. Even if Lesser had possessed the same power, it would have been unthinkable for her to escape that situation in one piece.

In that case.

What on earth had happened?

Was there really no logic to it?

Or…

6

Accelerator's vision flickered.

In his now-sideways field of vision was Last Order. She was still buried in the cold snow. Belatedly wanting to scowl at that fact now, Accelerator discovered someone squatting down right next to her.

That might have been enough for the Accelerator back when he'd entered Russia to be the trigger for murder.

But right now, he could no longer move.

The one bending beside Last Order was a spiky-haired boy. He'd been peering into the unconscious little girl's face, but eventually, he directed his right hand toward her forehead. The gesture was like checking the temperature of someone with a fever.

With only that, something happened.

A high-pitched noise, like a hard object breaking, rang out across the white Russian lands.

Accelerator couldn't comprehend what it meant.

His consciousness once again began to slip away.

When he next woke, he was in a vehicle.

It wasn't a common passenger car. It had no windows, much less furnishings for people to ride in it, so it may well have been the bed of a truck or something. The rough metal walls and floor aroused a sense of caution; he wondered if the Academy City shadow group had retrieved him.

A moment later, though, he figured it out: That spiky-haired boy had been in a motorcade made of several vehicles. Maybe the vehicle he, Accelerator, had been put into was one of them.

There were no vibrations, so the vehicle must have been stationary. Perhaps it had reached its destination?

But curiously, Last Order was lying next to him.

The earlier sweat dripping down her entire body was, for some reason, nowhere to be found. Right before he'd lost consciousness, the spiky-haired boy had touched her. Had his right hand applied some sort of effect?

However, no matter what kind of effect it was, Accelerator figured it was temporary.

His vector-transformation ability could accurately gauge even the agitation in a person's brain waves. When he used that sort of power to check Last Order's physical condition, he learned that the fundamental issue was unsolved.

She was stable for now, but she'd eventually relapse. Still, the fact of the matter was that the time he had to resolve the situation was now extended.

Accelerator, unsure of how he should interpret the situation, suddenly felt the rough texture of the parchment he'd put in his pocket. At about the same time, he noticed that someone had placed a small note right next to Last Order.

Given the timing, it was highly probable it was from that spiky-haired boy.

He picked the paper scrap up and unfolded it, and on it was written:

Index Librorum Prohibitorum.
The index of prohibited books.

Aiwass, who had defeated Accelerator just before leaving Academy City, had spouted something about remembering the word *index*.

Maybe it was connected.

Maybe the key to saving Last Order had been given to him in the form of a note.

And then, the truck's tailgate was thrown open from the outside.

Light poured in, revealing a tall man with blond hair and blue eyes. He addressed Accelerator and Last Order, the only two passengers inside.

"We invite you to the Elizalina Alliance of Independent Nations. I don't know how much we'll be able to do for you, but why don't we think of ways to heal that girl together?"

Accelerator didn't give a verbal response. He just hung his head low in front of Last Order, still gripping the note in both hands.

Almost like a white angel offering a prayer or something.

And thus, in the faraway city of science, a being who exceeded the extent of humanity was smiling.

Aiwass.

A regular person might have broken out into a greasy sweat at the sight of that expression. That was the sort of nuance this smile had to it. As he gave that smile, which nobody else would understand the actual meaning behind, he simply spoke.

"As I thought…His right hand is interesting."

It was unknown whether Aiwass deciding something was *interesting* truly benefited people who wished to live proper lives.

And Aiwass itself didn't possess the thought patterns to care about stunted human lifetimes.

This being only took action in accordance with its own interests.

"Perhaps I should have met with that boy as well before he left the City."

7

They'd lost the conifer woodland they'd used as cover, but one attack helicopter was still left.

They couldn't fool the attacks from the skies any longer. It was one-on-one, face-to-face. If they didn't shoot it down at this chance, the privateers' attack would slaughter all the people from the settlement running around trying to escape.

The immobile Rikou Takitsubo was included in that number. Hamazura and the others had to win, no matter what.

And yet.

"Ooooooooooooohhhhhhhhhhhhhhhhhhhhhhhhhhhhhhhhhhhh!!"

Someone gave a shout inside the cramped anti-air cannon. Hamazura and Digurv, who hadn't actually touched the trigger, were uplifted as well.

The attack helicopter approached.

A straight line of gunfire ran along the ground.

The attack helicopter, now committed to the attack, was incredibly fast. They wouldn't hit much if they took aim with the machine guns. They'd gotten a missile lock on it, but firing it now probably wouldn't do them any good. Normally, surface-to-air missiles were for shooting fleeing aircraft in the back. The chances of a direct hit on a flying object moving so fast right at them were slim. The ambush they'd pulled off using the conifers as cover had worked because their opponents never thought there would be a counterattack and were slow to take evasive action. That would be useless now that they were fully alert.

Grickin had said it would be a Wild West shoot-out. Their bullets would cross, and whoever pierced the other first would win.

Hamazura thought he was right, too.

However, the attack helicopter above had a staggering advantage over them.

Damn it...!!

Hamazura frantically worked the caterpillar treads, twisting the chassis's movement to get out of the approaching line of gunfire. But he wouldn't make it. The attack helicopter made a slight adjustment to its trajectory and approached, aiming to shoot through the anti-air tank.

It was over.

He unwittingly shouted Takitsubo's name—and then a sound that took his heart in an iron grip tore into his ears. It was the sound of thick metal plating being pierced.

He blanked out.

Completely unmetaphorically, he stopped breathing.

However—he didn't die.

In fact, the piercing, eardrum-hammering noise hadn't been the anti-air tank getting blown up at all.

The ghastly noise had come from the attack helicopter soaring in the sky.

The sound had been a giant sword, almost three and a half meters long, skewering it from the side.

"...Huh?"

The word on its side, *Ascalon*, was practically burned into his eyes.

Hamazura's dumb-sounding grunt had come out at the completely nonsensical sight. Despite his own life being saved, part of him didn't even try to acknowledge the phenomenon.

In the meantime, an even more absurd reality unfolded before his eyes.

Someone had jumped onto the attack helicopter, which was flying at over twenty meters in the air. Yes—someone had leaped up from the white ground. It was a tall man dressed in clothing that was mainly blue. Grabbing the grip of the sword he'd stabbed into the side of the helicopter, he whipped it around.

The king of the skies was tossed away with just that, like a toy hammer.

The tall man let gravity lower him, and he landed right in the middle of the snowfield. As he did, he slammed the sword into the ground. The attack helicopter exploded savagely, spraying orange flames all over the place.

"…To save others from meaningless atrocities, to quell the tears that have no need to flow, you stole the enemy's weapon and fought with all your might. You are a brilliant sight to behold."

A low male voice echoed out from the flames. He spoke in fluent English, on a level that allowed even Hamazura to manage to understand certain words.

A moment later, the flames burst out from within.

Around the man, possibly created when the snow melted, floated a mass of water. It moved in an unnatural way, like juice spilled in a space without gravity.

"I know not what transpired here, but would you allow me, Acqua of the Back, to offer what assistance I may?"

Several feelings intersected, and the protagonists' chance encounters gave way to even greater stories.

This was when their counterattack began.

As long as they continued to run through the giant, intensifying war without losing sight of their goals, this world, which had always created smiles for people, would never break so easily.

BATTLE REPORT

In a hospital in the city of Rome, a single one-person room, was enveloped by a strange air.

Tranquility.

It was a sight as though the image of the one sleeping there had permeated the entire room itself.

The one lying atop the bed was the Roman pope.

An old man, who was supposed to be cloistered away deep within the basilica in the Vatican, had been dressed in an operating gown and had had several tubes attached to his mouth and nose.

A young priest, right after entering the room, shook his head without meaning to.

Perhaps, somewhere in his heart, he'd been hoping: hoping that he would rise like someone from a legend at the chaos now engulfing the world.

"...No one can stop Fiamma's oppression...," said the young priest to him, wringing the words from his throat. "After seeing his power firsthand, all the cardinals have either bowed in fear or have chosen to obey out of personal desire. Of all the things, some have even stepped forth to suggest we choose a new pope in the middle of this war."

Only the young priest's words continued.

"A large magical battle appears to have broken out between the

United Kingdom and France as well. Fiamma is likely the one insti-
gating France…No, that is not the only place. At this very moment,
everywhere across the world, many battles are being waged now, all
in accordance to Fiamma's plans."

In other words, not a single response came back.

The young priest suddenly felt like crumpling at that fact. However, the situation wouldn't stop there. Another person, a nun, flew
into the hospital room, her breathing ragged.

"I-it's awful!!"

"We are in the presence of His Holiness!!" the young priest
scolded.

The nun flinched. However, her face was still pale as she continued to work her mouth like a beached fish. "Th-the people of Rome
have begun saying how sick they are of aiding this kind of war!! And
they're beginning to gather in the streets! They may start marching
on the Vatican!!"

On the surface, World War III was treated as a war between Russia
and Academy City. However, just as Academy City and the United
Kingdom were allies, civilians would have indistinctly realized that
Russia and the Roman Church were in a friendly relationship as
well. In fact, several units from the Italian military had already gone
to fight in this war.

The cardinals controlling the Roman Church had been captivated
by Fiamma's power and were now useless. Maybe, just maybe, the
normal people acting out of righteous anger held the power to better
change the course of history.

However.

"…We must stop them."

"Father?"

"Historically, several 'people's revolutions' have succeeded. But
those great undertakings only succeeded with painstaking advance
preparations! This sort of ad hoc riot will not change history! At this
rate, it will end with the Roman Church's security forces massacring
them!"

"Th-then what shall we do? What should we do?!"

"They earnestly have the Roman Church's future at heart. Therefore, we *must* stop them before they resort to violence. We cannot allow them to die like this."

The young priest and the nun hurried to rush out of the hospital room. However, the priest stopped once, right near the exit. Casting a short glance at the holy man on the bed, his words seemed to seep out of him.

"If only...If only you would show everyone your face and say a few words to them, we may have been able to cleanse their anxiety..."

The young priest shook his head as if to rid himself of impossibilities. After that, he headed off for the city of Rome, which was close to erupting into riots, in order to deal with the problem presented to him.

The tranquil air once again returned to the room.

And...

Something absolutely impossible happened.

With a twitch, the pope's fingertips moved.

Nothing but a tiny tremble. And then, as though that were the trigger for everything, the man's closed eyelids opened. He pulled out the tubes going into his mouth and nose, sat up on the bed, and looked around. The place held no grand papal attire; there was only a habit, both modest and trimmed down to the important elements, hanging up on the wall.

Picking up the remote control on the side table, the pope turned on the television. As he listened to the news playing on it, he removed his surgical gown and changed into the habit.

Tragedies were being reported.

A mother lamenting before unfair cruelty appeared. The commentator's words continued, almost as if to amplify the anxiety. The profile of a girl praying appeared. The report was that her father hadn't been seen ever since an explosion had gone off near their house. Somebody, somewhere, was crying, asking why this war had to happen.

For a time, the Roman pope was silent.

Before he took any definite next action, a magical communication came directly into his mind.

"Hiya, Mr. Dandy Gentleman. Should I assume you're still sitting in the Roman Papal seat?"

"Is that Vasilisa?"

Before, when he had gone for talks in order to strengthen his cooperative relationship with the head of the Russian Church, its patriarch, he'd secretly traded a means of communication with her.

"The cardinals seem to be attempting to carry out a papal conclave. They've probably decided already that my authority is lost. The words that come out of my mouth alone cannot stop the war, you know."

"But you still got up anyway. As long as I know that, everything's hunky-dory."

"What are you doing right now?"

"Hmm?"

A loud popping noise grated on the pope's mind.

He scowled.

That was clearly an explosion. Not one, not two—but many going off, intermittently. He heard angry yells with them. Vasilisa was probably having a magical death match against someone while making small talk.

"Would you like to know? I'm in the middle of making my rebellious subordinates cry. Ah-ha-ha—there's this perverted sorceress named Skogssnua, and her face is covered in snot right now. Weren't you the type to burst into tears if you heard about comrades killing each other?"

Vasilisa's tone didn't change.

From that alone, he understood just how one-sided the battle actually was.

"…Go easy on them. They *are* your subordinates."

"I thought you'd say that," said Vasilisa with a quiet giggle, in a tone that left it vague how serious she really was. *"But if you dislike this sort of thing, how in the world do you plan on ending this war?"*

"What? I'll just do what I need to," answered the pope simply.

"...Not as a pope leading two billion followers, however. I must only do what is needed as one more follower of the Roman Orthodox Church. Which is to work from within to halt any grave distortions that may lead us down the wrong path. I did promise that mercenary, after all."

After saying all that, the pope whispered the next part to himself alone.

"I contacted God's Right Seat as well, to save our followers more effectively, but it seems the Lord still intends to give me more trials."

The pope opened the hospital room window and, without hesitation, jumped out.

The curtain on a new battle was opening—for one old man.

Fiamma of the Right had returned to his base in Russian territory.

"Don't act so scared, Nikolai," he said with arrogant indifference as he walked.

An elderly man's voice came back to him from his communication Soul Arm, which was in the form of a book.

"You *started this war*."

"More accurately, I *proposed* it. You all were the ones who officially pulled the trigger, weren't you?"

"*Depending on how this war between the magic side and the science side progresses, Russia's standing after it's over will be unsatisfactory. You told us that, so we agreed to your proposal—and this is the result! I'm sure by now that you've heard something about the huge combat force partly composed of Academy City unmanned weapons and how good they've been doing!!*"

"I keep telling you not to act so scared."

"*If this state of affairs continues, you and I both will lose our bastions. I will not let you lie and say you don't understand what that means. And if I may, if you have no plan for dealing with this, then we're through. After we've eliminated you, we'll settle this war we started on our own terms. By searching for a way to end things with the least possible damage.*"

"Outlooks aren't so good on that one. You've been going about your preparations for war and keeping it secret from the patriarch—if that happened, the Russian Church would want *your* head, too."

Fiamma shrugged a tiny bit and smiled.

"Let's speak hypothetically. What if I had a card up my sleeve that could reverse everything in an instant?"

"What, have you gotten your hands on nuclear weapons? Unfortunately for you, Russia has those in great quantity."

Nikolai was speaking quickly, scornfully.

"But as far as we've done test firings of ballistic missiles through official routes, we are certain they won't ever reach Academy City or any of its satellite agencies. Switch out the warhead all you want—if you can't hit them, what's the point? With them intercepting one hundred percent of the missiles, bringing out nuclear weaponry won't lead to stopping them."

"The archangel Gabriel."

"?!"

With just those few quietly whispered words, Nikolai stopped talking.

"Or perhaps the name Misha Kreutzev is more familiar to you?"

"You've obtained it…?"

"I've secured the nun who had acted as its medium. What if I said I would use her as a basis to give form to the archangel and control it as my pawn? Just so you know, it would be ready to use at any moment. Anyway, would this state of the war, or what have you, that you've been so worried about not even budge a bit?"

In all likelihood, Nikolai Tolstoj, said to be a person who profiteered whenever some kind of conflict sprang up, had immediately started counting his chickens before they hatched. Fiamma heard him start speaking quickly and excitedly from the communication Soul Arm, but he wasn't listening much.

Ignoring the book-shaped Soul Arm, he muttered to himself alone, "…Well, my true goal in getting her was something else. The fact that I, of Michael, can make Gabriel's power my own—that ambiguity of the correspondence of aspects is one that should be detested."

Cutting off his monologue there, he once again spoke, as though announcing something to the world.

"Now then—it's time for the fun-filled Project Bethlehem to begin."

"What was that?"

Ekalielya A. Pronskaya, a Russian Air Force pilot continuing the fight in the skies over the Sea of Japan, frowned. Her communications device, connected with her helmet, delivered the words of the enemy Academy City superlarge fighter jet pilot.

"*I said, the Kremlin Report,*" the enemy soldier told her, sounding mildly annoyed, as they each flung their own top-of-the-line chunks of metal around. "*The most vital, top-priority procedure in the Russian defense forces. Anyone in the military must have at least heard of it.*"

"…"

She knew of it, but only by name.

But that hadn't been something she'd gained official viewing permission to see. It was more like a legend that had spread through those in the military. Nobody knew if it really existed or not. Ekalielya wasn't surprised by the Report itself, but at how their enemy had even grasped rumors of something that didn't (purportedly) exist in the public record.

"*Do you know what it entails?*"

"Do I need to answer that?"

"*A wall of bacteria.*"

Suddenly, the Academy City pilot veered the conversation elsewhere. That was how Ekalielya thought of the move—but she was wrong. Both thoughts were actually connected.

"*A killer virus transmitted through the air. The type that doesn't only infiltrate your respiratory organs—it can get inside your blood vessels from nothing but skin contact. And it effectively decomposes oils, to boot. It will stop animals from breathing while also poking holes in filters like masks and air ducts designed for use against biochemical weapons. Once they scatter it, the usual countermeasures won't be usable anymore."*

"What are you trying to say?"

"The Kremlin Report is a defensive procedure for nuclear weapon launch facilities...Should the nation suffer an invasion by an enemy force and those nuclear launch facilities be under threat of capture, the plan entails dispersing this bacterial wall around the facilities, precisely annihilating only the people, leaving the launch facilities unharmed. The procedure on how exactly to carry that out is the Kremlin Report."

"..."

"Naturally, they'll never send out an evacuation advisory for the Russian soldiers and civilians working at the facilities, nor the civilians living normal lives nearby. The procedure's only priority is to guarantee the nuclear launch facilities' safety. They still haven't completed a vaccine that can combat this bacterial wall. It has an extreme resistance even to heat treatment. Sure, there are reports saying you can obliterate the bacteria by using incredibly dense ozone, but... You know what would happen if they did something like that to the infected, suffering victims, don't you?"

Ekalielya's hands, gripping the flight yoke, quavered slightly.

If that was true, it would change the meaning of this war.

Academy City wouldn't be fighting to make the Russian people suffer. Russia's top officials had started this war on their own. They were about to greenlight an operation to cause further suffering to the Russian people they were meant to protect, who were fearful of the war's trends and saw how the situation had started to get out of hand...Didn't that mean Academy City would be fighting to stop that?

Ekalielya felt something central to her mind, her core, was about to break.

But she shook her head against it. She couldn't deny the possibility that this was propaganda designed to sap her fighting spirit.

"Words of an enemy nation. How could I believe something like that?! You're the ones *actually* using military force to invade our lands and point your weapons at our people!! Am I supposed to overlook this *real* invasion happening right now because of some idle chatter with no evidence?!"

"*I thought you'd say that,*" said the Academy City pilot, seeming somehow amused. "*So I brought something with me.*"

She heard a *bing!*

Modern fighter jet instruments had become digital monitors, able to display complex information from multiple angles. One of her many small LCD monitors had suddenly switched to a different screen.

It had forced her communication port open and was squeezing information through.

But that wasn't what Ekalielya was surprised about.

The values and sentences displayed on the screen almost stopped her heart in its tracks.

"*What do you make of that?*"

The Academy City pilot's question came to her.

"*Are your leaders really protecting the Russian people?*"

Britain's second princess, Carissa, had also spoken of the Kremlin Report.

The distance between her and the Femme Fatale had closed almost enough that they could ram their noses into each other. Their swords ground against each other, and their heads pushed past the blades.

The sword of light born of the Curtana Second's fragment and the French sword Durandal: As they pressed their weapons, each in the realm of legend, against each other, they traded words as well:

"...What was that?"

"You're the brains, aren't you? Considering Russia's circumstances and technology, and how Academy City's invasion is currently going, you should be able to tell whether I speak true or not. Or will you spout some trivial nonsense about not believing it until you see the Kremlin Report with your own eyes?"

A great force exploded between their blades.

Each withdrew by about ten meters.

The Femme Fatale, holding Durandal ready, told her quietly, "No matter how righteous the flag you fly, the fact is you're using French land as a stepping stone to interfere with Russia. And France, having matured this much under the patronage of the Roman Church, cannot allow itself to disobey their orders now. Even if what you say about the Kremlin Report is true, it isn't a reason for me to sheathe my blade."

"Are you being serious?"

"You're the one who caused a coup d'état to protect her own people and tried to destroy the Europeans, weren't you?"

"As much as was necessary."

Carissa didn't deny it.

She wouldn't utter only words convenient for her—she easily admitted to her own ugly faults.

And on top of that, she said, "But I don't plan on killing anyone I don't need to in order to protect my people. Not a single one."

"..."

"What connection is there between Russian people being made to suffer from the Kremlin Report's activation and you defending your French people?"

"It's..."

"The Roman Church's patronage? Did you really want that yourselves? Was it really protecting you? Right now, thanks to the pressure they put on you, you've caused a needless war and put your own people in a crisis, haven't you?"

The Femme Fatale stayed quiet for a moment.

Carissa quietly brought the Curtana Second's fragment, and the sword of light it created, to bear. "France is the only one mounting an actual magical offensive against the UK. Everyone else has figured it out—the Roman Church isn't behind this war; Fiamma is...And if not for this petty squabble, we could go to Russia, too. You have the chance, right now, to avoid the worst-case scenario."

She had no doubts.

She had no reason to have any.

"So what will you do? I don't remember France, the nation I've determined to be a long-standing rival, being *this* worthless."

Academy City, District 23.

In this school district, a conglomeration of aviation and space-related technology, waited all kinds of aircraft. Normally, passenger planes for transporting people and goods were common, but now, it was dyed in a more martial color. A myriad of fighter jets, bombers, and transport craft were lined up in rows, with staff for maintenance running around among them.

In their midst was one certain bomber.

The HsB-02 supersonic bomber.

Over eighty meters long. A top speed of a blistering seven thousand kilometers per hour—it was an aircraft that seemed to transcend physical limits of the earth's atmosphere.

A bomber.

However, not a single bomb was loaded inside that vast pile of high-spec machinery. Only an empty hold—but anyone who knew the circumstances would have felt their spine freeze. Something far more terrifying than mere bombs was on board.

"Hm-hm-hmm."

A woman's humming could be heard.

Along with the voice, filled with amused-sounding emotion, there was an audible cracking noise. One chair was placed there, and someone was sitting in it. A woman without a left arm and with a pulpy right eye. The edges of her yellow coat were charred black, and a pale-blue arm of flashing light extended from it. Countless medical devices were arrayed around her chair, and several tubes and cords were attached to the woman's body.

Shizuri Mugino.

Academy City's fourth-ranked Level Five, known as Meltdown.

The reason they'd decided to send her onto the front lines in Russian territory was a simple one.

"…I caaan't wait—can you, Haaamazuraaa?"

*   *   *

And another Level Five had boarded a different bomber.

"Wh-whoa! What, what is this?!"

The shout came from the bomber's pilot. Black-suited men were supposed to be on board this plane—a special force unit they'd be dropping into Russian skies by parachute. The team was ordered to confirm the movements of a Level Zero named Imagine Breaker and to quickly defeat him and knock him out if they could corroborate that he had allied himself with an enemy faction.

They weren't espers. However, they *were* a group of professionals, outfitted with the latest firearms and possessing the skill to precisely put down targets with inhuman motions. Supposedly.

But now.

Why was everyone in that massive cargo space unconscious?

And...

Who on earth was this girl, who looked like she was in middle school, standing in the center of them, sparks crackling every which way?

"Hello! You're gonna have to add another passenger to your list."

"...?!"

Every part of the pilot's body sensed danger. He tried to quickly leap outside the plane and raise his voice into a shout to inform others nearby of the crisis.

Before he could, though, sparks flew.

A high-tension current, regulated so that it wouldn't leave after-effects, forced the pilot's muscles to contract, leaving him unable to move a single finger, much less speak.

"Gah...?!"

"Sorry. I'm at the end of my rope at this point, so no guarantees I'll be able to hold back on the next one," she told the pilot as he wheezed.

Mikoto Misaka told him thus:

"To Russia, please. Do your original job, and I'll give you a pat on the back."

＊　　＊　　＊

"Now then, what will you do?"

Somewhere in Academy City, someone spoke—Aiwass.

Aiwass was not human.

And the one facing it, as if in concord, was not human, either.

"…"

Long hair, black, with a little bit of brown mixed in. Nervous eyes, visible through glasses. A girl with good proportions. That was how she looked—but in reality, she was an aggregate of AIM dispersion fields.

Hyouka Kazakiri.

Her eyes, as she confronted Aiwass, were not locked in her usual uneasy gaze.

In them was, though slight, a conviction—a will to fight.

To that girl, Aiwass spoke.

"A being similar to you has been confirmed in Russian territory, yes. An archangel—the POWER OF GOD. No, if I were to acknowledge its incompleteness as a trait, I suppose I should call it Misha Kreutzev. Either way, humanity currently does not have the technology or military force to do anything about it. Once the trample begins, tragedy is sure to visit all people of that land."

"Then you want me to fight it?"

"That is indeed a highly fascinating choice. Of course, you have no responsibility to make it."

"…"

"You've started to consider specific plans? Well, if you say you will, then there is no need for worry. We have a disposition to prefer this village, inundated as it is with AIM dispersion fields, but should we use the Sisters scattered throughout the world as a medium and grant directionality to the AIM dispersion fields, we could extend the belt-shaped field area from Academy City to deep within Russia for you."

"That would be…" Kazakiri stumbled over her words for a moment. "Would that mean sending a virus into their heads again?"

"If necessary," answered Aiwass simply. "But it likely will not be. Last Order is not with us, so it may be difficult, but your objective now probably aligns to the Sisters' benefit. Even without forcing the command tower to give the order, I would think the individual specimens would be cooperative."

"..."

"Now then, what will you do?"

"What will *you* do?"

"Nothing." Not even a second passed before Aiwass answered. "I only do things that I deem fascinating. The movements in Russia seem somewhat interesting, but I don't feel enough interest or value to fight for it."

Even if humanity died out and the world disappeared, Aiwass probably wouldn't bat an eye.

One built up intricate plans one by one for some grand goal, and one who had the power to destroy the world with one fingertip but never acted except on whims and fancies—which one of them was really more terrifying?

"You may go."

Kazakiri thought for a while, then said, "However, I have a condition."

"You would ask me? I'm not the one with a bombastic 'plan' in mind."

"Do not lay a hand on my friends, please."

"If they never whet my interest, then you may name any you like."

"...If you do, then I will turn against you both, even if we devour each other in the end."

"Still not enough to be called a threat." Aiwass smiled faintly. "Those very words could instead draw my interest, you know."

And the pilot of one of Academy City's supersonic fighters deployed over the Sea of Japan, for the first time since entering the battle, let out a desperate cry.

"?! Evade!! Turn right noooooooooooooooooooooooooooooooowwwwwwwwwwwwwwwwwwwwwwwwwwwwwwwwwwwwwwwwww!!"

"?"

Ekalielya, of the enemy Russian Air Force, frowned—but realized why a moment later.

Something.

A big hunk of *something* was hurtling straight through them, between each military's aircraft.

Roar!!

The explosion and shock wave tearing through the sky came later than the actual object. It shook the top-of-the-line fighter Ekalielya piloted like a tree branch. If it hadn't been a Russian plane with excellent mobility and stability, it would have stalled and fallen out of the sky. She looked and saw that even the Academy City–made titan, which was over eighty meters long, had almost lost its balance from the impact.

"What…?! What was that just now?!"

The new bogey had come from Academy City. It was probably *something* they'd developed. Considering the situation, it was highly possible it was another cutting-edge aircraft. But Ekalielya couldn't believe what she'd just seen. The object she'd witnessed a moment ago, with her own eyes, was clearly something that ignored all extant aviation sensibilities. It wasn't just a UFO. They were treated as metallic aircraft made of unknown technology—Ekalielya thought of them as mysteries—but mysteries on a level that humans could manage to accept. That was because they were vehicles, controlled on the inside by some sort of creature.

But that thing from earlier had been different.

For just an instant, that which had leaped into Ekalielya's vision was…

"An…angel…?" she murmured. "What on earth *was* that…?"

"Fuck, don't ask me…I'm just as surprised as you."

Though they had no way of knowing, it was a being called Fuse Kazakiri.

However.

She wasn't being controlled by a third party this time. Her own will shone clearly in her eyes. As she tore through the skies, something creaked and grew out of her right hand.

It was a sword. A mass of destructive force was created, one that was incredibly unsuitable for how she was normally.

It was almost like her will to fight had taken physical form.

Fuse Kazakiri flew through the Russian skies faster than any other airborne creature.

Her uncontainable desire to protect her "friends" would likely lead to a fierce battle, a direct confrontation between angels.

Yes:

Science and magic.

A battle between two angels created two wholly different ways.

Touma Kamijou was headed to the center of that battle.

He'd boarded one of the Elizalinan vehicles in the motorcade. He'd directed one of them to a different place in order to send off Accelerator, but the other vehicles were smoothly proceeding toward Fiamma's castle.

He'd found a bundle of parchment on the unconscious Accelerator.

He didn't carelessly touch it, since it might have been a magical item, but instead, he left him Index's name. The name of the girl who would tell him the parchment's meaning.

"...Yeah."

He smiled a little to himself.

The fight against Academy City's number one had been unexpected, but he'd gotten a lot out of it.

"I'm the one dawdling about, doing nothing but worrying. I didn't exactly have the right to talk big in front of Accelerator."

Lesser, who was sitting next to him, looked at the side of Kamijou's face.

He still had his eyes set forward, grinning, as he continued to talk to himself with such energy it was like he was beating the pulp out of his former self.

"Reasons? Justifications? I never needed any of those!! Do I have to have a logical motive to stand up for someone?! Index is suffering. And she can't give that smile she always does. Fight for that!! Isn't that enough?! Quit thinking up excuses!! Stop hesitating and hesitating and looking for more rational reasons!!"

Yes: Just like during the coup in London, when he'd wasted no time stepping up to the plate against the new queen with Curtana Original in hand, his voice had a strange kind of heart in it.

"Is leaving everything to Fiamma going to solve it all?! What the hell does it matter if you feel guilty toward Index?! No matter what that bastard says, is any of it a reason to stop wanting to rescue her?! It was never enough reason to stop me, was it?! No matter how grandiose he was being!!"

He'd returned.

The motivation granting this boy strength had settled back into its original position.

"I'm not protecting her because it's right!! I'm not saving her because the rulebook says I have to!! I just *want* to—me!! You don't need to stop for anything, asshole!! You don't need to debate whether it's right or wrong, and you don't need to look for clues to figure that out!!"

After letting his voice get loud, Kamijou forced himself to quiet down, until he continued softly, "...Yeah, I am the worst kind of person. I was lying to Index that whole time—I'm a garbage human. Maybe, with the life I've led, I can't proudly claim I've been protecting her."

Touma Kamijou.

Gripping his right fist once again, the boy, still looking ahead, said:

"But even so...that doesn't mean *Fiamma's* the one I need to be apologizing to."

London.

St. George's Cathedral had become a crucial and invisible base in this war. Many personnel—read: *sorcerers*—were moving about within, some to directly tackle the invading forces from France and others to indirectly end this great war itself. But among them, one person stood alone outside the general flow of things: Stiyl Magnus.

While he was one of Necessarius's combat personnel, he would never go to the battlefield. He wasn't interested in how this war turned out to begin with. Stiyl was in this cathedral as a bodyguard. For a girl in a large room who continued to sleep on a bed.

Index.

A nun who had 103,000 grimoires memorized and safely tucked away inside her brain.

It was something she'd done long ago, before the boy with the strange right hand had ever shown up.

And that was why...

"Don't yank my chain," asserted the sorcerer strongly, a cigarette coming out the corner of his mouth, glaring straight ahead.

A few meters away stood a woman with long blond hair. A woman whose golden locks seemed far *too* long—almost two and a half times her height.

Laura Stuart.

The archbishop of the English Church and simultaneously the head of Necessarius. Someone who possessed enough authority that, normally, Stiyl would have been forbidden to speak with her on equal footing.

But Stiyl's expression was dangerous.

It was like he laid eyes on an enemy.

Laura, in the meantime, wasn't of the inclination to admonish him for his rudeness and simply gave him a grin.

"Oh! This visit is merely to confirm my adorable subordinate's health, in such miserable suffering as she is. I've even come bearing some fruit."

"...There were *two* remote-control Soul Arms for her. Fiamma stole the one from the Royals, but the Puritans' is still in good shape. And it's obvious who has it."

Stiyl spoke softly in a low voice.

"You're using the Puritans' Soul Arm to interfere with Fiamma so he doesn't misuse the knowledge in her books, right? Currently, Fiamma has a much stronger connection, since he activated it first.

That's why you went so far as to consider messing around with her body and changing the command priority."

"A happy idea, a happy idea, indeed! I regret to say I noticed it not. If you are so inclined, would you like to consider the possibility?"

"I said *Don't yank my chain*! She's already tormented by a heavy burden— If you give her any more, you have no idea what could happen!!"

"Well. Even were your spuriousness on the mark...," teased Laura, "I *am* the rector of this organization, remember? I have countless personnel I can call upon with merely a flick of my chin or a fingertip. I wonder how long you will be able to hold them back by thyself."

"In that case..." Stiyl spat the cigarette in his mouth onto the sublime cathedral's floor.

The next thing she knew, he had several rune cards in his hand.

"...I'll take out their command tower right now, at the very least."

"Oh, I see, I see. Quite respectable indeed."

Laura Stuart shrugged, then removed a Soul Arm, small enough to fit in her palm, from the basket she'd brought the fruit in.

Stiyl's expression warped in rage, but Laura continued without him.

"But will the present situation last for long, I wonder?"

"Wh...what?"

Stiyl didn't even have time to repeat what she'd said.

Rustle.

From the bed behind him, someone had slowly gotten up.

Index Librorum Prohibitorum—the index of prohibited books. And the girl Stiyl Magnus wanted to protect most in this world. But she seemed different. She took one look around with emotionless, camera lenslike eyes, then moved her small lips.

"...Warning...*zz*...Chapter Four *ghghgh*...verse eight. Remote... user...connection, confirmed. *Ghghgee*...Data release, permit... Working-state, data...reception will be, blocked...Factors...presenting danger, beginning automatic removal..."

Bwoo!! A strange noise rang out, and several lights danced around Index.

In the blink of an eye, they'd begun drawing an intricate magic circle.

While placing an even greater load on the little girl's already exhausted body.

"What actions shall you take, Stiyl?" came Laura's amused voice, as if to further pressure Stiyl, who was already cornered.

While toying with history's worst Soul Arm in her hand.

"I shall grant you with a chance, so do *something* about this. If you can't, then I will."

"You don't need to..." Stiyl's teeth grated. "You don't need to tell me— This is the job I've always done!!"

The girl with machinelike eyes heard his shout and turned her head to face the flame sorcerer.

And so she said:

"Hostility, confirmed. Now...analyzing utilized spells and... commencing construction of a corresponding Local Weapon..."

AFTERWORD

To those of you who have purchased one book at a time, hello again.

To those of you who purchased all twenty-two volumes at once, it's nice to meet you.

I'm Kazuma Kamachi.

Finally, the war between science and sorcery! Last time we had a battle in a single country, but this time, the scope is one size larger.

Touma Kamijou, Accelerator, and Shiage Hamazura are each viewing the same war from different points of view. Apart from them, other people in the world, those who have had their hands full just living but would have never seen the light of day, are, just once, abandoning everything and risking their lives to fight. I changed the composition of this story slightly from being centered on a single protagonist because I wanted to emphasize how this is the story about a global conflict, and that no matter what one focuses on, the story will always be about a dangerous battle.

In the end of this story, the hearts of those who once fought against one another are, albeit a little at a time, beginning to gather toward one direction. Never stopping this flow. Never straying from one's own path, using this huge conflict as an excuse. That is probably the most important thing for so many protagonists, so that they can beat this all-too-great flow called war.

I would be deeply moved if you were to watch over their efforts and see whether they succeed or not.

Thanks to my illustrator, Haimura, and my editors, Miki and Fujiwara. The story is getting even *more* difficult to deal with. Science and sorcery, justice and evil, and what have you—so many different hues are mixing together, and I gather it was hard to give all the illustrations a singular direction. Thank you once again, so much, for meeting the unreasonable requests I make of you each time.

And thanks to all my readers. To be honest with you, with the first volume, I doubted whether you'd let me write this kind of story. Thank you very much for supporting an environment that allows me to do whatever I want.

Now then, as I have you close the pages here,
and as I pray you will open the pages again next time,
here and now, I lay down my pen.

How many protagonists *are* there anyway?

Kazuma Kamachi